HONEYMOON TO NOWHERE

By the same author

THE INFORMER (NO PATENT ON MURDER)

THE TATTOO MURDER CASE

Akimitsu Takagi

Honeymoon To Nowhere

Translated by
SADAKO MIZUGUCHI

HONEYMOON TO NOWHERE was first published in English
translation in Australia by the Anthos Publishing Company.

Originally published in Japanese as ZERO NO MITSUGETSU

Copyright © Akimitsu Takagi 1965

Published by
Soho Press, Inc.
853 Broadway
New York NY 10003

Library of Congress-in-Cataloging Data

Takagi, Akimitsu, 1920–1995
[Zero no mitsugetsu. English]
Honeymoon to nowhere / [Akimitsu Takagi: translated
by Sadako Mizuguohi.
        p.   cm.
"First published in English translation in Australia by the
Anthos Publishing Company; originally published in
Japanese as Zero no mitsugetsu"—T.p. verso.
ISBN 1-56947-154-1 (alk. paper)
I. Mizuguohi, Sadako.   II. Title.
PL882.A4Z2513   1985
895.6'35—dc21   98-31948
CIP

10 9 8 7 6 5 4 3 2 1

HONEYMOON TO NOWHERE

CHAPTER ONE

Etsuko Ogata was sweeping up dead leaves in the garden. She moved mechanically, biting her lip, her back toward the clear blue sky, her eyes on the black soil.

The sound of the piano next door pervaded the Sunday morning quiet. The girl's power of concentration was fantastic, Etsuko thought as she listened to the music. The neighbour's daughter was attending music school. Even during the recent Tokyo Olympic Games the piano had never stopped for a single day.

Right now she was playing Chopin's Étude No. 3 in E major, popularly known as the *Farewell Melody.* Etsuko wished the girl would switch to something else— this one was making her heart beat faster.

Sweet memories of love merged with the sorrow of farewell in the tune, and it was precisely this which upset her because she had no sweet memories at all of the parting with *him.* It had only left a wound, still fresh enough to start bleeding on any pretext. If it had to be a melody by Chopin, she thought, Sonata No. 2, the *Funeral March,* would be much more in keeping with the way she felt these days.

Etsuko squatted down in front of a small heap of fallen leaves until her buttocks touched her heels. She took out a box of matches and a square envelope from her apron pocket. Inside the envelope was an invitation to a wedding reception. She had declined it, of course.

She struck a match, lit the envelope and dropped it on the heap of dead leaves. The paper flared up and the leaves began to smoulder. She removed her glasses with one hand, and with the other raised her apron to her face to wipe her eyes.

She was angry—with herself, her own madness. How could she blame him? He probably wouldn't know to this day he had been anything more to her than the fiancé of her best friend. Love? The very idea was utterly ridiculous. It had been a crazy one-sided infatuation, the self-created agony of an imaginative woman of twenty-six whose chunky body was ready for a husband—for a gentle-hard man. That's what it was, and she knew it.

But even now, a year later, she only had to think of his face and his hand—especially his hand with those neatly patterned black hairs, those long, firm fingers— to feel a sudden weakness in her loins. As always, this disturbing sensation polarised into a sense of shame in her mind and an irritating hunger in her groin. It made her dizzy.

Still squatting, she shifted her weight till one heel was wedged between her thighs. She pressed down on it as hard as she could . . .

Then she felt better and began to gather some more dead leaves which looked easier to burn. She put another match to the heap, and this time it caught fire easily. She wished the orange flames would burn away her yearnings so that she could be left in peace.

"Etsu! He's leaving now. Will you see him off, please?"

It was Mrs. Ogata, her mother, calling out from the veranda.

See him off? Etsuko was puzzled. The visitor was Tetsuya Higuchi, a young lawyer who had long been a protégé of her father, himself a lawyer. Higuchi was a regular visitor to the house—quite capable of letting

10

himself out. So why all the fuss now?

But she couldn't be bothered thinking about it any further. She put away the garden broom, took off her apron and went around to the entrance. The girl next door was now playing a melody vibrant with passion. It was Chopin's Étude No. 12, *Revolutionary*.

Higuchi had just said goodbye to Mr. Ogata and was about to get into his car. He was only three years Etsuko's senior but looked older than his age. His appearance was always faultless, suggesting a perfectionist.

Etsuko tried to put on a pleasant face. "I'm sorry," she said. "I didn't know you were leaving so soon."

Higuchi bowed with a strange clumsiness. His narrow eyes, set deep behind his glasses, had a glow in them that was also unusual.

"Well," he said, almost stammering, "I've another engagement today . . . I'll call again soon . . ."

What on earth was wrong with him, Etsuko wondered. Being a lawyer he was a fluent speaker by training, but right now he sounded as if something was stuck in his throat.

Holding the car door, Higuchi seemed to hesitate for a moment before getting in. Then he said, "Etsuko," and then stopped again.

"Yes?"

"No, it doesn't matter . . ." He blushed and hurriedly switched on the motor.

She stood there dutifully until Higuchi's car turned at the corner towards Jiyugaoka station. Then she returned to the front entrance.

He had certainly been a bit queer today, she thought. Was he in some kind of trouble? Was that why he had come to see her father—to consult him?

But there was no sign of concern on her father's face. On the contrary, he smiled—a rare phenomenon these days.

"Come with me, Etsu, will you? I've something to tell you." The smile stayed on his pale lips as he spoke.

Etsuko looked at her father thoughtfully, wondering what he was up to. Then suddenly her own expression stiffened. But no, that was unthinkable . . . The black ashes of the invitation card she had just burnt began to drift across her mind.

When they reached the study he immediately settled into his swivel chair behind his desk. For the past thirty years of his life—more than twenty years as a prosecutor with the Criminal Affairs Division and nearly ten in his own private practice—Takuzo Ogata had spent most of his time in this room when he was at home. Etsuko often imagined that the whole study had been built of law books—each volume like a brick, each wall a different branch of the law.

He didn't waste any time on preliminaries. "As you may have guessed," he said, "Mr. Higuchi told me he'd like to marry you."

Etsuko suppressed a sigh and cast her eyes to the floor. She didn't say anything.

"I personally think this is excellent news, and your mother shares my opinion. She says this is a most desirable marriage proposal—just what we've been hoping for. Mr. Higuchi has been on intimate terms with our family for many years, and he has a very promising career. Not only does he possess a sharp brain; he is also diligent and ambitious. But you know all this, anyway—there's hardly any need for me to sing his praises to you . . . To be completely honest with you, I've been secretly hoping for some time that one day he'd marry you. Only I didn't want to raise the subject myself—I didn't want to create the impression I was determined to have my own way . . ."

Higuchi had lost his father while still a student, and ever since then Ogata had been looking after him. And because the old man was so upright in everything, he felt oddly constrained in the circumstances.

". . . Well, how do you feel about it? . . . I know marriage is one of life's biggest milestones and you may find it difficult to produce an answer straight away. But as Mr. Higuchi is almost one of the family, it should be much easier for you to judge him than some other man who might turn up with a marriage proposal. Don't you agree?"

Etsuko didn't look up and didn't answer, and her father was beginning to grow annoyed. "Say something for heaven's sake," he snapped. "Don't you like Mr. Higuchi?"

"I don't dislike him . . . But I can't say I particularly like him either."

Ogata heaved a sigh and lit a cigarette.

"Etsu," he said quietly after a little while, "you're already twenty-six, you know, and won't be getting any younger . . ."

She was conscious of her hips straining against her tight skirt—they seemed to be getting bigger every day. She must get back on her diet, she thought.

". . . You're well beyond the age of sweet romance, or dreamy love—call it whatever you like. Surely you're mature enough now to look at things more realistically . . . Affection between man and woman grows naturally once they're married. It was the same with us—your mother and me. What young people so fondly describe these days as love is not affection at all but fleeting passion that leaves nothing once it's gone. It's been proved statistically that the failure rate in so-called love-marriages is higher than in marriages contracted after a single meeting . . ."

Even though he was speaking now from a father's august position, it was impossible for him not to become argumentative. As a lawyer he had made his name and money by arguing for the past thirty years.

Etsuko heard every word but was busy with her own thoughts. There was no question about it—this marriage proposal made sense. At least she had to admit she would be aiming far too high if she hoped for anything more than this. Besides, it was quite natural for her father to try to establish a suitable successor. Against his wishes his only son Kazuaki had joined the Mitsuboshi Trading Company and was now working in New York.

If this had happened a couple of years ago, she might

have had more consideration for her father's feelings and accepted his argument without resistance. Yes, she might have nodded readily, then. But now, even if it had been only a one-sided infatuation, after tasting its heady violence, the idea of marrying a man she wasn't fond of seemed to her as tasteless as chewing sand.

And on top of that, after knowing *him,* she definitely didn't want a husband who belonged to the legal fraternity. Somehow, marrying a lawyer seemed taboo to her. She felt that such a match would only open her wound wider instead of helping to heal it . . . But she knew she would be quite unable to explain all this to her father so he could understand it, let alone accept it.

"Now look here, Etsu," he continued persuasively, "you're intelligent and good-hearted, and I'm quite sure you'll make an excellent wife and mother. I don't think I'm being a doting father for saying this. You're a fine girl with many good points, but unfortunately, your assets aren't readily visible to other men . . . Let me put it this way—a man who recognises your real value is obviously a keen observer. That's why I think you shouldn't miss this opportunity."

At last Etsuko raised her eyes and opened her mouth. "Father," she said, "I'm very grateful to Mr. Higuchi for his kind sentiments, and I do value your opinion. But I feel I'd need a little more time to think it over."

"But of course! You just take your time—think about it at your leisure . . . Will two or three days be enough, do you think?"

Etsuko sucked in her breath. What would be the use of buying two or three days? "I meant a little longer than that."

"A week then?"

"I——"

"For heaven's sake, Etsu, a marriage proposal isn't like a business offer one can chew over for a month or more. I hope you can understand that much." He glared at her. "Or do you want to turn him down? Is that what you'd like to do?"

"No, it's not that . . . It's just that my mind isn't prepared for marriage right now."

"Accepting his proposal doesn't mean you have to get married straight away. A normal six-month engagement period should give you all the time you need to get used to the idea."

"But father, I don't feel like getting married to anyone at present."

He knitted his eyebrows and held her gaze with total concentration.

She still got frightened of him every time he looked at her this way. Now she was doubly scared because he made her feel as if she were a hostile witness about to be relieved of her secret in one easy move.

"Etsu," he said slowly, "I'm your father, and I'm neither blind nor a fool. You don't have to tell me anything—I can guess what happened to you last autumn. And if I consider certain circumstances relating to that period, I think I can establish the identity of the man you fell secretly in love with . . . Well, I won't mention his name, and I do respect your feelings. Perhaps it was a rather harrowing experience for you . . . But you should get rid of that painful memory as soon as you can, don't you think? I believe those two will get married soon. You should make a special effort to find new happiness. What do you say?"

Etsuko was almost ready to cry. He was perfectly right. She herself had reached exactly the same conclusion before burning the invitation card with the dead leaves a little while ago. The only thing was—emotions of this kind couldn't be got rid of by reasoning.

Ogata said, "As you probably know, my health hasn't been the best lately. My blood pressure is fairly high, and I get tired very quickly. Sometimes I can't help being conscious of an ominous premonition . . . Anyway, I'd like to see you in bridal dress as soon as possible—while I'm still around. This is the thing foremost in my mind these days. And the older you get, Etsu, the more difficult it'll be for you to find a suitable match. Would you please try to make up your mind as soon as you can?"

Looking at her father Etsuko realised he had indeed

grown old all of a sudden. He had never been a robust man, living most of his life under the doctor's eye. But lately he looked as if the strain of the past thirty years had taken its toll of him in one big instalment. The truth —coming so openly from his own lips—made her heart turn over with compassion for him.

On the other hand, she couldn't bring herself to accept his advice without questioning it. This would be unfair, not only to herself but to Higuchi as well. She wondered if there was someone else somewhere she'd be more willing to marry, even if her affection for him wouldn't compare with what she had felt for *him*.

Her pale oval face was calm and resolute when finally she spoke up. "Father, I agree with everything you've said, but please give me at least three months to think it over. I wouldn't like to give Mr. Higuchi the promise of a lifetime without being fairly confident I can grow fond of him as time goes on."

Ogata softened his expression. "Yes, this seems reasonable enough . . . In other words, you'll keep company with Mr. Higuchi for the next three months, and then give him a definite answer. Is that it?"

No, that isn't it at all, she wanted to say, but didn't have the courage to do it. If she told him she didn't want to marry a lawyer under any circumstances and he hit the roof, who knew what might happen to him with his high blood pressure . . . She clearly remembered her father's distress when her brother Kazuaki had declared he wouldn't sit for the law entrance examination.

Finally she did the only thing she felt she could do— she nodded silently, and Ogata looked genuinely grateful.

He said, "Mr. Higuchi has visited this house a great many times over the years, but now that I think of it, there haven't been many occasions when the two of you talked alone. Yes, that makes your attitude certainly reasonable enough. Perhaps I've been too eager—I must be losing my touch."

Etsuko left her father's study feeling relieved and weighted down at the same time. *I don't dislike him, but I can't say I particularly like him either.* She had meant what she said at the time, but now that she was reconsidering it, the hand of the scale seemed to be leaning towards dislike.

Anyway, from now on she would have to go on dates with him whether she liked it or not. If during the next three months she managed to develop an interest in Higuchi, this at least might help her to forget about *him* . . .

Not that this was very likely to happen, though she wished it with all her heart. Even now she was vaguely conscious of that familiar weakness, just because she had thought of *him* . . . And would it be possible to grow fond of another man in three months—a man she had met constantly for years and hardly ever noticed?

But much as she tried, she could think of no other prospective suitor besides Higuchi. Her only real opportunity to meet eligible men was at parties held from time to time by the Kinome group which catered for single lawyers and the marriagable sons and daughters of legal families. But since she was determined not to marry a lawyer, members of this group were out of the question.

She had suggested a period of three months to her father, but wasn't at all sure anything would happen by the end of it . . .

It was two days later.

"Parcel, Miss Ogata," the postman called out at the front.

Etsuko went to the entry and saw a small parcel sitting on the bench. It seemed to contain something like a book. There had been occasions when authors of legal works had sent her father complimentary copies, but this package was addressed to her. She had a vague notion of having seen the name of the sender, Yoshihiro Tsukamoto, somewhere before, but couldn't place it at all.

She picked up the parcel and walked back with it to her room.

As she had thought, there was a book in it. It had the dull title, *An Introduction to Economics, Unabridged*

Edition, and acknowledged the joint authorship of five people. The sender was one of them.

In the *Contents* she found the line, *Industrial Management . . . . Yoshihiro Tsukamoto, Lecturer in Economics, Chiyoda University.*

Until now she had been mystified by the whole thing, but once she saw the characters of Chiyoda University, her fleshy lips twitched into a smile.

It had happened about six weeks ago.

On her way home from seeing off a girlfriend at Tokyo Station she had felt thirsty and gone into a tea house in one of those basement shopping arcades. The shop was crowded and she had to share a table with another customer.

Aged about thirty, he was so absorbed in a book, he never once looked up at her across the table. Then he glanced at his watch, jumped to his feet and rushed out of the shop in a great hurry.

He was hardly gone when Etsuko noticed a package in cloth wrapper left on the bench next to where he had been sitting. She naturally thought it must belong to him, so she picked it up, paid her bill, and went after him, but couldn't see him anywhere. He had already disappeared in the station crowd.

Wondering if she should take the package back to the tea house or deposit it at the station's lost property office, she finally looked at the label. *Research Section, Department of Economics, Chiyoda University,* it said, and the name *Yoshihiro Tsukamoto* was scribbled over it in black ink.

On her way home from Tokyo Station she would have to pass by Chiyoda University at Kanda, she thought. It seemed much more considerate to take the package there personally than hand it in at the station— it might be something important. Judging by the label, the man must be a tutor or a research assistant. She should be able to find him without much trouble if she inquired at the registrar's office.

Tsukamoto looked greatly relieved when she handed him the package.

"You don't know how grateful I am," he said excited-
ly. "I've been really worried about this for the past hour.
It's my stupid carelessness again, I guess, but I was so
busy thinking about something, I just left it behind
somehow. If I'd lost this I would've been in real trouble."
He patted the package. "A collection of data money
can't buy . . ."

Perversely, his carelessness appealed to Etsuko. It
seemed to her to be a sign of scholarly character. She
also liked his uninhibited self-reproach, and the way he
voiced his gratitude, like a big child.

" . . . Frankly, I didn't know where I'd left it. The tea
house did occur to me, but I couldn't recall the name of
the shop, so I couldn't check by phone . . . And I couldn't
immediately retrace my movements either because I was
already late for a conference."

After thanking her several more times, Tsukamoto
said a book of his would be published in the near future,
and it would contain some of the data he would've surely
lost but for her kindness, and he'd like to send her a
complimentary copy as an expression of his gratitude.

Thinking he might be offended if she refused, Etsuko
gave him her name and address before continuing on her
way home. And soon the whole episode was completely
forgotton.

Now she picked up the book and tried to recall
Yoshihiro Tsukamoto's face. His exact features escaped
her, but she could remember his shaggy head of hair, the
outline of his oval face, and his darting eyes which seemed
to be in contrast with his otherwise restrained scholarly
gestures. She decided her first impression of him hadn't
been unfavourable . . .

Etsuko kept turning the pages till she came to the part
he had written. Even the term *industrial management*
was completely new to her, but she felt that not to read
even a single page of it would be unfair to the writer who
had gone to the trouble of sending her the book.

Without any knowledge of management she found the
text a bit difficult to follow at times, even though it was
meant to be an introduction to the subject. But the

sentences themselves were lighter and wittier and the whole theme far more interesting than she had expected.

When she had read about ten pages she found a narrow strip of paper like a bookmark between the pages. Now, what was this supposed to be? It was a concert ticket with the date November 5 printed on it. That was the opening day of the London Symphony Orchestra's Tokyo season, one week ahead.

Well, he had done it again, Etsuko thought, feeling rather annoyed this time. How could a man be so absent-minded? He must have put the ticket in the book, then forgot it and sent it to her by mistake.

He was a damned nuisance, she thought as she dialled the number of Chiyoda University. He must have been in his room because he answered a few seconds after she had asked for him.

She thanked him for the book and then brought up the subject of the ticket, doing her best not to show her irritation.

"No, that wasn't an oversight," he said hesitantly. "It was just a small token of gratitude. Last time I saw you you had the biography of some famous musician in your shopping bag, didn't you?"

"I could've."

"That's why I thought you might have an interest in classical music."

"But I couldn't accept an expensive ticket like this."

"It hasn't cost me a single *sen*—its a complimentary ticket, so please accept it without qualms . . . I'm awfully sorry but you must excuse me now. I have a class waiting for me. Thank you very much for ringing. So long."

The phone clicked dead at the other end. She stood there for a while with a blank expression, trying to re-capture his words. Then she replaced the receiver. She had to admit she felt like going to the concert. On the other hand, she couldn't help thinking that the ticket, whether he had paid for it or not, was far too excessive a reward for what she had done for him. But returning it didn't seem the right thing to do either . . .

Just then the phone rang, and she lifted the receiver

20

again. "Hello," she said.

A male voice said, "May I speak to Miss Ogata, please?"

"Speaking."

"Oh, hello. This is Higuchi here."

Etsuko felt the skin tighten on her cheek-bones and temples.

Timidly he said, "I thought I should give you a ring and thank you for the other day . . . Incidentally, are you free on the evening of November 5? I've got hold of a couple of tickets to the Kabuki Theatre. Some new players will make their debut that evening, and I thought you might like to go . . ."

Her father must have told him she would date him for a while, she thought. He certainly didn't waste any time providing the opportunity.

"Thank you very much—it's kind of you to ask me. Unfortunately, I've a previous engagement for that evening." She was amazed how fast the words of refusal had rolled off her tongue. "I'm going to the opening performance of the London Symphony Orchestra . . . I'm terribly sorry."

"No, please don't worry about it . . . I'm naturally disappointed, but I'm also glad to hear you're interested in serious music . . . Anyway, there's always another time, so we'll just leave it till then, shall we?"

Being a gentleman, Higuchi didn't persist and ended the conversation without trying to fix an alternative date.

Etsuko put down the receiver and looked at the ticket in her hand. Would Yoshihiro Tsukamoto be at the concert? She had a feeling that he might . . .

Once more she tried to visualise his face, and a faint excitement began to stir in her. It gradually grew stronger, until it became the sweet weakness she knew so well. And she realised with a shock that the face conjured up in her mind no longer belonged to the young lecturer, but to *him*.

With some effort she shut off her mind and fought off the yearning in her flesh. And then she was ready to think of Yoshihiro Tsukamoto again. Could he, by any chance,

21

be the man she had been looking for? She knew she had to find out.

On the evening of November 5 she put on the silver-grey suit she liked best and went to the Tokyo Cultural Centre at Ueno. The throbbing of her heart was quite distinct as she approached the grounds.

Walking up the steep slope in Ueno Park she wondered what was wrong with her. Could she really be excited about a man she had seen only twice, each time for only a few minutes? Perhaps it was her subconscious reaction to the prospect of having to marry Higuchi. This seemed quite likely. After all, prior to Higuchi's proposal, Yoshihiro Tsukamoto had never once entered her mind . . .

But she must be careful. If she allowed herself to become obsessed with the idea that she had to find another man within three months, she might run into some unexpected danger . . . Not that she could imagine Tsukamoto as a lecher or a sadist, but he might be married already . . . And there was no guarantee at all he would turn up tonight, anyway . . .

She entered the foyer and bought herself a programme. It was unusual to find a *sonosheet* inside a concert programme. The disc was a performance by Pierre Monteux, the great French conductor who had planned to visit Japan at the head of this orchestra, but died last April.

Etsuko kept looking around the foyer for a while, but there was no sign of Tsukamoto. Finally she gave up and went inside to take her seat. A middle-aged woman was sitting on her right, but the seat on her left remained empty. It was still unoccupied when the performance started.

Sir Arthur Bliss, guest conductor of the orchestra, appeared on stage, and the British and Japanese national anthems were played. First item on the programme was a selection from the ballet *Checkmate*, Sir Arthur's own composition and one of his most admired works.

Etsuko had seen this ballet performed by the Royal

22

Ballet Company. Listening to the music now made her recall the previous stage scenes. Black and white chess figures blending in well devised confusion . . . the white
knight courting his queen . . . the dance of the black
queen—these scenes were coming back to her now as
clearly as if she had seen them only yesterday.

Then the music stopped and a storm of applause shook
the hall. The seventy-three-year-old veteran conductor answered the encores in his usual graceful manner. Etsuko
clapped enthusiastically.

The applause had died down when she realised Yoshihiro Tsukamoto was standing beside her.

"I'm sorry—I'm late," he whispered. "I tried to get here
on time but didn't quite make it, so I couldn't come up to
the seat. But I listened to it standing at the back." He spoke
hesitantly, as on the previous occasion.

His appearance was rather different from the picture
Etsuko had built up in her mind over the past few days. She
realised her imagination had been far too generous to him.
She had to force back a chuckle.

Admittedly, after watching Sir Arthur Bliss, this typical
British gentleman, she would be inclined to judge
Tsukamoto rather severely. But even so, she felt there was
no excuse for his hair to be as shaggy as before, and his tie
knot to be pushed to one side. And when she saw white
chalk powder on the end of his coat sleeve, and noticed
that his shoes which were supposed to be black were almost grey, she thought he could hardly be described as a
dandy.

Higuchi would be the last person to turn up at a concert
dressed like this.

But there was something else about Tsukamoto—something impossible to describe. He possessed a kind of natural warmth that made her pores open up to him. His
spontaneous friendliness had no hint of buried passions,
and this gave her a sense of comfort she could never experience in Higuchi's company.

Suddenly she remembered reading somewhere that
motherly women with large breasts were often attracted to
clumsy, untidy men, and she became conscious of her

own breasts straining in their harness under her blouse.

"Thank you for this lovely evening," she said, and was going to add something, but he interrupted her with a wave of his hand.

"It's nothing—I'm pleased you've come. The orchestra is better than I expected—quite colourful, and well balanced. The woodwinds are especially good, don't you think?"

"Yes. I've read your book." She was startled by her own words. She couldn't explain what had made her change the subject so abruptly, but Tsukamoto seemed very pleased.

"Thank you for making the effort—you must have found it pretty dry stuff. Or are you interested in management?"

"I wasn't till I read the book . . . I know a little about law because my father is a lawyer—a former prosecutor. In that I'm like a shopkeeper's errand boy who lives near a temple and learns to chant a sutra . . . But now I realise the study of management is much more fascinating than people generally imagine."

"Well, I couldn't wish for a more flattering comment. This will do wonders for the ego of the writer in me . . . Management as a study is in vogue at the moment, and the book is selling better than we expected. The publisher asked me specifically to use the simplest language possible to make it intelligible to laymen, but I wasn't sure if I succeeded."

"There were a few patches in it I found difficult to follow, but generally speaking it's rather amazing how you managed to present this complex subject with such clarity."

"What patches did you find difficult?"

She told him with complete honesty, and he listened thoughtfully, nodding every now and then.

After the intermission Colin Davis, an energetic young conductor, appeared on stage. Under his baton the orchestra played Beethoven's Symphony No. 1 in C major, followed by Dvořák's Symphony No. 7 in D minor. Etsuko was now able to abandon herself completely to the flow of the music. She was hardly aware Tsukamoto was sitting beside her.

When it was all over she rediscovered him, looking at him in wonder. If it had been Higuchi, she would have been conscious of him all the time and probably wouldn't have been able to enjoy the music at all. But with Tsukamoto she had felt completely relaxed. It had seemed natural that he should be there, sitting beside her. It had been as reassuring to her as the presence of a husband might be to his wife on a quiet evening at home.

They came out of the concert hall, walking side by side. The cold wind outside carried the loneliness of the deepening autumn. The pale glow of the neon lights added to a mood of unreality caused by the strange lines of the building.

"Miss Ogata . . ."

"Yes?"

"I've a confession to make. The ticket . . ."

"What about it?"

"I placed it well inside the book on purpose. If you had put the book away without looking through it, you wouldn't have noticed the ticket in it, would you? And since it's such a dry subject, I thought there was every chance this might actually happen."

Etsuko gazed at him wide-eyed. What was he trying to say? "And if I hadn't noticed it—what were you going to do then?"

Tsukamoto didn't answer. Standing there, his tall, lean figure vaguely outlined against the pale glow of the lights behind him, he seemed to be enveloped in some strange shadow of loneliness. Would this man, by any chance, have unhappy memories similar to her own, she wondered, the tenderness of compassion welling up in her.

He remained silent for a while, then said, "I come from the Kansai district—only been here since last spring and haven't got many friends . . . Would you meet me again some day?"

Etsuko cast her eyes to the ground. His unpolished shoes came into her sight, and her feminine instinct told

25

her he'd be still single—certainly without anyone to clean his shoes for him.

"All right," she said slowly as a few dry leaves scurried along the ground at their feet, scraping against the pavement.

CHAPTER TWO

It was exactly one week after the concert when Etsuko
Ogata saw Yoshihiro Tsukamoto for the fourth time.
They met at one o'clock in the afternoon in the Café
Pensées.

In the meantime she had also had a date with Higuchi,
and she couldn't help feeling it had been nothing more
than an unpleasant obligation. There was nothing wrong
with Higuchi, really, but likes and dislikes weren't things
that could be reasoned out. If she had been an extrovert
with a natural interest in people, she might have found
superficial pleasure in his company. She felt sorry for
her parents when she thought of this.

The Pensées was a café without any character or
mood, but at least it was quiet. This somehow atoned
for the proprietor's audacity in borrowing the name of
the famous work by Pascal. It certainly seemed to be the
kind of place suitable for meditation. Etsuko wasn't
surprised at all Tsukamoto had taken a fancy to it. And
the coffee was good.

He arrived a few minutes late with an apologetic grin
on his face. His hair was as unkempt as ever, but his

27

shoes had been cleaned, Etsuko noted. They weren't very shiny, but at least they looked black.

"This *is* a relief," he said. "I was a bit worried you mightn't turn up."

She couldn't help smiling. His words, utterly lacking in rhetorical flourish, washed through her consciousness like crystal-clear water.

She said, "Mr. Tsukamoto, is it all right for you to get away from work in the middle of the day, like this?"

"One advantage of being a university teacher is that I can use my time fairly freely, compared with other people. Today I'm free in the afternoon . . . By the way, since you're not one of my students, would you mind calling me by my first name? I'm not that old, you know."

She looked at him hesitantly, aware that this was only their fourth meeting, but couldn't resist his pleading eyes for long. She smiled and said, "All right."

"Thank you. And now that we've got this settled, what shall we do next? Where'd you like to go?"

"It's up to you—I don't mind."

"To be quite honest, I've been wondering about it since yesterday, but haven't been able to come up with anything. I'm not very good at this sort of thing, I'm afraid. If we were in Kyoto—there I know many spots we could go to, but Tokyo seems to be a terrible place for that."

"I agree."

"I spent a year in the United States, and while I was there I took some dancing lessons." He threw a despairing glance at the ceiling and sighed. "I'm hopeless . . . Furthermore, dance halls in Japan don't really cater for men of thirty, like me, and it's too early in the afternoon, anyway . . . You must think I'm completely devoid of ideas, but all I can think of is going somewhere out of the centre of the city where we can breathe some fresh air."

"That'll suit me fine. It's a nice day—and I don't particularly like crowded places."

"Well, what d'you say we go to Mukogaoka Recreation Grounds?"

"Okay, that'll do." She couldn't help feeling a bit

disappointed. If he had to find excuses from the start for not knowing what to do, what would happen later? Though perhaps it was natural he'd be over-anxious or supercautious, this being their first real date.

They went to Shinjuku station and caught an Odakyu-line train. On the way to the recreation grounds they said very little, and even on arrival walked around for a while in silence. Being a week-day, there weren't many people around.

Etsuko found his unsophisticated style oddly relaxing rather than awkward, and certainly not boring. She recalled her father's lecture about the difference between passion and affection, and decided her feeling for him, if any, didn't fit into either of those categories. But then, what was it? Friendship? Was that possible between a man and a woman who had only met three times before?

"Shall we sit down?" he asked and promptly flopped down on a bench.

Etsuko followed him. The sky was blue as far as she could see, the leaves on the trees were turning red, and the wind was already cold. He took out a packet of cigarettes and lit one with a queer-looking oil lighter that seemed to be a survivor from another age. There wasn't a soul around, and everything was quiet.

He slowly blew out the smoke, and said, "Have you ever been in love?"

"I guess so," she said, forcing a smile to cover up the stir caused by his unexpected question. She didn't feel like telling him a lie. "It was only a one-sided thing—hopeless from the start . . . Why do you ask?"

"I just had a feeling you might have been through something like that. Are you still concerned about him?"

She hesitated for a moment. "He's already married."

He smoked in silence for a while, then began to talk, almost in a whisper, pausing between each sentence as if thinking aloud.

"I myself have a rather unpleasant memory . . . I suppose it could be described as unrequited love for want of a better word . . . Soon afterwards I went to New York on a Fulbright scholarship. I thought it'd give me a chance to turn over a new leaf . . ." He laughed briefly but bitterly. A muscle in his cheek twitched, giving him a strangely twisted expression. "But I just couldn't patch up the hole in my mind . . . The United States is the home of management studies, and I was certainly learning a great deal, but somehow I never felt quite fulfilled . . . Of course, I was living in a strange country without friends, and had to rack my brains to produce even the simplest sentence in English—none of this helped. I can well understand why students studying abroad suffer breakdowns—even develop suicidal tendencies."

"Yes, it's not so hard to imagine how they must feel."

"So I used to go for long walks on my own whenever I had time to spare. I must have been trying to wear out my youth together with my shoe-soles . . . And I had this perverse desire to go into places like the slum areas of Harlem and the Bowery—places most people would want to keep well away from. Perhaps I could sniff the smell of tragedy in such places, watching people thwarted by fate shuffling on without hope . . ."

Listening to him Etsuko wondered if his morbid state of mind at the time could have been caused solely by that unhappy love affair. Perhaps there had been another, more compelling reason. It seemed to her that somewhere along the line his psyche must have absorbed a very severe blow. Otherwise why should a scholar—a man of reason and logic—allow himself to sink to such depths of despair after achieving his ambition to study in the United States?

He said, "Now that I think back, I might have been subconsciously trying to sustain my tragic mood. If you're exposed to grief long enough, you can become addicted to it, you know. You begin to feel something's missing whenever you're without sadness. And once this happens, sadness becomes a kind of queer delight . . ."

Etsuko began to feel strangely disturbed. Hadn't his words quite accurately described her own condition over the past year?

". . . I'm sure if I hadn't been able to snap out of it in time, I would've entered on a course of self-destruction.

But one day I discovered a marvellous remedy for unrequited love."

"A remedy for unrequited love?" She looked at him incredulously, her mouth slightly open.

"Yes," he said and quickly rose to his feet. "Would you like to come to my apartment at Setagaya? I'll give you that medicine—I've brought it back with me from the United States. It's really effective, not only against lovesickness, but against all sorts of other miseries as well."

"It wouldn't be alcohol, or some drug, by any chance?" Her smile, meant to prove she had a sense of humour, was laced with suspicion.

"No, it isn't the sort of thing you'd take into your mouth." He laughed, and the same muscle in his cheek oddly twitched again. "Let's go then."

Go to the apartment of a man she hardly knew? For a woman of her upbringing it was like leaping into the dark from the stage of Kiyomizu Temple.

Her mind was racing, trying to assess what he had just said. Did it have a double meaning? Was there a lewd allusion in it? The idea frightened her, but somehow it also made her excited. And above all, her curiosity was becoming uncontrollable. Finally she told herself this man wouldn't be capable of anything improper.

"All right, but only for a minute," she said in a low voice, and got up from the bench.

Yoshihiro Tsukamoto's apartment was about five minutes' walk from Setagaya Daita station on the Odakyu line. It was number 301, occupying the eastern corner of the top floor in a fairly new three-story concrete building.

"Please come in," he said. "It's in a mess, as usual."

Glancing around inside Etsuko thought he hadn't been exaggerating. There was general confusion in typical bachelor fashion. Obviously nobody had been doing any cleaning for days, but otherwise the place looked quite comfortable. It consisted of a Japanese room about twelve feet by nine feet, a western room of the same size, kitchen with dining nook, and a bathroom and toilet.

He picked up a couple of newspapers from an arm-chair in the western room and asked her to sit down.

"Quite a nice apartment you've got here," she said.

"Well, it may be a bit extravagant for a single man, but I thought it'd save me shifting again when I get married."

Suddenly there was a lump in her throat she couldn't swallow. "Are you getting married soon?" She gave a cool smile, but a quaver in her voice gave her away.

There was just a hint of amusement in his eyes as he gazed at her for a while. "It depends on her," he said slowly and meaningfully. "But I don't think she's quite ready for it yet."

She shifted her glance to the coarse carpet square on the floor. The lump was gone from her throat, and now she was conscious of her quickening heartbeat.

He said, "I haven't anything nice to offer, but would you like a cup of tea?"

"Yes, I'd love one."

"It won't take me a minute."

"Let me make it."

"Okay, if you insist . . . Tea bags and sugar are on the top shelf, cups and saucers in the cupboard. And while you're making it, I'll try to find that thing—the remedy for love-sickness."

He grinned mysteriously, and she liked the childish delight he took in whatever it was. As he opened the paper door to the Japanese room, she caught a glimpse of a low table covered with books and notepaper, and a heap of books stacked all along one side of the wall.

Then she was boiling the water in the kitchen, still conscious of the throbbing of her heart. A teacher of business management. Hm. He was so different from a lawyer. She could probably get along with him fine. Her nature seemed rather suited to the role of wife to a modest scholar . . .

The thought made her blush, but she couldn't control her imagination. She saw herself living with him in this apartment, listening to his voice on a quiet evening,

32

leaning against his arm outstretched on the back of the settee, his hand just around her shoulder, gently drawing her closer to him, and she yielding to his touch—his other hand, moving slowly along her thigh . . .

Then she felt that sweet weakness touching her loins again, until she had to press her knees together to stop them trembling. And suddenly she had the strange notion she had known Yoshihiro for a long time . . .

When she returned from the kitchen with the tea, she saw a little black doll on the table. It had a woeful expression on its face, and in its hand was a heart broken in two. She had never seen a doll like that before.

"Goodness me," she said, "where did you get this from?"

"This is the medicine I was talking about. It's powered by battery and is known as the heartbreak doll." He patted it affectionately on the cheek. "This is the sort of gimmick the Americans like. I bought it in a stall somewhere around Coney Island one night—to the ear-shattering accompaniment of *Heartbreak Hotel* by Elvis Presley."

The doll was sitting on a grey base which housed the battery and a tiny water tank. Yoshihiro switched on the mechanism, and the little Negro doll came to life. Big tear-drops fell from his eyes, some running down his miserable face, while his hands were frantically trying to put together the two halves of the broken heart.

"Isn't he clever? When I first saw him doing this I felt as if I was looking at my own ridiculous self, and I couldn't help laughing till tears were running from my own eyes." He opened his hands and awkwardly held them out towards the performing doll. "Just look at him—how he's trying to put his silly heart together."

His arms still outstretched, he slowly twisted his face into a grin in preparation for a chuckle, which soon swelled into full-blown laughter.

Etsuko couldn't quite see what was so funny about the doll, but she had an almost hysterical desire to adjust to his mood. She stared at him blankly for a moment and then, as if it had been a long time welling, began to laugh with him.

Then suddenly the laughter died on his lips and his face became hesitant and pleading. He turned his out-stretched arms towards her, as if asking for reassurance and comfort.

At that moment she was terribly conscious of how she looked, what she was wearing, how she stood there. She thought, *I don't know what made you take notice of me in the first place—what made you like me more than others—but I know I've been waiting to be touched by someone like you, to be held close* . . . She slipped into his arms and immediately put her hands up his back. Being so much shorter than he, her head just fitted in under his chin.

She didn't expect him to kiss her, and he didn't—he just held her tight, pressing her face against his chest. Her lips felt his skin through his shirt, and as she drew in the scent of his body, a flash of desire mixed with poignant affection swept through her, until her loins felt all weak and churned up, and she was aware of a dampness between her thighs.

"I don't think I need that doll any more," he whispered into her hair.

"Yoshihiro . . ." She took a deep breath, fighting off the urge to open her knees and wrap one leg around him.

Then the door-bell began to ring.

They pulled apart, almost guiltily, and she hurriedly adjusted her hair and dress while he went to answer the door.

"Who the hell is it, at this time of day?" His voice was vibrant with irritation. He walked through the dining area towards the entrance.

Etsuko watched him through the open door with maudlin eyes, her senses still in a turmoil, thinking it must be some bill collector, or perhaps the telegram boy. So she was surprised, even frightened, to see a man of twenty-seven or twenty-eight push Yoshihiro to one side and walk confidently into the apartment.

The man looked definitely unpleasant. His eyes were sharp and cold with a lot of white showing in them, his

34

lips were cruelly thin, and a knife scar like an earth-worm ran along his left cheek. It was the sort of face that would have fitted any Tokyo gangster, only Etsuko felt this one had an additional quality—somehow it radiated a corrupted intelligence that made it look even more uncanny.

"Aah, you have a visitor—and a lady at that?" The man spoke insolently, leering at her through the open door, "Well, well, what d'you know? I hope I'm not interrupting anything, am I?"

His glance made her flesh creep—she felt as if a centipede had just crawled over her bare breasts. Who was this man? What did he want? What was his relationship to Yoshihiro?

"You've certainly come at a most inconvenient time," Yoshihiro said, hardly able to control his anger. "Could you come back later—please?"

Etsuko couldn't see Yoshihiro's face from where she stood, but she sensed his distress from the tone of his voice.

"I'm sorry," the man said, "it'd be just as inconvenient for *me* to come back later. I'm about to leave town—I want to have a word with you *now*."

After that they lowered their voices, and Etsuko couldn't catch a single word. But a little later she noticed Yoshihiro take something out of his pocket and give it to the stranger.

Raising his voice now in mock apology, the man said, "I'm sorry to butt in like this." He looked at Etsuko with a lewd grin on his face. "Please forgive me, miss—and have a good time, huh?"

Then he was gone, and Yoshihiro returned to her, his shoulders sagging, his face still pale with anger. "I'm terribly sorry about this," he muttered.

"Who is he?"

"Hiroshi Watanabe, a distant relative of mine . . . He's a complete no-hoper—turns up every now and then to borrow money from me." He forced a bitter smile.

"Well, that's nothing unusual," she said soothingly. "Every family has its black sheep. I know this from my father who often has to deal with such people in his practice."

Her words were meant to reassure him, and perhaps they did, but they certainly didn't help her at all. Her mind was loaded with apprehension and doubt. If the man's relationship to him was what he had told her, then there was no reason for him to become so pale and upset. Moreover, the man had acted far too arrogantly for one who had only come to borrow some money . . .

Yoshihiro didn't offer any further information, and she decided to drop the subject. If he had been telling the truth, then there were certainly some queer characters in his family, she thought. But what right did she have at this stage to pry into his personal affairs, anyway?

She looked out the window into the gathering darkness and said, "It's getting late—I'd better be going . . . Thank you very much for the afternoon." By now her previous passionate mood was replaced by a deep chill.

Yoshihiro didn't try to stop her and merely offered to see her off to the station.

On her way home that evening Etsuko searched her soul with complete detachment—without being in any way influenced by her physical needs. And she discovered the tender beginnings of a new affection in one compartment, and the slow gathering of a poisonous suspicion in another.

Etsuko's third date with Yoshihiro went off without any mishap. This time the emphasis was on the mind, and theirs were duly drawn closer together. Meanwhile, to face Higuchi alone was becoming increasingly painful to her.

Her fourth date with Yoshihiro followed on November 26—again commencing at the Café Pensées, which was very close to Chiyoda University and was regularly used by the academic staff there.

When she entered the shop right on half past four, she found Yoshihiro already there, having a cup of coffee with a tall man about his own age. She hesitated for a moment, but he beckoned to her, and then she joined their table.

"This is Mr. Tatsuo Kawaji, a lecturer in the Department of Law at our university," Yoshihiro said. "We've been close friends ever since our student days. Among other things, we shared all the hardships of the boat club —always as reserves, never quite making the top . . ."

Etsuko thought Kawaji looked much more like a university lecturer than Yoshihiro. He was properly dressed, wore strongly framed glasses and had a rather stern expression. But when he smiled his face softened, and his voice was far more gentle than expected.

"How d'you do," he said. "Tsukamoto talks quite a lot about you—you seem to be always on his mind."

"I hope everything he says is good."

"Oh, naturally. He thinks there isn't another one like you in the whole world . . . By the way, he told me your father is Mr. Ogata, the former prosecutor."

"Yes, he resigned from the Criminal Affairs Division about ten years ago and has been in private practice ever since."

"I've met him once, but he wouldn't remember me, of course—I was only a kid then."

"Are you specialising in criminal law?"

"My special field is the Criminal Procedure Code, but I also have to lecture on the Criminal Code. At a private university they usually pay you less and make you work twice as hard." He smiled wryly and looked up, and then said, "Oh, no."

A woman of about forty, dressed in a gay kimono, wafted towards them. She had slanting eyes and looked quite beautiful for her age.

"Hello there," she called out in a strident voice. "Would you excuse me if I borrowed Mr. Tsukamoto for a few minutes? It's to do with the next function of the Economics Department's social committee."

Yoshihiro got up with badly disguised reluctance, and she immediately steered him away to a corner table.

"Who is she?" Etsuko asked.

"Mrs. Araki, wife of the professor in charge of management studies. And she's in charge of the professor . . ."

Kawaji sighed. "She has a dangerously sharp tongue, and lately she's developed a new hobby—men much younger than herself."

"Do you think she's got her eyes on Mr. Tsukamoto?"

"Probably, as on dozens of others, but I wouldn't worry about it if I were you. She wouldn't get to first base with Tsukamoto—he's too upright for this sort of hanky-panky. He's also smart enough to look after himself. He might act dumb at times, but I can assure you he's got a very good brain. Actually, he's far too good for Chiyoda University. Until last year he held a lecturer's post at Kyoraku University."

Kawaji suddenly fell silent, as if realising he had said too much.

Etsuko began wondering. It mightn't be fair to subject universities to an arbitrary classification, but there was no denying the fact they did vary a great deal in quality, ranging from top grade down to what was sometimes described as a 'station lunch university'. And in this respect Kyoraku University was definitely a grade or two above Chiyoda.

The movement of staff between tertiary institutions didn't always run to a set pattern. There were quite a few examples of tutors from a top-class university going to a lecturer's post at a second-class university. But it did seem rather strange that a lecturer from Kyoraku should move to Chiyoda at the same level.

Of course, Yoshihiro might have been offered some special incentive, Etsuko thought. There might be a difference in the waiting period for promotion. If he had been promised promotion from lecturer to senior lecturer after a fixed period of service, he might have decided to sacrifice academic pride for financial gain.

But she also realised that scholars were extremely jealous of their professional reputation. Furthermore, there was a great difference between first, second and third class universities in the research facilities they provided. Therefore it was common for academic staff in a top grade institution to remain there, even if it meant a longer wait for promotion.

If there *was* an acceptable reason for Yoshihiro's move to Chiyoda, then Kawaji must know about it. And if that was so, there had been no need for him to shut up in panic when the conversation touched on the subject . . . Was there something sinister in Yoshihiro's past? Had he run into some kind of trouble at Kyoraku University?

As she kept thinking about this, Etsuko became conscious of a growing tension in her temples. But the moment she saw Yoshihiro return to their table she managed to push her doubts out of her mind. Was she becoming hypersensitive about anything concerning him —because she was falling in love with him?

Kawaji watched Mrs. Araki float out of the shop, then turned to Yoshihiro. "I told Miss Ogata about her."

"Did you?" Yoshihiro grinned painfully. "She's a menace."

Kawaji fixed his eyes on his watch, and said, "Anyway, you should get married as soon as possible." Then he looked up, as if startled by his own words, and sheepishly added, "But what right do *I* have to suggest such a thing?"

They all began to laugh, rather half-heartedly, and Kawaji said, "Now I really must go. Please excuse me, will you?"

From then on their evening followed the usual pattern. Dinner at a quiet restaurant, watching a French musical comedy at the Sukara, strolling through the theatre district, and then a cup of tea—they trod the same path as tens of thousands of other young couples. And then the unexpected happened.

They were sitting in the upstairs tea room of the Amando, a European-style confectionery near Yurakucho station in Asahi Street. Yoshihiro was talking idly about unimportant things.

Listening to his warm, well modulated voice, Etsuko was as close to being completely happy as she had been for a long time. Mrs. Araki's unexpected appearance at the Pensées and Kawaji's disturbing words didn't bother

39

her any more. She watched him stroke his chin with those light fingers that promised her so much pleasure, and she remembered him holding her hand in the theatre, his presence pouring into her senses.

She didn't want to interrupt him—wanted to be with him for just five more minutes, though it was getting late. The only disturbing element was the problem of having to find another excuse when she got home. If her father found out she had been out with a man other than Higuchi, he'd be furious . . .

Then somebody screamed somewhere, and suddenly the street outside was noisy with voices. People around them in the tea room started shouting, too.

"Fire! Let's get out of here! Fire!"

In a moment pandemonium broke out. The customers grabbed their belongings and rushed towards the staircase, all at the same time. The shouting outside grew more violent. The heat and smoke and a crackling noise suggested the fire had now reached the shop.

"Yoshihiro!" she cried out in terror, looking at his face which to her seemed more frightful than the fire itself. He was on his feet but rooted to the ground, his hands at his throat, pulling off his tie and tearing at the white collar of his shirt. And despite the thickening smoke, she could clearly see an ugly red scar around the base of his neck.

His eyes were wide open but vacant. The colour of his lips had changed to purple, and he was trembling, as if about to go into a fit.

"Yoshihiro!" She grabbed him by the arms and frantically began to shake him.

This seemed to work. Slowly he came back to his senses and looked at her, sucking at the smoky air, his eyes running. "Etsuko," he said vaguely, almost as if surprised to find her there. Then the reality of the situation suddenly struck home, and he began to drag her towards the stairs.

For some time afterwards Etsuko felt as if she had been drained of all emotion. She just stood there on the footpath beside him and numbly watched the fire engines arrive and start fighting the blaze, hindered by the milling crowd around them. Then the roof of the building they had just left suddenly exploded, and multicoloured flames lept towards the black sky.

She looked at Yoshihiro and noticed that his eyes were fixed, unblinking, on the column of fire. There was something of that previous vacant expression on his face, and his hands were again fumbling at his throat.

It was obvious to her he must have been through some dreadful experience concerning fires sometime in the past. His reaction to the first shouting of the word 'fire' had been extraordinary—he had become almost paralysed with fear. And he had this red scar around his neck. Was his whole body like that? Had he been terribly burnt all over? That occasional twitch in his cheek—was that a legacy of plastic surgery?

Etsuko decided it was simply a case of pyrophobia. There must be many people like him, just as others suffered from hydrophobia, or claustrophobia. At least the morbid fear of fire, if caused by an unfortunate personal experience, was easier to understand than the dreading of water or confined spaces . . .

Gently she called his name again. He turned towards her slowly, and his tortured face broke into an embarrassed smile.

"I'm sorry," he said. "I must have been acting strangely . . . I have some shocking memories about fires. One day I'll tell you about it . . ."

His words sounded quite normal but contrasted strongly with what he did next. He embraced her roughly and held her very tight, paying no attention to other people around them. He gave the impression of being afraid she might run away if he let her go.

Enduring him helplessly, she was swept by compassion mixed with fear, until she was trembling in his arms.

Meanwhile, the fire was brought under control and the crowd began to disperse. A drunk made some vulgar comments as he tottered past them.

Then at last Yoshihiro released his iron grip on her. Silently they began to walk towards the station.

When she got home that night, Etsuko was still confused. She was aware of a gentle, slow-burning affection for him taking hold of her. That feeling of emptiness she had dreaded so much over the past year was completely gone when she was with Yoshihiro.

On the other hand, she couldn't help being frightened. What was that strange mist clinging so persistently to that lonely figure?

His relative Watanabe, his unexplained transfer to Chiyoda University, and tonight's incident at the fire— all these things might well be trifles hardly worth worrying about. Her fears could be completely groundless. But then why, after getting to know each other to this extent, had Yoshihiro said nothing about his transfer and made only the briefest of comments on Watanabe and his own reaction to fires? What on earth had he been through? And why didn't he tell her frankly about it?

She sat up in bed nervously and stared at the yellow flower pattern on the quilted cover. And then she realised that she herself was afraid of knowing the truth. That was why she didn't have the courage to put these questions to him point-blank.

But one thing was perfectly clear to her—Yoshihiro needed her. She felt it in her bones—especially now, after her experience with him at the fire—that at present she was the only comfort in his life. He needed the reassurance of her feminine warmth and softness, her accommodating gentleness . . . And she herself desperately needed to be needed by someone like him . . .

CHAPTER THREE

On Sunday morning, December 13, Etsuko was getting ready to go for a drive with Yoshihiro.

He had invited her on their last date four days earlier. "Next Sunday I'm going with friends on a car trip around Ashinoko. We may try a wild boar dish on the way back. Would you like to come?"

She hesitated for a moment, and he talked on awkwardly. "As a driver I'm quite hopeless, but my friends have their own car. While I was in the United States I once thought of taking some driving lessons. But over there everybody has his own car, so I decided it was quicker and easier to ask for a lift whenever I had to go somewhere. It was the lazy way out, I know, and now I'm still as bad as ever . . . Incidentally, have you ever tasted wild boar meat?"

"No, I haven't."

"Then you should come and try it. Some people wince at the very mention of it, but actually it's quite tasty. Other meats usually get tough when grilled too long, but this is just the opposite. The longer you grill it the more tender it gets."

"But if you're going to spend the day with your friends, wouldn't I be in the way?"

"No, not at all! Actually, your company will make things much easier for me. Those two have only been married about six months—since last May, I think. I just couldn't bear being exposed to their sweet mood all day."

"Who are they, anyway?"

"The husband is Shoichi Koike, a lawyer like your father. He's been a close friend of ours—I mean my brother and I—since childhood. I wanted to introduce him to you one day in any case."

"You have a brother?"

Yoshihiro looked at her unbelievingly. "Haven't I ever mentioned my brother, Nobumasa? Well I never . . . I'm sorry. He's two years older than me. He works in the chemical research laboratories of Toho Kasei—wrestling with those tortoise-shaped cores all the year round."

"Must be exciting . . . And what about other members of your family?"

An almost invisible shadow passed over his face. "My parents died a long time ago . . . My younger brother died late last year."

"Oh." Etsuko sighed as if in sympathy, but actually in relief. His elder brother was a research chemist with a big company, and he himself was a university lecturer. There was nothing there to be ashamed of, she thought. Everybody should be able to see he came from a talented family of considerable standing. The reason for not telling her anything about his people so far was simply that there hadn't been a suitable opportunity, and he was too modest to brag about it out of place . . .

She no longer had any doubts about the invitation. In fact, she was eager to accept it.

To think I've had my nerves on edge for weeks over this—I must have been out of my mind. Etsuko smiled as she now looked at her face in the mirror, touching up her make-up for the second time. Mr. and Mrs. Koike were picking them up at Yoshihiro's apartment at half

44

past nine, and she had promised to be there a few minutes early.

Then she saw her mother's face in the mirror. It could have been the angle of the light—the face looked delicately pale. A little startled, Etsuko turned around, but her mother's voice was the same as usual.

"Are you going out, Etsu?" she asked.

"Yes, I'm going for a drive."

"With Mr. Higuchi, I suppose?"

"Yes."

Mrs. Ogata paused for a moment, looking at her daughter with motherly concern. Then she said, "Your father has been anxious about your progress with Mr. Higuchi. You don't tell us anything of your dates with him when you come home."

Etsuko cast her eyes down. "Mother, I——"

"Lately a Mr. Tsukamoto has been asking for you on the phone every now and then. Would you mind telling me who he is?"

"He's a lecturer in economics at Chiyoda University, specialising in business management studies. I got acquainted with him by accident, but he's not the type of person you'd have to worry about."

"Well, then it's all right, I suppose . . . But why haven't you told me anything about him before this? I realise you're no longer a child—you don't have to tell your parents everything. But I'm still your mother, and quite frankly, these days I start worrying about you without any special reason whenever I look at you."

Etsuko felt like seizing this opportunity to tell her mother the whole story and then enlist her support. But even if she did that, she still couldn't be sure of her father's attitude, and at this stage she wasn't even sure of her own attitude towards Yoshihiro. Besides, she had to leave in a few minutes. Right now she just didn't have the time to explain it all.

"Look, mother," she said, "I'm quite sure of what I'm doing. There's nothing for you to worry about." She hadn't meant to sound so harsh, but that was how the words came out.

45

Mrs. Ogata took a deep breath and said, "Until now you've never told us a lie, have you, Estu?"

"A lie?"

"Yes. Mr. Higuchi is supposed to be going to a wedding reception today with your father. Or are you saying you're meeting him beforehand?"

"But mother . . ." Even the make-up couldn't hide her pallor now. "How could you trick me like that?"

"I haven't been married thirty years to a lawyer for nothing."

"Mother, I don't think I like you."

"Please don't misunderstand me, Etsu. All I want is seeing you happily married."

"I don't want to listen to you! Just leave me alone!" She grabbed her handbag and rushed out of the room. Her eyes were filled with tears as she put on her shoes in the entry. It was the first time she had ever spoken to her mother like this.

She felt quite sure if she firmly told her parents she didn't want to marry Higuchi, they wouldn't try to force her. And if she could find another respectable man, they would accept him . . .

No one had to be ashamed to see his daughter marry a university lecturer, and her father had always been very fond of her. He was unlikely to insist she should marry a lawyer at any cost. But she couldn't help feeling he would object to Yoshihiro . . .

Until a short while ago her day had been radiant with anticipation, but now the morning no longer looked bright to her. As she headed for Yoshihiro's apartment her heart was weighed down with misery.

She was about to press the button on the door-bell when her finger sprang back, as if it had touched live wire. She heard voices, coming sharply and violently from inside.

You can say what you like, but when they find out about it——

Stop talking rubbish!

46

The last three angry words belonged to Yoshihiro.

Etsuko didn't want to eavesdrop. She walked to the stairwell side of the hallway and leaned against the railing. As the indistinguishable din of the argument kept filtering through to her, she just stood there, filled with apprehension. Why was Yoshihiro so furious? Whom was he arguing with?

Suddenly the door was flung open and a man marched out with shoulders raised, hands in pockets. It was Watanabe, Yoshihiro's relative.

He looked at her, his mouth spreading in a slow grin. "Aah, I see," he said. He turned his head and threw a caustic glance at Yoshihiro who had just appeared in the doorway. "I *thought* you were acting like a racehorse just before the barrier rise. Now I——"

"That's enough! Get out of here before I throw you out!"

"Okay, okay—I'll try again some other time . . ." His eyes worked over Etsuko's body and stopped on her belly. "What's that saying about the man who tried to squeeze in between two lovers?" He gave a lewd cackle and was off, taking two steps at a time on the way down.

With a hang-dog look on his face Yoshihiro asked Etsuko to come inside.

"Whenever you visit me I manage to have an ugly scene put on for your entertainment." He spoke with bitter self-scorn. "Aren't you getting sick of it all? Haven't you had enough of me yet?"

"No, but . . ." She couldn't hold back her tears. The moment she was in his arms, feeling his tense body, her pent-up emotions breached her self-control and gushed freely out of her. "But why can't you get rid of this awful man, even if he *is* your relative?" she asked with sobs in her voice.

Yoshihiro bit his lip and stared at a corner of the ceiling with vacant eyes. "Yes," he said gloomily, "that's what everybody would expect me to do. And to be quite frank, there *are* certain things about him I can't tolerate. But the fact is, I owe my life to him."

"Owe your life to him?" She looked up at him, her

47

mouth open.

"That's right. It happened during the war—we were still young children then. At that time Watanabe was just an ordinary boy. I don't think anyone could've guessed what sort of man he'd become twenty years later, though he did have a tendency to boss the other girls around."

"The war . . . Was it something to do with an air raid?"

"Yes, it *was* during a raid. An incendiary bomb landed very close to our shelter, and soon the whole area was turned into a sea of fire. Everybody was running, crazed with fear. Somehow in the confusion I took the wrong direction. Then I broke my leg. I've never been able to recall how it happened—I was in such a panic—but I couldn't go on . . ." For a moment he seemed to look through the distance of twenty years. "I tried to crawl, but the blaze was all around, closing in on me. Then suddenly I stopped being scared. Calmly I thought this was the end of me—I'd be dead in another minute."

"It was then that Watanabe saved you?"

"Yes. He dragged me onto a bicycle trailer left nearby and began to push me through that inferno, risking his own life . . . Because of Watanabe, I'm alive today."

Etsuko's mind began to clear. It was like the morning mist being lifted by a fresh wind.

Yoshihiro sighed and said, "It depends on how you look at it, I guess. I *could* say I've already repaid my debt to him many times over. I've often helped him out with money over the years, right up to this day . . . But can money pay for life? This may sound strange to you, but I still can't turn him away, even today."

What a warm-hearted person he was, Etsuko thought, deeply touched. Her eyes became misty again.

"I'm so sorry," she whispered. "Without knowing this part of your past, I've been thinking and saying a lot of silly things . . . I've been aware of that scar around your neck since the other day. Is it a reminder of that dreadful day during the war?"

"No," he said, hesitating for a moment. "Since then I've been through another terrible experience in a fire. The scar around my neck belongs to the second fire."

48

"Oh, dear." She sighed deeply. Was it any wonder he had a morbid fear of fire when he had been trapped in it twice?

"Okay," he said, "let's forget about it for now. Koike and his wife will be here any minute . . . Wait, I think they're here now."

The bell rang and Yoshihiro went to the entrance. He opened the door and was faced by a uniformed policeman.

"Excuse me," the policeman said, raising his hand to his cap. "May I come in for a moment?" He stepped inside.

"What *is* it?" Yoshihiro asked, and Etsuko was surprised by the strange tension in his voice and the stiffening of his face. He joined his hands behind his back, and she noticed that his left thumb was twitching.

"This is just a routine check, sir. Some goods were stolen from two ground-floor apartments here last night. You've nothing missing, have you, sir?"

Yoshihiro's face relaxed and his thumb stopped twitching. "No, I don't think so," he said.

"Haven't heard any unusual noise last night?"

"No."

"Or seen any stranger acting suspiciously on the premises?"

"No."

"Well, that's all then. Excuse me for the intrusion, sir." At the door the policeman added, "Please make sure your doors and windows are securely locked when you go out, sir. There've been quite a few thefts reported in this area in the past few days."

He saluted and left, and almost at the same time Mr. and Mrs. Koike walked in. Now completely relaxed and smiling, Yoshihiro introduced Etsuko to them.

Shoichi Koike was about Yoshihiro's age, with a body that looked masculine and energetic. Despite his youth he was a man of commanding presence, and Etsuko thought he must be a very competent lawyer.

His wife, Reiko, was the type of beauty who made even women stop and stare. She was about twenty-four—

49

twenty-five at the most—and was dressed according to the latest whim of the season. She looked as if she had just sneaked out of a fashion parade. Her diamond ring must have cost him at least a few hundred thousand yen. In her presence Etsuko was painfully aware of her own lack of height and excess weight.

"Well, this *is* a pleasure," Koike said cordially, with an easy smile on his strong, handsome face. "You are Mr. Ogata's daughter, aren't you?"

"Yes."

"I've great respect for your father—faced him once in a civil action, two or three years ago. He was senior counsel for the plaintiff, and I was junior counsel for the defendant. This may sound funny, but I was greatly impressed by his performance, even though he was representing the other side. I was a raw youngster at the time and had the depressing feeling he was altogether too good for us. We lost, of course . . ."

Etsuko went through the motions—answering questions, paying compliments, smiling cheerfully always at the right time, laughing at jokes—but her heart was not in it. Whenever she had a moment to herself she kept thinking of the scene which had taken place just before the Koike's arrival. Yoshihiro's reaction to the appearance of that policeman had been most unusual . . .

Admittedly, some people felt uncomfortable in the presence of a policeman even if they didn't have a guilty conscience. But Yoshihiro's behaviour had suggested he was *afraid* of the police. When he had realised the policeman's business concerned a simple stealing incident, his tenseness eased immediately . . .

Would he by any chance have a criminal record? The idea cropped up unexpectedly, and she immediately dismissed it. If he had a record, he couldn't work as a lecturer at a fairly well known university.

But she could think of no other reason for him to be afraid of the police . . . This was torture. Her doubts were like a crazy balloon that kept expanding and deflating all the time.

Sitting beside him in the car, Etsuko glanced at Yoshihiro's profile. Certainly there was a shadow lurking there somewhere. But even when she tried to look at him with the most critical eyes, she simply couldn't believe he was a bad man . . .

The Koike couple in the front seat looked perfectly blissful. Somehow they gave Etsuko the impression that every single cell in their bodies was thoroughly enjoying the new married state. If she became Yoshihiro's wife, could they be as happy as those two? She felt that strange anxiety gnawing at her again.

On the evening of December 19 Etsuko and Yoshihiro were sitting in a Chinese restaurant, enjoying a special dish. It was after seven o'clock, and to her relief their day together had passed without any disturbing incident. This *was* a change, she thought wryly, feeling that at last she was beginning to regain her peace of mind.

They were about to get up and leave when once again the unexpected happened. But this time it was Etsuko, not Yoshihiro, who turned pale. The moment she saw the two men walk into the restaurant the blood began to drain from her face.

One of them was an old man of about sixty, wearing *haori* and *hakama*—the full Japanese dress. She didn't know him, but she knew only too well his companion, Tetsuya Higuchi . . .

Higuchi noticed her immediately. He stopped at the entrance for a moment and shot her a sharp glance. She closed her eyes without being conscious of it. If this had happened any other time she mightn't have panicked so much, but only that morning she had asked him on the phone to postpone their date till tomorrow, giving him a plausible excuse. Now she felt as if she had been caught red-handed . . .

She imagined Higuchi boil up inside with rage, march over to their table, demand to know who her companion was, and then run straight to her father and tell him all about it. It was sure to happen, she thought, but there was nothing she could do about it now.

Well, too bad . . . She decided she couldn't care less and opened her eyes.

Higuchi seemed to have just made up his mind—he began to walk towards them. Then to Etsuko's amazement the old man in full dress called out, "Hey, is that you, Yoshihiro?"

Yoshihiro awkwardly rose to his feet and made one or two half-hearted steps towards the man.

"I'm glad to see you, Mr. Kumagaya," he mumbled as they met.

"How are you, my boy? Haven't seen you for ages! You've changed so much—look so respectable—that's why I didn't recognise you straight away."

"You are looking well, Mr. Kumagaya." Yoshihiro's politeness couldn't hide his discomfort.

Etsuko thought he was either embarrassed by the old man's emotional approach, or just wasn't very keen to meet him for some reason. She would have liked to listen to their conversation, but Higuchi had just reached her. He kept his eyes on her but didn't say anything, and she decided to take the initiative.

She stood up and said, "I'll introduce you."

She touched Yoshihiro on the shoulder, and he stopped half way through a sentence and turned from the old man towards them. It was all very sudden and awkward. Yoshihiro looked confused, and she felt her cheeks flush. Only Higuchi remained completely calm.

"Mr. Yoshihiro Tsukamoto, lecturer in economics at Chiyoda University . . . Mr. Tetsuya Higuchi, junior partner in my father's law firm."

"How d'you do," Higuchi said, looking at Yoshihiro like a prosecutor.

"How d'you do," Yoshihiro echoed, and for a moment there was an ominous silence. Then, as if he had read her mind, he added, "Now, you must excuse us—we have to be on our way . . . Hope to see you again, Mr. Kumagaya, some other time." He began to walk towards the entrance, his hand firmly planted on Etsuko's shoulder.

Outside in the chilly night air a little later, she shivered and he tightened his arm around her.

He said, "Isn't this a queer coincidence? Mr. Kumagaya knew my late father, and the fellow with him happens to be in your father's firm. It's a small world, isn't it?"

"Was Mr. Kumagaya an acquaintance of your father?"

"Yes . . ."

She felt he wanted to say some more but held back for some reason. For her part, she was ready to tell him about Higuchi.

"Yoshihiro," she said resolutely, "my father wants me to marry Mr. Higuchi."

She waited for his reaction with bated breath, hoping the next few words would change the course of her life, but nothing happened. He just tightened his arm around her shoulders a bit more and gazed at the neon lights ahead, as if hypnotised by them. She looked up at his face and saw an oddly twisted expression on it, suggesting a conflict in his mind. Or was it just blind anger?

Etsuko felt like bursting into tears. She would have loved to sob, to cry out loudly, to make shrill noises . . .

That night she hardly slept at all, and throughout the following morning kept toying with the idea of calling off her date with Higuchi, pretending to be ill, though she realised this would be a rather transparent excuse. Finally she began to dress. She was ready when Higuchi called in the afternoon.

As she got into his car she was waiting for his questions about Yoshihiro, but he didn't even raise the subject. He acted as if he had completely forgotten about the whole thing.

If his idea was to punish her by keeping her in suspense, he certainly was succeeding, Etsuko thought. Throughout the afternoon she felt as if she were sitting and walking on pins and needles.

It was not until they had settled down to dinner in a restaurant on the Ginza that he first mentioned the previous night's incident.

"This Mr. Tsukamoto I met last night—is he really a lecturer in economics at a university?"

"Yes, of course."

"I wonder."

"But why?" Etsuko looked at him wide-eyed.

"Well," Higuchi said, "for a university lecturer he has some strange friends, I must say . . . Do you know who that old man is?"

"No."

"He's Sogo Kumagaya, leader of a fairly well known right-wing extremist group."

"A political group?"

"Yes, and it's not one of those newfangled terrorist gangs that specialise in blackmail and other criminal rackets. Kumagaya has been right-wing to the core since pre-war days. His organisation is called Kokoku Dojinkai. To this day it displays mottoes of the movement which attempted to restore direct imperial rule in the early part of the Showa period. In other words, they're hopelessly outdated. They claim to be a party concerned only with ideology and high principles, but in their actions they're not very different from all the other right-wing ratbags. During the U.S.-Japan security pact riot, Kumagaya was seen dashing about at the head of his young followers, wearing a white head-band."

"But what business do *you* have with a man like that?"

"Not so long ago some of his supporters got themselves into trouble, and I was asked to undertake their defence. So it was necessary for Mr. Kumagaya to brief me on background and some of the facts. I can't say I'm very enthusiastic about this case—it's pretty hopeless, anyway—but as you know, I'm duty-bound to do all I can for my clients." He paused for two gulps of water, lifting the glass to his lips in his best bar-table manner. "What happened was that three chaps from his group were walking past a factory where a strike was being held. A few nasty words were exchanged, and then the young bloods assaulted some of the workers forming the picket line . . . These fellows are like fighting bulls—as soon as they see something red they go for it . . . Well, there isn't very much I can do for them, really. I was going to base their defence on provocation by the factory workers, but to my dismay the old man ordered me to put the emphasis on 'activation by an intense spirit of patriotism' . . ."

Etsuko was too impatient to pay much attention to Higuchi. What had been his father's connection with this eccentric old man? Had they been close friends? As she asked these questions, her doubts about Yoshihiro began to inflate again.

Higuchi said, "Except for some very old men, most academics have connections with left-wing groups, if anything. When it comes to right-wing extremists, they certainly prefer to remain at a respectable distance. Tsukamoto is quite unusual in this, I'd say."

"Didn't you ask Mr. Kumagaya about their relationship?"

"Of course I did, but the old man gave an evasive answer, revealing very little. I gained the impression he might be under some obligation to the Tsukamoto family. And he might have decided it wouldn't be to Tsukamoto's advantage if he told me about their relationship. In the matter of personal loyalty no one can beat these right-wing people. I don't think I would've got any further with him if he'd been in the box under oath."

Higuchi's every word was a hammer blow, driving the wedge a little further between Yoshihiro and Etsuko. The waiter had just served the soup, but she was hardly aware of its taste.

When they were having coffee at the end of the meal, Higuchi knitted his brows and lowered his voice till it was almost inaudible.

"Etsuko," he said, "this may sound a little out of place here, but I'm sure we could establish a fine home together . . . With your assistance as my wife, I think I could become a very successful lawyer . . ." This was the first time since they had started going out together that he spelt out his intentions so clearly. His face seemed to be lit up by the spirit of contest. "My decision to ask you to

55

become my wife isn't based on reckless impulse or obstinacy. I've reached the conclusion there's no other woman as suitable as you are to become my life partner . . ."

Etsuko didn't answer. Higuchi was a stiff man, she thought, but he was also steady and totally reliable. As a husband his average would be higher than Yoshihiro's. On the other hand, she couldn't help feeling that everything he did was based on calculation, and there was no warmth in him at all.

". . . Therefore I'm going to stick it out till you say yes, no matter how long it'll take. I'll never give up, no matter what you may feel or have on your mind at the moment." He raised his cup and drank the rest of his coffee, then once again fixed her with his sharp eyes. "And should a rival appear on the scene, I'm ready to engage him—and he'll lose his footing in the end." He roughly slammed down the cup on the saucer, almost breaking it.

CHAPTER FOUR

Two days later Etsuko was spending the evening at the home of Takako Shibazaki.

Takako was one of Etsuko's friends in the Kinome group. Early last year she had married an official of the diplomatic service, and now he had been suddenly transferred to Paris. They were to leave for the new post at the beginning of the new year, and this was Takako's farewell party.

Etsuko arrived a little late. All the other women were already there.

Takako came to the entrance to meet her. "This is going to be a real chin-wag session," she said. "My husband will only stay a few minutes before escaping to his book upstairs. Then the girls can really let their hair down."

"I'm sorry I won't be able to see you for years, but isn't it wonderful—going to Paris? I'm very happy for you."

"It's not as wonderful as it sounds. My French is terrible, so I've already got a headache. I took some panic lessons, and also tried to practise with linguaphone records, but it's too late, I'm afraid."

They reached the visitors' room. Seven young women were sitting around, and one of them was Kyoko Kirishima, *his* wife . . .

Etsuko knew Kyoko would be there. She was both prepared for it and afraid of it, and now she was amazed she could take it so well. Yoshihiro's appearance on the scene since she had burnt Kyoko's wedding invitation not quite two months ago must have worked wonders, she thought. She had imagined that on meeting her friend again, waves of affection and envy would crash, sending up sprays of emotion. But now she only felt ashamed of having hurt Kyoko by avoiding her for more than a year.

"Glad I can repeat my good wishes in person," Etsuko whispered when they had a chance to exchange a few private words.

"Thanks." For just a fleeting moment Kyoko's eyes clouded with regret, but almost immediately the warm, good-natured smile returned to her round face. After only two months of married life she hadn't quite lost her girlishness yet, but she already seemed to possess a new calm and self-confidence. "I was longing to see you, Etsu."

Her words were so obviously genuine, they made Etsuko's heart fill with tenderness. Impulsively she took Kyoko's hand—and felt she had found her dear friend again. She knew she still wouldn't want to meet Saburo Kirishima—not yet, anyway—but she also knew Kyoko had permanently re-entered her life.

"Let's have a good yarn after the party," she suggested.

"Mm-hm," Kyoko nodded and gave an impish smile.

They stopped at a coffee shop on their way home, and Etsuko immediately launched into a recital of her problems. She had been wrestling with them on her own for so many weeks now—the mere telling of them to someone was a great relief to her.

"So that's it," Kyoko said as Etsuko stopped talking. "Somehow I sensed you had something on your mind

. . . Yes, it must be awful having to go through day after day doubting him when you're so fond of him." She gave a prolonged sigh. "It's easy enough for me to use my common sense, because I'm not involved. Well, the safest thing to do would be to marry Mr. Higuchi, I'd say. I'm not surprised your parents are encouraging you to do that. But I couldn't bring myself to give you the same advice at this stage. If things remain as they are at present and you marry Mr. Higuchi, you'll be left with a lingering affection for Mr. Tsukamoto, and that'd be dangerous, don't you think?"

Etsuko nodded. "I wish I could have complete faith in him regardless of what other people might say . . ."

"That's not easy, especially when you've only known him a short time . . . On the other hand, it's so easy for people to become estranged, even hostile, over trifles. They often regret it afterwards when it's too late, realising they allowed a happy relationship to be ruined by small misunderstandings. You too could find later that either your doubts have been without foundation, or his shortcomings have been vastly exaggerated in your mind."

"This may be so, only in his case——"

"As I was listening to you I couldn't help recalling the case of a man who nearly went to the gallows on a false charge earlier this year. You probably remember it—my husband was the investigating prosecutor, and I myself got caught up in it in the end."

"Of course I remember. Wasn't the man's name Segawa?"

"That's right. Well, the case against him began with a number of small doubts that gradually grew into an overwhelming suspicion."

Etsuko looked at Kyoko hopefully. "Do you think the same might apply to Yoshihiro—small, unimportant doubts coming together by coincidence?"

"Well, I can't be sure, of course . . . But I wouldn't be surprised at all if some of your doubts could be removed simply by taking a good look at them."

"For instance?"

59

"For instance the fact that Mr. Tsukamoto moved from Kyoraku University to Chiyoda without promotion. Outsiders may imagine that university people rely on their academic ability alone for advancement. But once you're on the inside, you realise the place is crawling with sycophants, and departmental heads often try to act as if they were feudal lords. Now, supposing Mr. Tsukamoto had clashed with his professor over something, and felt his chances of promotion at that university had been ruined forever? Wouldn't it be natural for him to try to make a fresh start at another university which happened to offer him a post? And if this *was* the case, I don't think anybody at Kyoraku University would admit it. Mr. Tsukamoto himself would probably be reluctant to talk about it."

Etsuko raised her hand and mechanically began to stroke her upswept hair, as if to gather loose strands. "Yes, this makes sense," she said. "But then why did his friend, Mr. Kawaji, stop talking about it so suddenly?"

"He might have realised he shouldn't talk about something given him in confidence. Or perhaps he thought you might misunderstand him. You must remember this was the first time he'd met you—he didn't have much idea of your level of intelligence."

"Yes, that's true . . . But what if——"

"If Mr. Tsukamoto did commit an offence, or do something improper as a scholar, he wouldn't have been offered a lecturer's post at Chiyoda University. As far as I know, university authorities are very strict about such things."

"I think so, too," Etsuko said, still frowning but feeling somewhat relieved.

Kyoko took a long breath before going on. "So far as this right-wing man is concerned, there's no reason to doubt Mr. Tsukamoto's word that Mr. Kumagaya was an acquaintance of his late father. The point here is that the word 'acquaintance' covers a very wide range of relationships. Supposing you were walking down the street with an acquaintance. Suddenly an underworld boss with six criminal convictions came up to you and said he was greatly indebted to your father. What would your acquaintance think of that?"

"You're presupposing, of course, that my acquaintance happened to recognise the underworld boss but didn't know my father was a lawyer."

"That's right . . . Well, the chances are your acquaintance would be anxious to say goodbye to you as soon as possible, thinking you might be the daughter of an even bigger underworld boss with *eight* criminal convictions."

Etsuko couldn't help bursting into laughter. This further relieved the tension in her mind. She thought she had done the right thing consulting Kyoko.

But Kyoko maintained her serious, questioning expression. "On the other hand," she said, "it's just as easy to go to the opposite extreme and interpret everything to Mr. Tsukamoto's advantage. To get rid of your doubts forever, I think the best thing for you to do would be to go straight to Mr. Tsukamoto and put all your questions to him. Don't you agree?"

"Yes, I thought of that myself many times, but somehow I was always reluctant to broach the subject . . . To be quite honest with you, I think I was afraid of learning the truth."

"I appreciate how you feel. Anyone would be reluctant to ask awkward questions of the man she likes. But if you're thinking of marrying Mr. Tsukamoto, you'll just have to make the effort one day, won't you? Besides, it's not necessary to throw all your doubts at him at once. You can clear them up one by one over a period of time, can't you? You've already asked him about his relative, Mr. Watanabe. Well, in the same way, you can bring up each of the other things as the opportunity presents itself."

"You're probably right . . ." Etsuko stared into her cup for a while. Gradually her face became resolute. "Okay, I'll try. And Kyoko, thank you so much for your help."

At last her mind was at ease. She knew that for the first time in a week she would sleep well that night.

No definite conclusion had been reached one way or

the other, but at least the need for taking more time—the fact that there was no other alternative at this stage—had been established. This in itself was very reassuring to her.

At the same time she was amazed by the growth of Kyoko's personality. She had always fancied herself as an elder sister to Kyoko, but now she felt their roles had been reversed. Admittedly, personal involvement did affect one's behaviour—it made one timid, even blind. But she sensed that the change in Kyoko—her mature outlook—was due to more than detachment. It had to do with her happiness in marriage.

Early in the new year suddenly a turning point was reached in Etsuko's relationship with Yoshihiro.

He had been away in the Kansai district for the last few days of December and the first week in January, showing around an American professor he had worked under during his Fulbright scholarship year.

When Etsuko met him again on January 10, Yoshihiro was so busy he didn't even have time for a leisurely talk. Higuchi had paid a visit to the family on January 2, but after that there had been no sign of him either. He had told her that immediately on resuming work after the holidays he would have to attend a court hearing at Kyoto. Etsuko couldn't care less about it.

On January 15, a public holiday, she was to meet Yoshihiro in the Café Étude at Shibuya. This time he was with a man a little older than himself and about the same height and build.

"Etsuko, this is my elder brother Nobumasa," Yoshihiro said. "He had some business around here, so we came together."

She wasn't fooled by him—his eyes were telling a different story. Obviously, he had arranged this meeting.

The features of the two brothers had very little in common. Against Yoshihiro's rather boyish face, Nobumasa had heavy eyebrows, steady eyes, a pointed nose and prominent chin. His whole face was made up of acute angles. He certainly looked very sharp, Etsuko thought. And his skin seemed to radiate some strange energy.

She was awed by him at first, but in the course of the conversation her apprehension gradually dissolved. Nobumasa himself seemed to be developing a friendly feeling towards her.

"Yoshihiro has his share of shortcomings," he said, "but I do hope you'll go on putting up with him. Whether he has any talent as an economist I wouldn't know, since I'm a chemist. He's supposed to be an expert on management, but in some respects he seems to do a lot worse than I in managing his own affairs . . . Well, this may be due to the difference between people who work for business enterprise and those who lock themselves away in ivory towers."

Yoshihiro gave a slow, sardonic smile. "My brother surprises me," he said. "He has always been able to twist me around his little finger, but as far as I can remember, this is the first time he has ever praised me."

From their bantering tone Etsuko deducted the two were very close.

"Well," Nobumasa said condescendingly, "I do recognise your good points, of course. I could list them in no time, but what good would that do? Being your elder brother I feel I should concentrate on your numerous faults so that Etsuko could file them away in her memory and launch a corrective programme in due course."

Etsuko nodded in mock agreement and thought Nobumasa was thoroughly enjoying himself at Yoshihiro's expense.

He said, "To begin with, my brother doesn't know how to get along with people, nor does he have the knack of getting the most out of life. To give you a simple example —if only he paid a little more attention to his appearance, he'd create a much better impression all round, but despite my repeated pleas, he remains completely hopeless in this. He's also too good-natured, too modest, and this puts him at a disadvantage. These days even a scholar must have some push, some cheek—a willingness to play to the audience . . . Etsuko, I hope you can help him wake up to himself."

My brother doesn't know how to get along with people. The words got stuck in Etsuko's mind. She thought it was quite possible Yoshihiro had moved from Kyoraku University to Chiyoda because of a clash with his professor, as Kyoko had suggested. It might have been entirely his own fault, but if it wasn't, then it indicated uprightness and sincerity . . .

Later Nobumasa invited them to lunch and took them to a Russian restaurant. By the time they were choosing the hors d'oeuvre after finishing a bottle of beer, Etsuko had a definite liking for Nobumasa.

"And what've you been doing lately, brother?" Yoshihiro asked.

"I'm working with those so-called highly polymerised compounds. There are vast unexplored areas in this field, hence the world-wide interest in it. I hope I don't sound too pompous, but this is the type of research which is currently expanding the frontiers of modern chemistry."

"Highly polymerised compounds?" Yoshihiro gave Etsuko a sideways glance and made his mouth droop at the corners. "Would you mind giving us an example—something that might have a name we can understand?"

"Well, you must have seen words like polyurethane, polyester, polyethylene and so on. Do you know what the prefix 'poly' means?"

"Yes, big brother," he said schoolboyishly. "It derives from the Greek 'polus', meaning 'many'. In music, 'polyphony' means a composition in which two or more melodies blend in harmony."

"I believe you—music has never been my strong point. Well, in chemistry every word beginning with 'poly' denotes a highly polymerised compound known as a polymer, which has the same percentage composition as some other compound but a different molecular weight. Have I made myself clear? . . . So far as polyester is concerned, it divides into resins—my special interest—and fibres, like tetron. The resin system is the more complicated. There is alkyd polyester, unsaturated polyester and——" He stopped suddenly and looked at Etsuko. "I think that's enough—Yoshihiro is making a very unpleasant face."

Nobumasa finished his meal in high spirits and later said goodbye to them in front of the restaurant.

"You've got a nice brother," Etsuko said, looking at Nobumasa's receding back.

"He's all right, though he likes to bung it on a bit . . . He told you I didn't have the knack of getting the most out of life, but funnily enough he himself has a king-size blind spot."

"Concerning what?"

"Women."

"How come?"

"Some time ago he had an affair, and rightly or wrongly, the woman blamed him for the result and tried to force him to marry her. It was a tight squeeze for him for a while, and ever since he's been pretty sour on women generally. That's why I was so surprised to see him open up to you as he did today. Normally he sticks to absolute essentials when he meets somebody for the first time, especially if it's a woman."

That evening Yoshihiro had to write an article for *Management,* so they ended their date early and Etsuko returned home. She was very pleased about meeting Nobumasa. It suggested Yoshihiro might gradually come around to discussing with her the things she wanted to ask.

But her happy mood didn't last long.

Straight after dinner her father looked at her sternly and said, "Etsu, I want to have a talk with you. Let's go into the study."

She winced inside, remembering from childhood that whenever he put on that face he was about to upbraid her, or at least say something very unpleasant. Following him into the study she felt as if her feet were dragging a chain.

Right from the start his voice was harsh and unyield-

65

ing. "You've been going out with a Yoshihiro Tsukamoto, haven't you?"

She bit her lip and nodded.

"Are you in love with him?"

"Yes."

Ogata wiped his forehead and stared at the blotter on his desk.

"I'm your father," he said quietly, "and I want to respect your feelings. I've no intention of forcing you to marry Mr. Higuchi. A university lecturer may be a suitable match." He paused and looked up at her. "But Mr. Tsukamoto is a special case. Any suggestion of your marrying him is firmly opposed, not only by me, but also by your mother."

"But why?" She felt her throat tighten. Her doubts about Yoshihiro's past began to rise like a black storm cloud.

"Listen, Etsu—listen carefully. An individual may be perfectly respectable when looked at in isolation, but when it comes to marriage, his family background must be considered. A girl blinded by love may think this is unfair, even ridiculous, but after a while—once her head is clear again—those same considerations may well lead her to divorce . . . Please don't misunderstand me. I'm not suggesting your future husband should come from a family of outstanding lineage or wealth. But unless he meets at least the minimum requirement demanded by common sense, I simply can't allow my daughter to marry him."

"But why shouldn't he meet this minimum requirement, as you call it? He himself is a Master of Economics, and his brother is a Doctor of Chemical Engineering, working in the research laboratories of Toho Kasei."

"There's nothing wrong with him or his brother. But hasn't he ever told you anything about his father?"

Etsuko had no answer. When she thought of it, Yoshihiro had hardly said anything about his parents. Both were dead—that was all . . . Lamely she shook her head.

"I thought so. He didn't have the guts to tell you the

66

truth. His father, Shinnosuke Tsukamoto, died in prison."

"Died in prison?" The words floored her. Her dull repetition of them carried a warning of hysteria. She had the illusion of her father's face dividing into three and glaring at her from three different angles.

"That's right," he said sadly. "Young people of your generation may not know this, but Shinnosuke Tsukamoto was a fairly well known figure in his own time. He was a scholar of Japanese history with a fanatical ultra-nationalistic viewpoint. He had been on friendly terms with men like Shumei Ookawa and others branded as criminals at the Tokyo war trials. His philosophy, an adaptation of Nazism with some ancestor worship added, had a fairly strong influence on young soldiers. As the war dragged on, his followers started a witch hunt against suspected internationalists and pacifists, and soon they earned themselves the nickname 'Private Political Police' . . ."

Ogata shifted in his chair and lowered his voice. "Well, to a man like him the sudden end of the war must have been a much greater shock than to others. On August 14, 1945, the eve of the Japanese surrender, he was involved in the well known revolt by junior officers. They tried to force their way into the Imperial Palace and seize the recording of the Emperor's surrender broadcast, after killing the comanding officer of the guards. He was also present, leading dozens of civilians, when the private home of the then Prime Minister, Kantaro Suzuki, was set on fire. I think he must have lost his reason by then . . ."

Etsuko listened with mounting excitement. So this was the source of that persistent shadow surrounding Yoshi-hiro. His fate of being saddled with a father like that must be playing on his mind all the time . . .

". . . The revolt was put down overnight. Its leader, Major Hatanaka, killed himself in front of the Imperial Palace. Most of the civilians involved also committed suicide at Atagoyama or Yoyogi. But Shinnosuke Tsukamoto didn't try to end his own life. Instead, he went into hiding and was arrested three months later. It was a period of confusion just after the end of the war, and the old criminal law was still in force. Even before a preliminary hearing could be arranged, he died of illness in prison, so no conviction was ever recorded against him . . ."

Ogata poured himself a glass of water and slowly drank it, looking into the distance through the window. Then he said, "Naturally, this type of offence is different from an ordinary crime. Even the former Prime Minister, Mr. Yoshida, was put into a military lockup during the war. There were many examples of consciencious objectors dying in prison. If we could look upon Tsukamoto's case as simply the opposite extreme, then we could leave the matter at that. Yes, considering the frenzied atmosphere of those days, we could almost sympathise with him—except for one thing. Why didn't he commit suicide together with his followers? Why did he allow himself to be labelled a coward, as well as a fanatic?"

"But father——"

"Wait a minute," Ogata said, raising his hand. "This business about his father is not the only problem your friend's got. There's a very good reason for his resignation from Kyoraku University and his transfer to Chiyoda . . . At the end of the year before last he went to a hot spring resort far up in the mountains of the Sanin district. One night the inn he stayed at was gutted by fire and he suffered serious burns, narrowly escaping death. His younger brother, who was with him, was burnt to death."

So this was the second fire he had been through, Etsuko thought. But why didn't he tell her he had lost his younger brother in it? She felt her brain slowly going numb and her nerves tightening at the same time.

"Your friend was soon restored to health, I understand, but somehow he has never been quite the same since. At the end of last March he himself decided to move to Tokyo."

"The shock of losing his brother would explain this, wouldn't it?"

"Yes, but the matter seems to be a bit more complicated than that. There's something fishy about his dead brother, too. It has been suggested he was on the wrong side of the law—we're looking into that right now. Anyway, it's most unlikely your friend would've changed his place of work just because of his brother's accidental death. No, there was another reason . . . I understand about three years ago he fell in love with the daughter of a company president who wields considerable influence in the Kansai business world. At first the girl's parents were quite enthusiastic about Mr. Tsukamoto, but just before the engagement the whole thing was suddenly called off. And I'm told that while the father's history did have a bearing on it, the main reason was the doings of the younger brother."

Ogata's every word tore into her, until she was on the verge of tears. How much Yoshihiro had to suffer through no fault of his own . . .

"He's not responsible for any of those things," she said with a quiver in her voice. "He can't be blamed for everything . . ."

"You're quite right," he said soothingly. "I too have sympathy for Mr. Tsukamoto. Had I made his acquaintance by chance and subsequently discovered those unsavoury facts about his family, I certainly wouldn't have broken with him on that account. But when it comes to marriage, things just can't be taken so lightly. One black sheep is bad enough, but he has two in his family. One can't help thinking there must be an ominous streak in him, too. It's often said that only a thin line separates genius from madness. The two living brothers may be fine people with outstanding ability, but how can you be sure the insanity of their dead father and brother isn't in their blood?"

Ogata made his voice as soft as he could. "Etsu, dear, I know it'll be hard for you to give him up. You've had one heartbreak fairly recently, and now this—but I'm sure you'll get over it soon enough. While there are plenty of eligible men about, there's no reason why you should marry one with a black cloud hanging around him. Admittedly, his questionable father and brother are both dead, so they wouldn't personally cause any trouble, but there's every possibility the mad streak in them would show up in your children. And if that happened, the trouble would persist, not only through your own lifetime, but right through to your grandchildren's generation and beyond . . ."

Etsuko no longer could control the tears which had been glistening behind her glasses for some time—they slowly began to roll down her cheeks. Her father's words had been most reasonable. Faced with so many unfavourable factors, no parent in his right mind could do anything but oppose this marriage proposal.

And yet, her father's words had produced in her a feeling which was directly opposite to what he would have expected. She felt relieved because her doubts about Yoshihiro had been completely removed.

Now it didn't look at all strange to her that he had a natural dislike for the police. Because of his younger brother, there must have been many occasions in the past when he had to contact the police, much as he would have despised the idea. Being afraid to reveal anything about his dead brother, it was also natural for him to avoid going into details about the second fire, which had involved that brother. It had also been quite reasonable for Kawaji to fall suddenly silent when the conversation had touched on Yoshihiro's transfer. And since his father had been that kind of man, it was understandable he had been associated with a person like Sogo Kumagaya . . .

Suddenly she recalled the scene at the fire when Yoshihiro had embraced her so tightly, as if afraid she might run away. Her instinct had been right—he needed her. After years of loneliness and quiet suffering, at last he had found relief and reassurance in her feminine warmth and softness, her understanding gentleness.

She knew her father had no idea how she felt. That's why he looked so self-satisfied.

"So far as the dead brother is concerned," Ogata said, "I know the story isn't complete, but soon we'll have the full information. On the last occasion there wasn't enough time to investigate—Mr. Higuchi could only use his off-duty hours while in Kyoto."

"Mr. Higuchi?" The mention of the name set off in her an explosion that sent her to her feet. It shattered her previous conclusion that her father's words had been reasonable. She could see Higuchi now—sitting opposite her in the restaurant, declaring war on Yoshihiro—and felt the blood rush to her neck and cheeks.

Ogata seemed to realise he had made a mistake and looked uncertain for a moment, but soon he regained his composure. He said, "I hope you're not suggesting Mr. Higuchi has deliberately distorted the facts? He'd be incapable of such meanness, I can assure you. His sole concern is for your——"

"Stop it, father! I've had enough of Mr. Higuchi!" Her own shrill voice helped to whip up her anger. "Even if all you've said is true, I'm still going to marry Mr. Tsukamoto! Nothing you've told me has anything to do with him at all . . . What if his father *was* an ultra-nationalist? I'm hardly qualified to condemn Mr. Tsukamoto for that. I myself have a father who willingly served the military as a prosecutor during the war."

"Etsu!" He turned red in the face and the veins began to bulge in his temples, but he managed to control his anger. "You'd better be more careful. You can't say such things without knowing the actual circumstances. I did all I could at the time to uphold the dignity of the law in the face of absurd demands by the military. But you wouldn't know this, of course, and I will not tolerate your insolent remarks."

"Oh, yes," she said spitefully, "when the war was over, suddenly everybody became an anti-militarist. They all started talking about democracy, turning up their palms and pretending they knew nothing about the war years. Compared with them, I think Shinnosuke Tsukamoto was an admirable person, even if he was wrong. And who can say he was wrong, anyway?"

Ogata looked weary, and very angry. Quietly he said, "Despite all I've told you—all I've explained to you so clearly—you still go on talking rubbish."

She babbled on for a while, hardly knowing what she

was saying, or what she was going to say next. Then she caved in and began to cry, quietly at first but quickly working up into a state of hysteria. And then, amid the harsh sobs, a preposterous idea was born.

She lifted her tear-stained face and said, with sobs in her voice, "Father, it's no use . . . I can't marry anyone but him . . . I'm carrying his child."

"What?" His eyes narrowed. There was a white line around his tight lips. He got up, walked around his desk and slapped her across the face, the force of the blow sending her reeling against the wall. "You fool! I didn't bring you up for this!"

She was leaning against the wall, holding her face, thinking that her father had never hit her before.

Ogata became deadly pale. Still standing there in front of his desk, he began to tremble. He looked as if he had suddenly aged ten years.

His wife was now by his side, assisting him back to his chair. "I'm sorry, Takuzo," she whispered. "I should've watched her more carefully . . . What can we do now? . . . We'll have to think about it . . . We must apoligise to Mr. Higuchi . . ."

Etsuko walked out of the room. They didn't try to stop her—just watched her in silent grief.

CHAPTER FIVE

For a moment Yoshihiro was lost for words when he opened his front door and found Etsuko standing there, shivering in her coat, her eyes swollen from crying.

"You? . . . At this time of night, with a face like that? . . . What happened?"

She didn't answer, and he pulled her inside.

As soon as she had her shoes and coat off she went into his arms and started crying again, her cheek pressed against the thick cloth of his winter kimono.

"Come on, let's go inside—it's too cold in here."

He led her into the Japanese room which looked cosy with the glow of an electric heater in one corner. A desk-lamp threw its light on sheets of paper scattered on the low-slung table, leaving the rest of the room almost in semi-darkness. There was a stack of three or four heavy volumes on the floor between the table and a set of bedding laid out alongside the wall.

"I was about to go to bed with a book," he said, pointing to the bed-clothes on the *tatami*-covered floor. "The place is in the usual mess."

She ignored his comments and once more moved into

his arms. The tears started rolling down her cheeks again.

"What's wrong?" Impatiently he took her face into his hands and forced her to look up at him.

"Had a quarrel with my father."

"Ah. I see."

Suddenly she put her arms around his neck and said, "Yoshihiro, would you marry me?"

He winced. "Of course I would, but——"

"I told my father a lie. I said I was carrying your child."

"You what?" He stared at her in disbelief. "But why?"

"I had to do it . . . Will you marry me?"

"I—I've been dreaming about it but——"

"Are you worrying about your father and younger brother? Well, don't—I already know all about them. My father told me the whole story tonight."

His face stiffened. Gently but firmly he removed her arms from around his neck and made her settle down on a cushion beside the table. He sat down in his usual place.

"Tell me about it," he said evenly.

Etsuko repeated the whole conversation with her father as faithfully as she could.

He listened without interrupting her. As he lit a cigarette, the flame of the lighter sharpened the concentrated furrows on his face.

When she stopped talking, he said, "I'm sorry . . . *I* should've told you all this, but I didn't have the courage to do it. I was afraid of losing you—wanted to hold on to you as long as I could. That's why I kept putting it off . . ."

She reached out and placed her hand over his. He looked at her silently for a while.

"So far as my father's concerned, there's nothing more I can add, except that I've no interest whatsoever in right-wing politics—or any politics, for that matter . . . Phew. What my brother and I had to go through because of my father . . . Nobumasa swore he'd never have anything to do with ideologies, right or left. That's why he became a chemist, and that's why I plunged into business management studies—something that wasn't tainted with ideologies."

His face looked handsome with its tight frown, Etsuko thought as she listened to him. Still shaken with the emotional upheaval of the past few hours, she now felt a physical desire for him. As she kept holding his hand, the touch of his fingers began to send waves of reverberating tremors through her. She wanted to be touched by him all over.

"And now I must tell you something more about my younger brother," he said. "To begin with, all my maternal uncles died in the war. To maintain the family name Yasuda, my mother's parents formally adopted my brother while still a small child. So he became Tada-aki Yasuda . . . My father's death in prison was a greater shock to him than to anyone else. Nobumasa and I were already old enough to understand he didn't die as an ordinary criminal but as a political prisoner. But a boy in the second or third grade of primary school was quite incapable of seeing the difference. It was the beginning of a fundamental change in Tadaaki's personality . . ."

This time Etsuko listened intently. For the moment she ignored the blind and immediate physical attraction she felt for him. She had been a small girl when the war ended and the wild winds of democratisation began to blow. It was quite beyond her to conjure up the boyhood days of Yoshihiro and his brothers.

"It wasn't so bad while my mother was alive—she encouraged Tadaaki to continue his studies. Gradually things settled down and my father's disgrace began to fade from people's memory. Tadaaki entered university. Then my mother suffered a heart attack and died, and at that point my younger brother seemed to change completely."

Yoshihiro gave a helpless sigh. "I'm no psychologist, so I can't really explain what went on in his mind. Perhaps the shock of losing his mother, combined with the memory of his father, produced in him a revulsion against a society that was strongly coloured by leftist ideals at the time. That's the only thing I can think of

75

. . . Anyway, we were really surprised by his odd behaviour and the little speeches he subjected us to. He
defended my father's theories, only his arguments weren't
based on logic but sprang from his distorted feelings. He
began to hang around with members of a notorious
right-wing group, and from then on it was a fast downhill
ride for him, I'm afraid."

Etsuko moved her hand till their fingers firmly inter-
locked. It was strangely thrilling, she thought, sitting
here with him in the intimate cosiness of this dimly lit
room, at this time of night. She felt a warm. enveloping
glow.

"Well," he said, "the rest is rather ugly. Somehow or
another Tadaaki managed to get through university, and
then got himself a job with a small company. Next thing
he helped himself to some company money and ran off
with it. On that occasion my elder brother replaced the
missing amount and the company didn't go to the police.
But after that Tadaaki couldn't be helped any more . . .
There was some suggestion he might have got himself
mixed up with a mob of smugglers or some other criminal
element. We didn't have any direct evidence of this . . .
Then he killed somebody and went into hiding again . . .
I don't know how it happened, or whether the dead man
had been a gangster, or belonged to the right-wing
extremists . . ."

Yoshihiro spoke quickly now, in a highly agitated
voice. He gave Etsuko the impression he was trying to
get rid of all the bitterness in him in one long breath.

"At the end of the year before last I wanted to use my
winter holidays to complete my thesis, so I went to stay
at a hot spring inn up in the mountains in Tottori
Prefecture. But on my third day there, Tadaaki turned
up unexpectedly. He said he was broke and sick of hiding.
He had called at my flat in Kyoto and was told where I
was staying, so he followed me . . . By this time my elder
brother wouldn't have anything to do with him, but I'm
not as tough as Nobumasa, and Tadaaki could be very
persuasive. I just couldn't refuse to let him in . . . I tried
to convince him he should give himself up to the police

76

and wipe his slate clean. He said he'd think about it during the night, and I felt quite relieved."

"And that's when the fire broke out?" She increased the pressure of her hand.

He nodded. "When I woke during the night, the room was already filled with smoke. Half choked and crazed with fear, I rushed out and through the fire—and that's as far as I can remember. I was in hospital when I regained consciousness, and was immediately aware that I had saved my own skin but left my brother there to burn . . ."

The lost, broken look on his face made her melt with compassion for him. "You're being unfair to yourself," she said. "There was hardly enough time to save your own life."

He shook his head, and his face became more distorted. "I was well aware Tadaaki was in the next room, asleep, dead drunk. I could've yelled out to warn him—but I didn't. The awful thought crossed my mind that a hopeless brother like him was better off dead—that my career was doomed while he was alive . . . As a matter of fact, his very existence had ruined my marriage plans."

Now she understood his strange behaviour during the café fire. It hadn't only been fear but also a sense of guilt. And she decided he was crazy to blame himself. What he might have *thought* at the time had nothing to do with the real lack of opportunity to save his brother. Yelling out to him? What difference would that have made amid the roar of the fire, with Tadaaki deep in a drunken sleep? She felt a stir of affection for him so quick and sharp, it made her reach out and take hold of his other hand as well.

Looking very pale, Yoshihiro said, "After learning of his death I was tormented by my conscience for days. So when a story of his death and his criminal background appeared in the local paper, and it became impossible for me to remain in Kyoto as a university lecturer any longer, I felt I well deserved what was coming to me. But my professor was kind enough to use his influence to get me another job. That's how I was able to transfer to Chiyoda

University. Even that would've probably been impossible if my brother's family name hadn't been changed to Yasuda . . ."

He fell silent, and she kept clasping his hands, conscious of a mounting excitement in her brought on by the notion that her life was leaking away, and no matter what he said, he was the only one to stop the leak—she had to make him do it.

"Well, now you know," he said, giving a short laugh that choked in self-contempt. "My brother was a killer and, in a sense, my father was one, too. And I myself let my brother die without lifting a finger . . . And I'm reminded of all this every day of the year by the ugly scars all over me . . . For a while after I met you I thought perhaps these things could be forgotten, but of course they can't—they are there, burnt into me forever." He swallowed hard. "As your father said, I'm the last person you'd want to marry, and now our friendship's finished, too. So just forget about me." He tried to take his hands away from her, but she wouldn't let him. "Look, it's no use . . . Go home, please."

As if obeying his order she stood up quickly, almost lifted on the tide of her emotion, still clasping his hands, forcing him to rise with her. "I'm going to be your wife," she said.

He gaped at her, stunned into silence.

She let his hands go and reached up, linking her arms around his neck, trying in vain to make him bring his lips closer to hers, till she was standing on tiptoe.

Stiff-necked and still staring at her, he said, "You want a man like me?"

"Yes, I want a man like you." Her voice was tense with anticipation that made her pulse race and left her short of breath. "I want you now."

This made him gape again, but at last he lowered his head enough for her to reach him. She sealed his parted lips with her own and immediately slipped her tongue into his mouth.

His reaction was tantalising—all his restraint was gone in an instant. With the greediness of a baby he began to suck on her tongue until it was fully drawn, and she felt him stiffen quickly against her belly, for she was so much shorter than he. She put one foot on the stack of books beside them to raise herself, and wrapped her other leg around his thigh to accomodate him. Delicious shivers began to run through her in waves, in rhythm with the instinctive movement of his hips.

"Oh, Yoshihiro," she sighed, her cheek now against his ear, her eyes closed. She felt she was all belly and buttocks and thighs, ready to open to him. Violently she pressed herself against him and lost her balance. The heavy volumes began to slide from under her foot. She hung on to him with all her weight, and together they sagged and rolled down to the bedding on the *tatami*-covered floor, almost oblivious to the change in their position.

Impatiently, as if anxious to atone for the lie she had told her father a few hours ago, she slid her hand inside his kimono. He gave a gasp as she took hold of him. Immediately his hands began to urge away her clothing. She straightened her thighs for a moment and raised herself to help him. Then she felt him touch her wet flesh. In a wave of heat she flung her legs around him. She felt every nerve in her body exposed to him, every pore enlarged to receive him.

Her first coital spasm came even before he could fully enter her, only to be eclipsed by a new rush of mounting passion for him. Then his quickening beat warned her of his approaching climax, and instinctively she tightened her grip on him to heighten the roar of his satisfaction. Its coming flooded her with such indescribable pleasure she nearly passed out.

It took minutes for the turmoil inside her to subside and for her breath to recover enough to take his lips again.

"I'm going to see your father," he said, "tomorrow morning."

Yoshihiro took Shoichi Koike, his friend and legal

adviser, along with him to the Ogata house the next morning, not for his own protection but out of consideration for Etsuko's father. Discussing wedding arrangements with another lawyer would be easier for Ogata, he thought.

Etsuko was a bundle of joy and nerves when Yoshihiro looked at her for the first time since she had given herself to him. Wondering if his estimate of her had changed either way, she half avoided his eyes till he reassured her by saying, "You look lovely this morning." And she did feel marvellously well. The tensions and constant weariness of the past year—and especially of the past few weeks—were completely gone.

Ogata seemed to be resigned to the inevitable. Etsuko's lie about being pregnant had shattered his resistance. His wife had produced some arguments in Yoshihiro's favour during the night, but he didn't need much persuasion to agree to give his consent to the marriage.

"I'll be frank with you," he told Yoshihiro. "I don't like to be forced into a position of having to approve, but it's too late now to complain. So let bygones be bygones, and let's concentrate on what's ahead . . . I hope you can make my daughter happy." He spoke stiffly, and his voice carried a trace of indifference.

Etsuko sensed Yoshihiro's discomfort. In her mind she begged him to forgive her for having to carry on with the deception she had initiated last night.

"I'm sorry if I caused you any anxiety," Yoshihiro said, bowing obediently. "I'll do my best to make Etsuko happy for the rest of her life—please accept my word on this." He swallowed. "By the way, now that things have gone this far, I'd naturally like her to be my wife as soon as possible. I realise the usual arrangements will have to be made on both sides, and this will take some time, but perhaps it wouldn't be unrealistic to aim at a wedding date in February."

Ogata cast a sly sideward glance at Etsuko's stomach, and said, "That should do."

"Then would you mind if I leave all discussions about the ceremony, reception and other details to my lawyer,

Mr. Koike?"

"No, I've no objection."

Yoshihiro gave Etsuko a nod, and she went to bring in Koike from the visitors' room.

Koike quickly got through the formal greetings and congratulations, and then said, "I'll be happy to accept the role of liaison man and organiser. You can rest assured I'll do my best. I can't see any special problems, except that because of the limited time available, it may be difficult to arrange the wedding for one of those lucky days according to custom."

"That won't make any difference in *this* case," Ogata said wryly. "I'll leave it to your judgment."

Etsuko felt her cheeks flush. She shifted her eyes to Yoshihiro. He seemed to be steadfastly studying his right shoe.

"Well," Koike said, "the next thing is the official witness. I'm sure you have many suitable acquaintances, Mr. Ogata, but I wonder if you'd go along with Mr. Tsukamoto's desire to have the dean of his department, Professor Kuwajima?"

Koike was acting in a businesslike manner, and Ogata had no cause for any ill feeling towards him, so he softened his expression. "That seems to be a sensible suggestion," he said, "quite acceptable to me. After all, as the wife of a scholar my daughter will live a life connected with the university."

"Thank you," Koike said politely. "And now, there's one more thing. Mr. Tsukamoto hopes the wedding could be solemnised in a non-religious style. As you probably know, his father was a prominent exponent of Shintoism. Because of his tragic fate, it's quite understandable Mr. Tsukamoto wouldn't be very keen on a ceremony performed according to Shinto rites. On the other hand, he feels Buddhist rites are associated with an overwhelming smell of incense, and he's not a Christian. So a non-religious ceremony would appear best suited to his present frame of mind."

"I see." Ogata thought for a moment, then forced a joyless smile. "This reminds me of the time when the

81

present constitution was being drawn up. One school of thought was that it should be written in modern language instead of the traditional legal style. Under normal circumstances this would've created a prolonged argument. But in this case the contents themselves were so revolutionary that the revolution in phraseology didn't really matter, so the idea was adopted without fuss . . . I think this example illustrates my present feelings on the question of non-religious rites. Anyway, they've been gaining in popularity in recent years, I understand . . . I'm quite prepared to leave the matter to you."

Koike said, "Then I'll discuss this with Mr. Tsukamoto's friend, Mr. Kawaji, who's a lecturer in law at Chiyoda University. We'll formulate a tentative programme, and then present it to you for your approval . . ."

For some minutes past Etsuko hadn't been properly listening to the discussion, and now her mind wandered off completely. She imagined her bridal outfit—the delicately patterned white material, the red lining, the gold-braided hood—and saw herself wearing it, standing beside Yoshihiro's tall figure . . .

Now the days were passing very quickly, but every so often they managed to find time for themselves. Sometimes during the day and sometimes in the evening, depending on the opportunity, Etsuko would sneak up to Yoshihiro's apartment, and then for an hour or so they would lose themselves in each other, oblivious to the world outside.

Koike was organising things with his customary energy. He managed to book the Old Boys' Association Hall at Hitotsubashi University for Monday, February 15. This was a bit close, but it was decided that too soon was better than too late. According to the calendar, February 15 was a 'neutral' day—neither good nor bad for getting married—and nobody objected. It was agreed that the marriage ceremony, to be attended by close relatives only, would take place around midday, and the reception would follow at four o'clock.

So far as the honeymoon was concerned, the middle of February was the end of the academic year, with all the exam papers to be processed. Yoshihiro wouldn't be able to get away for long, so they decided on a one-week stay at Kyoto, returning to Tokyo the following Sunday. Etsuko thought that tripping around Kyoto together, looking at places associated with Yoshihiro's bad memories, contrasting the happy present with the unhappy past—this might be the way to cure his mind completely.

Koike looked after the honeymoon bookings, too, with businesslike thoroughness. Yoshihiro would have been lost without him. When it came to practical things like studying bus timetables and choosing the right inns, the management expert much preferred someone else to do the managing for him.

Reporting to Etsuko on tentative arrangements for the honeymoon, Koike said, "It'll be at least six o'clock by the time you get away from the wedding reception. Speaking from personal experience, you'll be pretty tired by then. Setting out for Kyoto straight away would be far too much for you. That's why I thought you should stay at a hotel in Tokyo overnight and leave for Kyoto on the super-express early next morning. How does that sound to you?"

"Sounds fine," Etsuko said, thinking that Koike was not only thorough but also very considerate. "I'm really grateful to you for your help."

"Don't mention it. For a young lawyer like me buzzing around like a blue fly is normal everyday exercise, and I actually enjoy it. And Yoshihiro is one of my closest friends from way back, so please just tell me whatever you want, and I'll do my best to fix it for you."

Etsuko was delighted with Koike's helpfulness and courtesy, and was always pleased to see him. It was the other young lawyer, Higuchi, she wanted to avoid. But one day, soon after the date of the wedding had been fixed, he buttonholed her in the street. She had just left home to do some shopping when his car pulled into the curb right beside her, and he got out with a stiff face.

"Your father has told me everything," he said. "My disappointment must be obvious to you. In fact, I don't feel like congratulating you—not at the moment, anyway."

Her conscience made her look away from him. Whether she liked him or not, she had been unfair to him—there was no question about that. "I'm sorry," she whispered. "Please forgive me."

"There's no need to apologise," he said bitterly, shrugging his shoulders. "I'm only angry with myself for not being able to win over your mind. I've no ill will towards you. And I'm man enough to know when to withdraw." He took a deep breath. "All I can do now is wish you happiness and ask you to look upon me as one of your friends. If by any chance you meet any problems in the future, remember I'm always willing to help you to the best of my ability . . ."

Higuchi's emotional attitude made Etsuko realise he was still fond of her. She felt sorry for him, but then she thought of his tenacity, and this produced goose-pimples all over her.

"Now, let's say goodbye," he said and put out his hand.

Hesitantly she offered hers, and he held it tightly for a few seconds. Then he bowed and got into his car. He drove off without looking at her again.

On January 26 something else happened that would have made a superstitious person uneasy. Yoshihiro's brother Nobumasa was struck by a motor-cycle and broke his left arm and left leg.

Etsuko turned pale when she heard of it and immediately went to the hospital with Yoshihiro. But Nobumasa was much more cheerful than she had expected, despite his pathetic appearance in white bandages.

"I'm sorry I had to finish up like this just before the happy event," he said with a grin. "That's my carelessness for you . . . I'll be allowed to leave the hospital in

84

about a week, but they tell me it'll be at least another three weeks before I'm fit enough to go back to work. So I may not be able to attend your wedding, but I'm sure nobody will miss me."

Yoshihiro was greatly relieved when he realised his brother hadn't been badly hurt.

"I'll miss you all right," he said, "but I'd rather do without you than see you strain yourself and get worse . . . Actually, I think you were very lucky—your head didn't get hit, and your doctor says you're not likely to be left with any deformity."

"Well, I've been rather overworked lately. The gods might have decided I was due for a rest. I'll be stretching myself lazily at home, so please enjoy your honeymoon without giving me a thought."

"But how will you manage on your own at home after leaving the hospital?" Etsuko asked.

"That's no problem at all. I'll ask the charwoman to come every day for the time being, and there's a doctor nearby. I'd much rather be staying at home, where I have the stereogram and other things, than being cooped up in hospital. But thanks for asking, anyway . . ."

"Just don't strain yourself, brother," Yoshihiro said. "I really think you should get married."

"That's enough of you! Don't you think it's a bit too soon for you to give me a lecture on marital bliss?"

Listening to them Etsuko felt completely happy. How that ominous shadow surrounding Yoshihiro had vanished as soon as they decided to get married! She managed to pull him out of the depths of despair. The idea made her proud, and flooded her heart with love for him.

"Would you like me to come up—just for a little while?" she asked him on their way back from the hospital.

"A completely superfluous question," he said, and took her hand. "Incidentally, do you remember Watanabe—the man who used to butt in, always at the wrong time?"

"Your relative?"

"Yes. Well, at last he seems to have made up his mind

85

to turn over a new leaf. He's getting a job in Hokkaido, so I don't think he'll bother us for a while."

"Oh, that's wonderful." She looked up at the clear winter sky and felt like laughing. Watanabe had been the last remaining worry on her mind. It would have been unbearable if a man like that turned up every now and then to invade the intimacy of their home. But now he would be gone, and with him her final worry would disappear.

In his hurry to get to the hospital Yoshihiro had forgotten to switch off the electric heater in the Japanese room. So it was nice and warm when they got back to his apartment.

Less than five minutes later they were in bed, locked in embrace. In the ten days since they had started it, their love-making had already achieved the ease of familiarity which allowed them to enjoy it to the full. Especially in his case, the shedding of all inhibitions seemed to heighten his pleasure enormously, and this in turn moved her to new plateaus of ecstasy. She was almost glad he had been shy to begin with.

When she got home that evening, Etsuko once again looked at the guest list, and then took from her desk an unfilled wedding invitation card. She wrote on it the names she had left till last—*Mr. and Mrs. Saburo Kirishima*.

She examined the eight *kanji* characters, and burst out laughing. It seemed incredible that only three months ago she had been so upset by a wedding invitation card coming from the same people.

The next nineteen days really raced by, what with preparations for the wedding, meeting Yoshihiro in secret, and dreaming about him in between. Her dreams ranged from the virginally romantic to the wildly erotic that made her wake up in the middle of the night.

Then it was February 14, the eve of the wedding. She was sitting at the dining table with her mother and father. Suddenly she realised this was her last night alone with them—the end of twenty-six years of girlhood. The thought made her heart twist with pity, not for herself but for them.

Lately her father hadn't been complaining so much. He had met Yoshihiro a number of times over the past few weeks. Perhaps he had discovered that Yoshihiro wasn't such a bad match after all.

Now he started lecturing her again on the duties of a good wife. This might be his strange way of demonstrating his fatherly affection, she thought tenderly.

After dinner Etsuko was busy in her room when her mother appeared in the doorway.

"Etsu," she said nervously, "I don't know if I need to ask you this, in this day and age, but do you know what to do tomorrow night?"

She looked at her mother wide-eyed. "What d'you mean?"

"Come now, Etsu, how long do you think you can deceive me?"

"Mother, I——"

"It isn't true you're pregnant, is it? It's just the opposite—there hasn't been anything between you, has there?"

Etsuko embraced her mother tightly. Love and poignant pity for her made the tears rush to her eyes. "I'm sorry," she whispered. "Please forgive me."

"It's all right, my little one . . ." She began to weep with her daughter without really knowing why.

The wedding ceremony went off without a hitch, ending just before one o'clock in the afternoon. It was solemn and dignified despite the absence of religion. Following the marriage vows there was the exchange of rings, the drinking of wine from the nuptial cup, and the signing of the official papers.

Immediately after the ceremony Yoshihiro went to the ward office to get the papers registered. Etsuko, radiant in her bridal outfit, stayed behind among the admiring relatives.

The wedding reception commenced at four o'clock as planned. It was a fairly large affair, following the usual pattern. Kawaji proved a capable master of ceremonies. Kirishima didn't show up, but his wife Kyoko was there, offering her formal congratulations as representative of the bride's friends.

The newly-weds reached room 322 in the New Tokyo Hotel in Akasaka just after seven o'clock.

Etsuko felt physically tired but explosively happy. She shuddered with excitement as they kissed, and almost immediately undressed, watching Yoshihiro do the same. Then she let her long shiny hair down and impishly covered her breasts with it.

He ran his fingers through her hair, and then tenderly took hold of her and kissed her on the top of the head. She looked up at him lovingly, trembling a little from excitement and weariness in the legs. He explored her body as if for the first time.

They made love gently, without a sound. As he reached his climax, whispering "Etsu . . . Etsu," she felt that for those few seconds she was the most beautiful woman in the world.

Afterwards they clung together fervently, without moving or saying anything. And it wasn't long before they coupled again, this time with more violence than tenderness. Finally, damp with fatigue, they held each other loosely, their bodies sated but their minds still greedy for more.

"I'd better go and have a bath," she said.

He kissed her gently. "Okay, that'll give me time to catch my breath." He lay on his back and looked as if he might fall asleep any minute.

But when she got up to go into the bathroom, he came alive again, turned and watched her back. Her loose black hair reached down almost to her full buttocks. Her legs were also a little heavy but well shaped and firm all the way up, except where they joined in a rhythmic combination of curves. As she disappeared, he looked at his watch. It was just after nine o'clock. The night was young . . .

Etsuko ran the water, adjusting the taps and testing the temperature with her fingers. Then she stepped into the bath and carefully lowered herself into the steaming water. Finally she lay back and thought how lucky she was, and what a wonderful day this had been. She almost wished she was thirty years older, so she could look back nostalgically on these golden hours of her life . . .

Now she relaxed completely, letting her mind become delightfully blank. The caressing warmth of the water was luring her slowly into sleep. Then she heard the phone ring, and sat up in the bath with a jolt. What could that be? Perhaps the usual wedding night prank by one of his friends. She heard Yoshihiro talk on the phone but couldn't make out what he was saying.

When his face appeared in the bathroom door he looked annoyed. "This is preposterous," he said. "I've just got a call from the university—they can't find the last batch of exam papers I've marked . . . I know I've put them in the safe in the dean's office—there's no question about that. I just can't understand . . ."

For a moment she thought she could see a trace of that old shadow across his face. "They'll be found in the morning," she said hopefully. "How could they get lost?"

"They couldn't. They are there in the safe. I put them there myself. This isn't something I could forget—I've been working on those papers for days."

"But isn't this rather inconsiderate of them? They know you just got married. Why do they have to bother you on your wedding night?"

Yoshihiro sighed heavily. "That's just it. They know I'll be away on my honeymoon till Sunday, and all the exam results must be put on the computer this week."

"Oh, I see." She was no longer conscious of being in the bath, naked.

The frown on his face deepened. "Etsu," he said almost guiltily, "they want me to go over there to look for the papers."

She stared at him in disbelief. "Go over there tonight —*now*?"

"Yes, but it'll only take an hour at the most. I know

89

where I put those papers, and I'll use taxis both ways
. . . I'll be just about back by the time you finish your
bath."

Suppressing her uneasiness, she said, "All right. I
don't suppose you can do much about it . . ." She smiled
wryly. "At least we've had the first two hours of our
married life to ourselves . . . But you'll try to get back
as quickly as you can, won't you?"

Yoshihiro bent down to her and kissed her lips. Then
he kissed her steaming face, her neck and her nipples,
one after the other. She held his head, trembling in the
warm water . . .

"I won't be long," he whispered.

She was reluctant to let his head go, and felt a pang
of fear as the bathroom door clicked shut behind him.
But she soon adjusted to being alone, and the previous
glow of satisfaction returned.

She began to re-live the previous two hours, realising
as she moved from episode to episode that their love-
making had been none the less exciting because it was
no longer stolen fruit. How long would it remain that
way? How long would their elation last? She smiled at
her face in the mirror. Right now she was as sure of their
happiness as she was sure of her love for him.

Carefully she dried her face and put make-up on it.
She let her hair down again and brushed it. Then she
switched off the bathroom light, returnd to the bedroom,
and opened her suitcase. Neatly folded on top was the
mauve negligée she had bought specially for the wedding
night. It was almost transparent, hiding nothing—the
sort of thing she would never again wear after tonight.
Her mother would go into a fit if she saw her in it—the
poor thing. She had meant to put it on immediately after
their arrival at the hotel, but somehow the urgency of
their love had left no time for it.

Etsuko slipped on the negligée and looked at herself
in the wall mirror. It clearly revealed every detail of her
chunky body. Adjusting the black lace on it, she thought
it looked very suggestive. It was totally against her own
taste, but she felt sure Yoshihiro would like it. It would

remind him the night was not yet over . . .

At half past ten, just about an hour after Yoshihiro had left, Etsuko was sitting on the big double bed with knees drawn up, her arms around her legs. She was looking at nothing in particular, but her ears were tuned to pick up any noise outside in the corridor. She was waiting for the door to open. He would be back soon— any minute now . . .

At eleven o'clock there was still no sign of him. Her brow furrowed and her eyes became misty as she fought back her tears. All her nerves strained towards the phone, waiting for its ring to break the silence. She wanted to hear his voice at the other end . . .

At half past eleven she got off the bed and stood facing the door—a pathetically lonely figure in the transparent negligée. She removed her glasses as her eyes filled with blinding tears. All she could see now in the room was a blur of light—the reflection of the bedside lamp in the mirror.

She took off the negligée and got fully dressed, just in case. She could feel herself sinking, drowning in panic. What could have happened to him? Had he met with an accident?

At half past twelve she threw herself on the bed and began to cry helplessly, releasing the harsh sobs that had been gathering for the past two hours. She stayed there, face down, until the last spasms of grief had been drained from her.

Then she reached for the phone to dial the police emergency number, but changed her mind at the last moment. No, she thought, steeling herself, she was Etsuko Tsukamoto now, and she would do what was expected of her. She would wait.

An eerie quiet filled the room. Absently she shifted

her bloodshot eyes towards the window. The eastern sky was already growing lighter. Her eyelids were still swollen, but the tears had dried up a long time ago. She felt tired, terribly tired, but couldn't go to sleep .

CHAPTER SIX

Since their wedding three and a half months ago, the Kirishimas had been living at Tokiwamatsu in a house left to Kyoko by her late father. It was far too big for the two of them, but thinking of the future they decided to stay in it.

For State Prosecutor Saburo Kirishima the morning of February 16 began like any other. He had just finished his breakfast of bacon and eggs and was looking at the paper, sipping his coffee.

Almost the entire local news page was filled with a report on a man who had gone berserk with a rifle at Nagoya, after putting a bomb on the express train.

"Hmm. He was supposed to be a quiet man," Kirishima said as he handed the paper to Kyoko. "Then suddenly some little thing set him off . . . Yes, I've often heard people say, 'Who would've thought he'd be capable of such a thing'."

"It's frightening, isn't it? The things that can lie hidden in a man's mind."

"He himself was probably unaware of it."

Kirishima was finishing his coffee when the phone

rang.

Kyoko got up to answer it.

A few minutes later she came back to the dining room, her face turned to stone.

"What's wrong?"

"That was Etsuko . . ."

"Etsuko? Isn't she supposed to be on her honeymoon?"

"She was so upset—almost incoherent. I couldn't quite follow her, but her husband seems to have disappeared."

"What?" Kirishima sat upright and stubbed out his cigarette. "Disappeared?"

"Yes."

"But how?"

"I can't make it out."

"You told me they were supposed to stay at some hotel overnight and leave for Kyoto this morning?"

"That's right."

"But surely he couldn't have gone on a spree on his wedding night, leaving her in the hotel?"

"I wouldn't know . . . Anyway, she asked me to go and see her at the New Tokyo Hotel. Her parents had been opposed to her marriage to Mr. Tsukamoto—maybe that's why she contacted me."

Kirishima knitted his eyebrows. "Has she reported him missing to the police?"

"Judging by her manner, I don't think so."

"All right. You'd better go to her straight away. And once you get the full story, give her father a ring. You could contact the police if you think it's necessary."

"Okay, I'll get dressed."

"You can ring me at the office later and let me know what's up."

"Okay."

"Oh, and one more thing. Just remember you're now the wife of a prosecutor. So don't do anything adventurous, will you?"

Kyoko's face broke into a smile. "Don't worry, fussybody, I'll uphold your dignity at all costs . . . Now, I must be off. See you later." She dashed out of the room.

Kirishima folded his arms and drifted into thought. A university lecturer was usually a reliable person of some standing in the community, possessing considerable self-confidence. It was most unlikely he'd run away from his wife on the first night of their married life . . . No, Tsukamoto's disappearance looked most unusual, to say the least . . .

As for Etsuko, he wasn't particularly keen to meet her. Over the past twelve months Kyoko had repeatedly hinted at the reason for the Ogata girl's conspicuous absence from their company. Not that *he* had anything to do with it—he certainly hadn't encouraged her in any way. Still, it could become a little embarrassing . . . He sincerely hoped Tsukamoto would turn up soon, hale and hearty.

It was about half past ten in the morning when Saburo Kirishima was summoned to the office of Renji Sanada, chief of the Criminal Affairs Division.

Sanada's face was expressionless, as always. He said, "Body of Yoshihiro Tsukamoto, lecturer, Chiyoda University. Found at Kitamicho, Setagaya ward. Report received from police headquarters." His voice totally lacked modulation. It was part of his job to utter sentences like these all the year round. To him it was the most natural thing in the world. One more corpse wasn't likely to make him either surprised or excited.

But the name Tsukamoto made Kirishima grow slightly pale in the face, even if the information wasn't entirely unexpected. "I see," he said softly.

"Inspector Yoshioka from the homicide squad has been assigned to the job. He went out to the scene early this morning and has already made certain arrangements at Seijo police station. But I understand he'll direct the investigation from police headquarters." Sanada took out his handkerchief and elaborately blew his nose before adding, "Kirishima, will you take charge of the case, like a good lad?"

"Yes, sir. I'll make contact with police headquarters

straight away." He bowed lightly and left the chief's office.

But on his way back to his own room he grew increasingly uncomfortable. This was one case he could well do without, he thought.

His clerk, Kitahara, was holding the phone for him when he reached his desk. "It's your wife, Mr. Prosecutor."

Kirishima took the receiver. "Yes. How's Etsuko?"

"Terrible—almost out of her mind. I called a doctor and asked him to give her a sedative."

"Do you know what time her husband left last night?"

"Around half past nine," Kyoko said. "Told her he had to go to the university."

"What about Mr. and Mrs. Ogata?"

"They're already here. Mr. Ogata is making enquiries on the phone. He says if he can't locate Mr. Tsukamoto privately, he'll contact the police."

"He's a bit late for that, I'm afraid," Kirishima said. "I've already been put in charge of the case."

"Oh, no!" Kyoko gave a woeful sigh. "Have they found his body?"

"Yes . . . Where are you ringing from?"

"From the ground-floor lobby. Mr. Ogata is using the phone in the room upstairs. Anyway, I didn't want to talk in front of them."

"That was wise . . . I've no details yet, but I'm sure the police are checking at his apartment and at the university right now. Sooner or later they'll learn he stayed at that hotel last night. It won't be long before they get there."

"Then *I* don't have to break the news to her, do I?"

"Of course not—it's not your responsibility. In any case, I want you to stay out of it from now on. Her parents can look after her."

"I'd like to see Etsuko once more."

"You can do that later—perhaps during the afternoon. I don't want you to be there when I make the official inspection later this morning."

"I see."

"So you just go home straight away, and I'll see you before going back to the office."

"Okay then."

Replacing the receiver Kirishima was conscious of the questioning eyes of the clerk, Kitahara. The nosy old badger wanted to be in on the act, and it would have been impracticable to keep him out. Not only was he Kirishima's memory bank, but also the one who made the difference between order and chaos in his office.

So Kirishima told him about the latest case in a few words.

"Miss Etsuko Ogata . . . I think I remember her." Kitahara screwed up his ruddy face. "We met her in Kobe last year, didn't we?"

"If you say so."

"Yes, she *was* a rather strange girl, wasn't she? The way she kept looking at you all the time, Mr. Prosecutor."

The cunning old soak didn't miss much, Kirishima thought, turning to the book-shelf and reaching for a volume to hide his embarrassment. Then he sat down behind his desk and dialled the number of police headquarters.

Inspector Yoshioka was a fast talker. "I'll give you the details later," he said. "There's one interesting point— Tsukamoto got married only a few hours before his death. He was staying with his bride in the New Tokyo Hotel last night. They were to leave for Kyoto on the super-express at nine o'clock this morning. She's still in the hotel—very close to a nervous breakdown, I understand. I'll be going there shortly."

"I'll go with you," Kirishima said.

For a moment Yoshioka remained silent at the other end. Perhaps he was surprised Kirishima wanted to move in so quickly—even before the police had a chance to complete the preliminary investigations.

Then he said, "If you can spare the time, Mr. Prosecutor, it'll be a great help to us. I've been told the bride's father is a lawyer, so he may feel more inclined to talk to you about any of the more delicate details . . . Well, then perhaps you'd like to come in my car—I could give

97

you the details on the way."

"That'll be fine," Kirishima said.

"Okay then. I'll be there shortly."

Twenty minutes later Kirishima was sitting in the police car, listening to Inspector Yoshioka's report. Kitahara was following in the departmental car.

The body had been discovered by a milkman on the bank of an irrigation canal at Kitamicho just before seven o'clock in the morning. The cause of death was strangulation. A preliminary estimate placed the time of death between ten o'clock and midnight. It was not yet clear whether the crime had been committed where the body was found. The body could have been taken there to be dumped. A search of the immediate area and inquiries in the neighbourhood were still in progress.

Identifying the victim had presented no problem. A wallet containing name cards and two round-trip tickets had been found beside the body. There was no money in it.

The detective visiting the victim's apartment had learnt from the caretaker that Tsukamoto and his bride were to go on a honeymoon. But even after searching the apartment the detective was unable to establish the name and address of the bride's parents. Then Chiyoda University was contacted, and a Professor Kuwajima, who had been official witness at the wedding ceremony, told police the newly-weds had been staying at the New Tokyo Hotel overnight.

It had taken nearly three hours to get this far, partly because of the morning rush hour, Yoshioka told Kirishima. He was still talking when the police car pulled up in front of the New Tokyo Hotel.

As Kirishima and Yoshioka walked into the hotel lobby, two men rose from their seats at the far end. One looked like a detective, the other was Takuzo Ogata.

Kirishima immediately recognised him—they had

fought in court once, some years ago. But now Ogata looked like an old man of seventy or more.

When Ogata saw Kirishima, his face became even more gloomy. He must have thought of his daughter's feelings. "*You* are in charge of this case?" he asked, without really expecting an answer. "The detective here has told me what happened."

"Please accept my deepest sympathy, Mr. Ogata," Kirishima said formally. Because of his official position he couldn't say much more. "This is Inspector Yoshioka from police headquarters."

Yoshioka quickly mumbled his stock phrase of condolence and then added, almost in the same breath, "How's your daughter?"

"We put her to bed. My wife's looking after her. She's been fairly calm since the doctor gave her an injection."

"Does she know?"

"I think she realised it when she saw the detective. We didn't have the courage to tell her. It was a great shock to us, too . . . If only I'd opposed this marriage with a little more determination——" He stopped in mid-sentence.

Yoshioka's eyebrows imperceptively moved upwards, but he must have decided not to pursue the matter at this stage. "Since the wedding took place only yesterday afternoon," he said, "I imagine the papers wouldn't yet be registered at the ward office. So legally your daughter is still unmarried and may continue to use her maiden name."

"That would've been a tiny piece of luck amid all the misfortune," Ogata said dryly, "but in fact the papers were handed in yesterday—largely because it was one of those newfangled non-religious ceremonies."

"Aah, I see." Yoshioka was a seasoned crime investigator, but he seemed genuinely sorry for the poor girl.

Kirishima felt the same way, only more strongly. Etsuko had at last found happiness, and now this. He thought of Section 733 of the Civil Code which provided that a woman whose marriage had been terminated by the husband's death or by divorce couldn't remarry for six months. This was to ensure the proper identification of the father of any child. The provision would apply to Etsuko even if she happened to be still a virgin.

Breaking the silence, Yoshioka said, "Was it a love-marriage?"

Ogata nodded without comment.

"Well, as you know, Mr. Ogata, I'll have to ask you some further questions later on, but would you first take us to your daughter, please?"

"She has suffered a very severe shock. You'll keep that in mind, won't you?" Ogata cast a pleading glance at the inspector and then at Kirishima before walking to the lift.

When they entered the hotel room, Etsuko was sitting in an armchair in one corner. Her face was stiff like a mask, and she looked as if she had become insensitive to everything.

As she recognised Kirishima her swollen eyes widened and her mouth twitched a couple of times, but then she compressed her lips and turned her eyes away from him. Who could've imagined he'd have to see her like this?

"Etsu," Ogata said, "this is State Prosecutor Kirishima, and this is Inspector Yoshioka from police headquarters."

Silently she bowed.

Kirishima signalled the inspector with his eyes. It was normal procedure to leave the first step in an investigation entirely to the police, and he was especially glad of this now.

When Yoshioka began with a casual "Miss Ogata", for the first time Etsuko's face came alive.

"I'm Mrs. Tsukamoto," she said with resentment in her voice.

"Oh, I'm sorry—just a slip of the tongue." He cleared his throat. "Mrs. Tsukamoto, you may already know this—your husband was found dead this morning."

Her eyelids fluttered, but she didn't say anything.

Yoshioka then trotted out the formal sentence. "I fully appreciate how you feel but must ask you to co-operate with us so that the deceased may rest in peace."

She gave a tiny nod.

"Thank you . . . And now, would you please tell us first about your husband's relatives and close friends?"

"He has a brother, Nobumasa Tsukamoto. He's a chemist, working in the research laboratories of Toho Kasei."

After what she must have been through last night, her voice was remarkably firm, Kirishima thought.

"What's the brother's home address?"

"4-1017, Shimotakaido, Suginami . . . He was injured in a street accident at the end of last month. He also has a severe cold at present and is under medical treatment at his home, I think."

"He didn't attend the wedding then?"

"No." The mention of the wedding seemed to heighten her distress.

"Were there any other relatives of his at the ceremony?"

There was a lost, destroyed expression on her face, but she managed to take hold of herself. "Three or four of his relatives were there, but he hardly had any contact with them at other times. I met them for the first time yesterday."

"What about his friends?"

She mentioned Koike and Kawaji.

Yoshioka wrote down the names in his notebook and then turned to Ogata. "Have you already advised the victim's brother and friends, by any chance?"

"No, I haven't," Ogata said. "After I got here I rang three different places to check, but I simply asked if they'd received a phone call from the honeymoon couple. I pretended I was just a nervous father wondering how his daughter was faring. I didn't want to give them the impression something might be seriously wrong."

Nodding, Yoshioka turned to Etsuko again. "Mrs. Tsukamoto, would you mind telling us now, as fully as you can, what happened just before your husband left you last night?"

As a rule, women in her situation were so upset, the

only way to obtain a coherent account from them was to ask them the same questions over and over again during a long interview. But her story was quite clear. She spoke in an orderly manner and sounded almost indifferent, showing no emotion at all. Yoshioka looked a little surprised, but Kirishima recognised in her that deep-seated, unrelieved grief that kept grinding away at a person's sensibilities until they became paper-thin.

"I see," Yoshioka said. "Then at the time of the telephone call you weren't with your husband?"

"That's right."

"He told you he had to go over to the university to locate some missing exam papers, but he didn't say who had telephoned?"

"No, he didn't."

Yoshioka signalled to one of the detectives in the room. The man left immediately, obviously to check with the university.

"And he promised he'd be back within an hour?"

"Yes."

"Did he take anything with him?"

"Nothing special that I can think of."

"How much money do you think he had in his wallet?"

"It must have been sufficient for the trip."

Kirishima thought it was quite natural for a bride of a few hours not to know how much money her new husband had on him.

"As he was about to leave, did you notice any change in his manner?" Yoshioka asked.

"Perhaps he looked slightly worried . . . I'm not sure."

"What sort of worry?"

"I naturally thought it had to do with the missing exam papers."

"Mrs. Tsukamoto, I'll ask you now to try to cast your mind back to your association with your husband before your marriage. Did you ever get the feeling he was worrying over something, or somebody—an enemy, perhaps?"

She hesitated for a moment. Then she said, quite firmly, "I didn't notice anything."

"Have you any idea at all who might have killed your husband?"

"No."

"Or what might have been the motive for his murder?"

"I've no idea."

Yoshioka might have thought it was futile to expect answers to questions like these from a woman who had been married to the victim only a few hours. Whatever he thought, he didn't pursue the matter and turned to Kirishima. "Mr. Prosecutor, would you like to ask anything?"

"No, not at this stage," Kirishima said.

Just then Etsuko got up unsteadily and gazed at him. There was such a strange glow in her eyes—it made him feel embarrassed, even afraid she might say something absurd in front of the inspector.

But then she slowly shifted her gaze to Yoshioka and said, in a wooden voice, "When will you be ready to return my husband's body to me?"

The inspector's sun-tanned face seemed to be losing some of its colour. "The post mortem should be completed today."

"As his wife, I'll naturally have to arrange for his funeral."

"I see," Yoshioka muttered. "I'll let you know . . . We'll also have to make an official inspection of your husband's apartment. This will include an examination of his belongings for possible clues . . . Well, Mrs. Tsukamoto, thank you very much for your co-operation."

Etsuko bowed curtly and glanced in Kirishima's direction, but almost immediately turned away, as if the people in the room no longer existed. Only the slight quivering of her fingers revealed there was still some tension left in her.

Kirishima eagerly led the way out of the room.

Ogata followed them into the corridor, apparently to see them off.

Yoshioka turned to him and said, "Mr. Ogata, forgive me for asking this at such a time, but couldn't there be some other man interested in your daughter, by any

103

chance?" When Ogata gave him a frosty look, he hurriedly added, "I hope you appreciate I'm not suggesting anything improper. I'm thinking of the possibility of a one-sided infatuation, which isn't uncommon, as you know."

Ogata said, "As you can see for yourself, my daughter isn't a beautiful woman by any stretch of the imagination, and she's rather conservative in her outlook. In fact, she had very little to do with the opposite sex until she met Tsukamoto. The only thing—well, you'll find this out sooner or later, so I might as well tell you now. The man I would've liked my daughter to marry wasn't Tsukamoto."

"Whom did you have in mind?"

"Tetsuya Higuchi, my junior partner."

The three men were standing in front of the lift. Now it seemed Ogata meant to accompany them to the ground-floor lobby because he stepped into the lift with them.

"Then at one time she would've been associated with Higuchi to some extent?" Yoshioka spoke casually but hurriedly, with the air of a man to whom every minute was precious.

"That's correct. Of course, Higuchi is a very respectable man. You can take it from me he had nothing to do with Tsukamoto's death. This would be quite unthinkable."

"Naturally, he'd still have a lingering affection for your daughter?"

"That I couldn't answer. Anyway, much as I tried to talk her out of it, my daughter insisted on marrying Tsukamoto. There was nothing I could do, so I apologised to Higuchi, and he gave her up with good grace."

The lift reached the ground floor, but Yoshioka no longer seemed to be in a hurry. He suggested Ogata might like to sit with them in the lobby for a while. He found a sofa in a corner. "Did you have any special reason to oppose her marriage to Tsukamoto?" he asked.

"Yes, indeed," Ogata said grimly. "And since we are on the subject, I'll give you the whole story. It may help

104

you with your inquiries."

He began with Yoshihiro's father, and then went on to the younger brother on whom he now had the full information. He didn't leave anything out. When he had finished, he said, "Father and younger brother—they were the reasons for my objection to the marriage. Of course, they can't have any direct bearing on this incident, since both have been dead for some time."

"Yes, of course," Yoshioka said solicitously. "Well, Mr. Ogata, we do appreciate your help." He thought for a moment. "Oh, and what about the funeral? Naturally, I couldn't take your daughter seriously, but I didn't want to hurt her feelings."

"Yes, I understood . . . Well, she'll be chief mourner, so I suppose we must do all that has to be done in consultation with the victim's elder brother." He blinked a couple of times. Perhaps he thought of his daughter wearing black mourning clothes only a few days after she had been standing there, radiant in her white bridal outfit.

"Then we'll advise you about the release of the body as soon as we can," Yoshioka said. "And thank you very much for your co-operation." He stood up and bowed, and watched Ogata's tired figure disappear into the lift. Then he asked Kirishima if he'd like to return to his office in the police car.

"No thank you. I have some other business to attend to."

"Well then, I'd better get on with it, I suppose . . . I'd like to keep in touch with you though, if I may."

"Yes, of course. Just contact me whenever you wish, especially when things get a bit further advanced. At this stage I've nothing special to ask."

"Thank you, Mr. Prosecutor." Yoshioka turned to leave, then stopped suddenly and said, "This is a sad business, isn't it? I myself have a daughter of nineteen."

Before returning to the office Kirishima called at his home. He invited his clerk inside, but Kitahara insisted

105

on waiting for him in the car. As he walked in, he marvelled at his clerk's unpredictable leaps between the heights of tactfulness and indiscretion.

Kyoko was already making a cup of coffee for him. She looked at him inquiringly, but Kirishima didn't have the time to satisfy her curiosity. It was he who wanted some answers from her.

"Towards the end of last year you told me Etsuko sought your advice concerning her relationship with Tsukamoto."

"That's right."

"I wasn't very interested in her problems at the time— I even asked you not to go into detail."

"Do you want me to do it now?"

"Yes. Try to recall everything she told you."

"I met her once more after they got engaged. That's when she told me how she tricked her father into giving his consent, with the lie about her pregnancy."

"Just start at the beginning, and try not to leave anything out."

Ten minutes later, when Kyoko had finished, Kirishima said, "It sounds reasonable enough . . . The only thing that bothers me is that character Watanabe. Etsuko didn't say a word about him during the interview this morning."

"Well, he's supposed to have gone to Hokkaido. Perhaps she just didn't think of him."

"Yes, that's possible. She was very upset."

"Should I suggest to her that she tell the police about him?"

"No, I don't think it'd make any difference. It won't be long before they learn about him anyway . . ." He lit a cigarette and slowly inhaled the smoke. "And now, will you try to recall everything Etsuko said when you first met her this morning?"

Kyoko obligingly repeated the conversation between them, and Kirishima noted that Etsuko's account to the police was identical with what she had told Kyoko.

"But hasn't she already told the same thing to the police?" Kyoko asked.

"Yes, she has. I just wanted to double-check it, since it's such a queer story. That urgent call from the university—I'm pretty sure it was a lie. The police will know soon."

"You mean the killer told Mr. Tsukamoto a lie to lure him out of the hotel?"

"That's one possibility. Another is that Tsukamoto told Etsuko a lie. And a third one is that Etsuko told *us* a lie."

"But surely Etsuko wouldn't . . ."

"Look, as a prosecutor I must treat her as if I met her for the first time today. Your friendship with her doesn't enter into this, so far as I'm concerned. To me she's just the wife of the victim, and an important witness."

"Yes, yes, I know," Kyoko said unpleasantly.

"But just to put your heart at rest, it's not very likely Etsuko would've lied to you. She was terribly upset at the time. I don't believe she could've thought up a clever story while in that condition, let alone told it to you with any semblance of conviction."

They finished their coffee and sat in silence for a few minutes. Kirishima kept drawing on his cigarette, his eyes half closed with concentration. Kyoko didn't even try to guess what he was thinking.

Then he got up to go, and she saw him out to the front door, as might be expected of a wife of three and a half months.

But he failed rather miserably in his role as the enthusiastic young husband. Instead of some tender words of farewell, he looked at Kyoko vacantly, and said, "No, it isn't Etsuko who told a lie."

CHAPTER SEVEN

Kirishima had been right. Less than five minutes after his arrival back at the office, he was told by Inspector Yoshioka on the phone that no one at the university had called the victim last night.

"My man checked with a number of people in Tsukamoto's department," Yoshioka said. "They all agreed it was nonsense . . . I had my own doubts from the start."

"I felt the same way."

"They said that while they might be a bunch of egg-heads noted for their tactlessness, they wouldn't go that far—they wouldn't drag a colleague out of bed on his wedding night without a compelling reason. And at the registrar's office my man was told a young lecturer would never be required to go to the university at that time of night, not even in an emergency. If Tsukamoto had been the vice-chancellor or the dean of a department, that would've been a different matter . . . But the clincher is that not a single exam paper's missing. They're all in the safe, just as Tsukamoto left them there . . ."

Well, that was that, Kirishima thought as he replaced the receiver after listening to the rest of Yoshioka's report. It looked as if this would be all for the day—and it wasn't very much. He had the uneasy feeling this might turn out to be another one of those hard-to-crack jobs.

On his way home in the car that evening he recalled that strange glow in Etsuko's eyes. Soon it would be his turn to question her . . . He drew a long breath and tried to keep his mind on the traffic.

The front of his house was enveloped in darkness, but he could imagine its colour, pleasantly subdued by the years. Only the plate at the entrance, bearing his name, was new and shiny.

"Hello," he said, handing his brief-case and overcoat to Kyoko who had come to meet him in the entry.

While taking off his shoes, he said, "Did you go to see Etsuko again this afternoon?"

"Yes." She took his coat as they walked into the living room. "There was more trouble."

"What trouble?"

"Etsuko's parents tried to take her home with them, but she didn't want to go. She said she was now Mrs. Yoshihiro Tsukamoto, and insisted on going to the apartment at Setagaya Daita where they were to live after the honeymoon."

Kirishima recalled Etsuko's resentment when Yoshioka called her Miss Ogata by mistake. "It might have been her parents' opposition to the marriage that made her so obstinate."

"That's part of it, no doubt, but isn't the only reason. She's had a taste of independence, so now she wants to live her own life. I think I'd feel the same way in her place."

Kirishima changed into a winter kimono and sat down to warm his feet in the *kotatsu*. "I see what you mean," he said, "but her married life only lasted a couple of hours—hardly long enough to make her feel like a married woman."

Instead of answering Kyoko busied herself with his clothes. Finally she said, changing the subject, "Etsuko is a very quiet, even-tempered girl, but she has a will of her own. Once she makes up her mind about something, she'll stubbornly persist. That explains her daring lie about being pregnant, though normally she's a very truthful person."

"Hmm . . . And what happened in the end?"

"Her parents kept coaxing her, trying every trick they knew, and finally she agreed to go home with them, for a couple of days anyway. Her father said the apartment would be in disorder because the police had just searched it, and it wouldn't be large enough for the wake service. And her mother insisted they now looked upon her dead husband as their own son, and their mind would never be at peace if they weren't allowed to give him a proper funeral."

"I can sympathise with her parents. Apart from everything else, they're probably worried she might try to commit suicide if left on her own in that apartment."

"I never thought of that," Kyoko said anxiously. "It could happen quite easily, couldn't it? She keeps saying she'd move into the apartment immediately after the funeral."

"Well, that's something to think about when the time comes. All they can do at the moment is try to solve their immediate problems, one at a time."

Early next morning Inspector Yoshioka called on Kirishima at his office.

First he handed over the post mortem report. It contained nothing unusual. Congestion in the abdominal region indicated the victim had been rendered unconscious with a *karate* blow before being strangled. The time of death was placed somewhere between 10 p.m. and 11 p.m. This meant Tsukamoto had been murdered approximately one hour after leaving the hotel.

Yoshioka then reported on the result of inquiries made at the hotel. One of the bell-boys had seen Tsukamoto leave via the front entrance at about half past nine, but wasn't sure if he had engaged a taxi. This was being checked with all the taxi companies at present. It would take some time.

As to the victim's belongings at the hotel, there was a suitcase and a camera. The suitcase was filled with the usual things required for a one-week trip. No money was found in it, and he hadn't deposited any for safe-keeping at the hotel. This suggested he had all the money for the trip in his wallet when he went out, and it was taken by the killer. It was unthinkable a man going on his honeymoon would have been without any money.

A search of the victim's apartment didn't yield much, Yoshioka said. The only valuables found in it were a savings bank book with a balance of 558,650 yen, and a life insurance policy for 1,500,000 yen. From the savings account 400,000 yen had been withdrawn a few days earlier. This seemed to be a reasonable amount to cover the cost of the wedding ceremony and the honeymoon trip.

Listening to the inspector Kirishima thought the money in the victim's account was rather more than one would have expected. A thirty-year-old lecturer at a private university wouldn't be earning very much. Many academics of this class had to supplement their income by teaching elsewhere in their spare time, or by writing magazine articles for small fees. Even if Tsukamoto had been very careful with money during his bachelor years, it would have been difficult for him to save up nearly 1,000,000 yen by the age of thirty. This seemed to be a point worth looking into.

Yoshioka said the beneficiary of the life insurance policy was the victim's elder brother. It had been taken out about two years ago. At that time the victim wouldn't have known his bride. It would have been natural for him to make his brother the beneficiary.

As expected, the detectives didn't find any jewellery or share certificates in the apartment. There were quite a lot of books, but no valuable collector's items among them. And according to Koike, the victim's lawyer, Tsukamoto had no real estate or any other property apart from his personal effects and some copyrights.

When finally Yoshioka came to the search of the area where the body had been found, he looked slightly uncomfortable. "So far we haven't found a thing," he said, "but we're still looking."

This was the end of his report on the facts. He only stopped to light a cigarette before eagerly moving into the field of opinions and theories.

"On the basis of what we have to date, I'm inclined to rule out money as a motive. The only two people to profit from Tsukamoto's death are his wife and his brother. If he had been worth hundreds of millions of yen, then the position would be entirely different. But it's unthinkable that for something like 1,000,000 yen she would've joined in a plot to marry him and then get him murdered on the wedding night. Nor do I believe his brother would've killed him for an insurance of only 1,500,000 yen. Actually, Koike told me the brother had repeatedly asked the victim to change the policy, making his fiancée the beneficiary. And at the wake service last night, he told Ogata he intended to hand over the whole insurance money to the widow. He said this was the least he could do in compensation for all she had to endure."

Kirishima nodded a couple of times. When it came to inheritance, it wasn't uncommon for relatives to start wrangling, but Tsukamoto's brother was obviously a kind-hearted, unselfish man. No, inheritance seemed to have no bearing on this case.

Yoshioka said, "I've no idea how much money he had in his wallet—it could've been anything between 50,000 and 100,000 yen, perhaps more. Whatever it was, it wasn't nearly enough to make somebody want to murder him for it. I know there are quite a few examples of people getting knocked on the head for 10,000 yen or less, but in all such cases the attacker hoped for more, the victim being a stranger to him. Furthermore, these crimes are invariably committed by people of poor intelligence. But this time the killer was clever enough to lure the victim out of the hotel on his wedding night . . . I think the money was taken in an attempt to throw us off the scent."

Kirishima was impressed with the inspector's reasoning. The way he eliminated one unlikely motive after another revealed him as an experienced investigator of considerable common sense.

"Well now," Yoshioka said, "this brings us to the question of grudge. This could well be the motive we are looking for. And the person to come immediately to mind is Higuchi, Ogata's junior partner. Being a lawyer, he's sure to prove a difficult customer. He was away in Chiba yesterday, so today is my first opportunity to take a good look at him. But I can assure you, Mr. Prosecutor, I'll be keeping an eye on him from now on . . . I also heard the victim had some connection with Kokoku Dojinkai, one of those right-wing extremist groups. My men are checking on this at the moment. The leader of the group, an old fellow called Kumagaya, has been away on a trip, I understand. There seems to be no reason for him to have any ill feeling towards the victim, though you never can tell with people like him . . . Besides Higuchi and Kumagaya, we're looking at all the victim's friends and his past relationships with women. We just might come across somebody with a secret grudge against him."

As he spoke, Yoshioka's sun-tanned face beamed with vitality. Kirishima thought once this inspector had a clue in his claws, he'd hold on to it like a mud-crab.

"The most baffling aspect of this case, Mr. Prosecutor, is the strange behaviour of the victim himself. Imagine anybody being prepared to leave his bride in the middle of their wedding night!"

"Agreed," Kirishima said. "And there's something else. Most newly-weds who spend their first night in a hotel won't disclose where they're staying to avoid teasing telephone calls. So the person who made this call must have been very close to the victim to know it. What d'you think?"

"I'd go along with that, except for one thing. In his speech at the wedding reception Koike let the cat out of the bag by announcing the couple would spend the night at the New Tokyo Hotel and leave for Kyoto on the super-express the following morning. Yesterday he was eating his heart out over this slip of the tongue, but actually the victim's honeymoon plans had been common knowledge days before the wedding. All his students—even his girl students—knew the name of the hotel, as we found out. They had been told by the victim himself. So we can't narrow the field of suspects to those who attended the wedding reception. In any case, I'd say the killer could've easily obtained this information if he wanted to."

Yoshioka drew on his cigarette and blew out the smoke like a steam whistle. "Moreover, the switchboard attendant at the hotel told us that the caller—a male voice—hadn't specified the number of the room but inquired if there was a Yoshihiro Tsukamoto staying there, and then asked to be connected to his room. This again suggests we shouldn't try to narrow the field too quickly, or we might miss the man we want, or end up with the wrong one."

Kirishima suppressed a smile. It was supposed to be the prosecutor's duty to stop the police from jumping to conclusions. But now things seemed to be the other way round, he thought wryly.

"Now, concerning this telephone call," Yoshioka said, "I think there are three possibilities to consider. The first and most unlikely one is that the killer cleverly deceived the victim by impersonating somebody at the university. To do this he would've had to imitate not only the voice but also the speaking manner of that person. In addition, he would've had to dream up a situation at the university which would've looked sufficiently convincing to the victim . . . No, that's too much. It might have been possible for the killer to bring off such a stunt if the person to be imitated had been met by the victim only once or twice before. But to impersonate successfully someone who had been almost in daily contact with him?" He slowly shook his head.

"I think your argument is quite sound," Kirishima said. "But we mustn't discount the possibility that the killer is actually a member of the university staff."

"You mean, he used his name openly, and only lied about the exam papers? But Mr. Prosecutor, in that case there would've been every chance of Tsukamoto revealing the caller's name to his wife before leaving, don't you think? How could the killer have taken such a risk?"

"He might have calculated that nobody would believe he had made the call in his own name."

For a moment the inspector seemed to struggle to conceal his scorn at this idea, but then he bowed and said, "I follow. You want me to take a close look at people at the university who had been associated with the victim. I'll certainly do that . . . Now, the second of the three possibles is that Tsukamoto himself told his wife a lie. Personally, I think this is the most likely thing to have happened . . . The third is obvious."

"Mrs. Tsukamoto told *us* a lie. Is that it?"

"Exactly. Supposing Mrs. Tsukamoto overheard the phone conversation, or the victim told her the caller's name. And supposing the caller was someone she couldn't put into police hands, or someone she wouldn't believe could commit murder. What then?"

Kirishima drew a deep breath. Until now this frightful theory hadn't occurred to him. What if Ogata had a reason to prevent this marriage at all costs? And what if he had learnt of that reason as late as the day of the wedding, perhaps only at the reception? This would make a desperate act by him appear more feasible . . .

Yoshioka lit another cigarette, and said, "As I've already suggested, the most probable alternative is that the victim himself told a lie. And if that was so, then it wouldn't be unreasonable to assume he had a secret known to the killer, who made clever use of it."

"Yes, this is logical enough . . . It may be too soon to guess at the secret, but if it did exist, then it's not unthinkable the victim unknowingly set himself up for the murder by sneaking out somewhere during the night."

"Well," Yoshioka said, "if we assume there was a secret, the killer could've made use of it in two different ways. Either he convinced the victim a sudden emergency had developed concerning his secret, or else he simply threatened to disclose the secret unless the victim did as he was told. But somehow I don't think it was a threat."

"Why not?"

"Because it's rare for a person threatened to be actually murdered. The only case I can think of is when the victim plucks up enough courage to attack his blackmailer, and gets killed for it. But on this occasion the victim had been enjoying some of the happiest hours of his life. He was hardly in a mood to do something desperate regardless of the consequences."

"That's true," Kirishima said absently. "A lot would depend on the nature of the secret, I'd imagine . . ." He scratched the back of his head for a while, then sat up and looked the inspector in the face. "Mr. Yoshioka, the various theories you've advanced are all interesting and logical. But before we go any further, I feel we should try to find an answer to a basic question."

"What's that?"

"Assuming this was a premeditated murder, why did the killer choose that particular night?"

"Hmm." Yoshioka stared at Kirishima rather stupidly. The question seemed to have thrown him completely off balance.

"Whether he was going to use a threat or some clever lie, he must have known it'd be pretty hard to lure a man out of bed in the middle of his wedding night. Furthermore, he knew very well that on that night, of all nights, the bride would be very close to the victim most of the time."

"Quite so," Yoshioka muttered. "If Mrs. Tsukamoto is telling the truth and she was in the bathroom when the call came through, well, that was a piece of luck the killer couldn't have counted on."

"That's right. Undoubtedly, he would've been ready with an excuse in case it was Mrs. Tsukamoto who took the call. Even so, if he was known to her, he still would've run the risk of being recognised by her."

"If only she'd been there when the victim answered that phone," Yoshioka said wistfully. "Even if he only said two or three words, the tone of his voice might have suggested to her whether he was talking to a friend, a superior, stranger, or what."

"Let's forget about the might-have-beens and try to look at this thing from the killer's point of view, shall we?" Kirishima could hardly conceal his impatience. "Anyone planning to lure another man into a death trap would naturally try to make contact when he knew the other was alone. Who would want a witness to murder? Until the wedding day the victim was living on his own as a bachelor, so the killer had plenty of better and safer opportunities to carry out his crime. Why then did he choose the wedding night—a night when there was a ninety-nine-percent chance of the victim *not* being alone?"

"It's strange all right," Yoshioka said, biting his lip. "This problem is so basic—that's why I didn't think of it, I suppose . . . Well, there must be a reason why the killer didn't act before the wedding day. Perhaps he'd been away from Tokyo?"

"Surely that wouldn't have stopped him. By using a plane he could've got back to Tokyo within a few hours from the northern tip of Hokkaido or the southern end of Kyushu . . . But suppose he couldn't have acted before the wedding. Why didn't he then wait for the couple to return from their honeymoon? He would've had plenty of opportunities afterwards. Why did he have to pick that most unsuitable night?"

"Isn't it possible he was afraid that during the honeymoon Tsukamoto might tell his wife something she shouldn't know? So to prevent this . . ." Yoshioka stopped and shook his head, frowning. "No, that doesn't make sense either. If that was the case, he could've murdered Tsukamoto long before the wedding."

"Well," Kirishima said with a smile, "it's a well known fact that sex partners love to launch into true confessions after their first session together."

For a while neither of them said any more. Kirishima kept twirling his pen between his fingers, and the inspector looked increasingly uncomfortable, as if the silence was becoming suffocating for him.

After a few minutes he took a deep, mournful breath, and said, "I've certainly made a bad blue missing this

117

point . . . Have you any suggestion, Mr. Prosecutor?"

Slowly Kirishima shook his head. "No, I've no idea at all. But I do feel that once we find the answer to this question, we'll have no trouble identifying the killer . . . I think at this stage we should work on the assumption that he had deliberately planned to strike a few hours after the couple became man and wife. He must have had a very good reason for doing that. I could be wrong, of course, but I feel that once we discover that reason, we'll have the case solved."

CHAPTER EIGHT

Kyoko Kirishima looked out the window. The clear winter sky was dazzlingly blue again that day. But inside the building the atmosphere seemed to be damp and gloomy. Perhaps it was only her own state of mind.

There were about twenty people in the anteroom of Nishihara Crematorium, waiting in small groups for the deceased to make his final journey through the flames. Soon Yoshihiro Tsukamoto would be reduced to a handful of ashes and placed in an urn inside a small wooden box.

Kyoko sighed and glanced around the room. Etsuko was sitting between her parents, still as a statue. Behind her glasses her eyes looked so swollen, she must have found it difficult to see through them.

Only thirty minutes ago the coffin had disappeared on its way to the furnace. That moment must have burnt into Etsuko's mind. She had placed both hands on the coffin for the last time and muttered something in a quavering whisper that could hardly be called a sound. The tears were running down her cheeks.

Not far from Etsuko, the deceased's brother,

Nobumasa, and his lawyer, Koike, were sitting together.

Nobumasa hadn't made the wedding, but he had managed to drag himself to the funeral. He looked just as pathetic as Etsuko, but in a different way. His left arm was in a sling, and a walking stick was placed against his chair—a reminder of his heavy limp. His face seemed feverish. A white gauze mask covered his mouth, and every now and then he coughed painfully. He must have contracted the current flu which was just reaching the height of its fury, Kyoko thought.

Koike looked rather worn out, too. After completing the business of the wedding, he had hardly had time to catch his breath before being called upon to organise the funeral. Even today he had to receive the mourners, look after Nobumasa, act as pall-bearer, and do a thousand other things. But now it was all over, and for the first time in days he had an opportunity to sit down and think of the death of his client, who had also been one of his closest friends. No wonder his face looked hollow with grief, Kyoko thought.

Perhaps it was natural that Higuchi wasn't at the funeral and hadn't turned up at the wake ceremony either. To him Yoshihiro Tsukamoto had been a complete stranger who had taken away from him the woman he wanted to marry. And in any case, it would have been rather awkward for him to face Etsuko at a time like this. But he did send her a telegram. Kyoko had been sitting with Etsuko at the wake last night when she opened the black-bordered piece of paper and then quickly put it aside as she recognised the name of the sender.

Sitting in a group at the rear were some university people, including Kawaji, the deceased's personal friend, and Professor Araki, head of the business management section. Professor Kuwajima, dean of the Department of Economics, who had been official witness at the wedding, had to depart early for another engagement but left his wife behind to pay her respects on his behalf.

Apart from Etsuko and Nobumasa, it was Kawaji who looked most upset by Yoshihiro's death. His naturally harsh face was broken and pale. In offering Etsuko his sympathy he had revealed a depth of sorrow not often seen in a man. Even now he seemed to be almost on the verge of tears as he kept watching her. His expression was in odd contrast with that of Professor Araki, who appeared to be peeved by the unpleasant taste of his cigarette.

Kyoko turned with a start when she felt a hand on her shoulder. It was Mr. Ogata. She hadn't seen him leave his seat.

"We're indebted to you for your kindness, Mrs. Kirishima," he whispered. His pleading attitude suggested he had something to tell her, but couldn't do it in front of the others.

Kyoko stood up and followed him out into the corridor, feeling sorry for him. It was all too obvious the past two days had taken their toll of him.

"For forty-nine days—until the ashes are committed to the grave—Etsuko herself wants to keep watch over them," he said. "It's perfectly natural for a young widow to want to do this—we appreciate how she feels. But she wants to take the ashes with her to the apartment at Setagaya, and we can't agree to this under any circumstances. We're afraid something terrible might happen to her if she's allowed to brood over them all alone in her dead husband's home."

"I thought she had given up the idea?"

"No, far from it. She's becoming more and more obstinate. She now insists on going over there tomorrow night . . . I wonder if you'd try to persuade her not to go? She might take more notice of a close friend . . ."

"Yes, I understand," Kyoko said, feeling even more sorry for the old man now. "I'll try . . ." She herself was definitely against the idea of Etsuko living on her own in that apartment.

She returned to the anteroom and gently took the chair beside Etsuko, previously occupied by Mr. Ogata. But before she had time to collect her thoughts, Etsuko turned and glared at her like never before in all the years they had known each other.

"I know what you're going to tell me," she snapped.

"You've been talking to my father, haven't you?"

"Please listen to me, Etsu. I know how you feel but——"

"And I know how you and my parents feel. You're worried about me, and I'm grateful to you for that. But this is one occasion when you'll just have to stay out of my way, that's all. At least for the first forty-nine days I'm going to live in that apartment on my own, thinking about my husband, re-living our happiest hours together . . . What's wrong with that? Isn't it perfectly natural for a widow to do that?"

"Yes, but——"

"Are you worried I might try to kill myself?" Etsuko was talking in whispers, but there was a stiff determination in her voice. "Well, stop worrying—that's what I've been telling my parents for the past twenty-four hours. You should know me better than that—I'm not that kind of woman. And even if I *were* crazy enough to want to commit suicide, I could never do it till my husband's killer is caught and I hear judgment passed on him with my own ears."

"But Etsu, I only——"

"Look, I promise you I'll return to my parents' home without fail at the end of forty-nine days. It may take six months or more even to catch the killer, let alone convict him. So you can rest assured I'll be perfectly safe on my own for the next seven weeks."

Listening to her Kyoko became conscious of a new doubt in her mind. Perhaps there was no danger of Etsuko committing suicide, but what if she was thinking of doing some other preposterous thing? What if she set out to track down the killer herself, and then take her own revenge? Being a young woman whose happiness in marriage had been nipped in the bud, it wouldn't be at all surprising if she was bitter enough to entertain such ideas.

"All the same, Etsu," Kyoko said, "I beg you to consider it carefully once more. My husband's worried about you, too, but for a different reason. He says so far he's been unable to establish an acceptable motive for the

122

crime. So how can we be sure the killer hasn't picked you for his next target? By living on your own in that apartment you'd be unnecessarily exposing yourself to danger, I feel."

"I can't recall incurring anybody's grudge, and I can't see that anybody would gain anything by killing me. Even if my husband had left behind a vast estate—and you know he hasn't—in the event of my death it would pass on to my parents. I know that much . . ." Suddenly she shot Kyoko a sharp glance. "Surely you don't think my father and mother would murder me for money, do you?"

Kyoko thought the conversation was becoming absurd, with Etsuko's voice growing more hysterical with every additional word. But she decided to try again, dabbing at the base of her throat with her handkerchief.

"Please stop talking nonsense, Etsu," she said. "Isn't it possible your husband's killer is insane? He may be doing things without any reason at all."

"Come now, Kyoko," Etsuko said impatiently. "Once we start on this, we can go on forever. If he *is* insane and wants to kill me, what will stop him even if I remain at my parents' home? He can murder my whole family if he wants to, in a number of ways. And next time he may even go for *you*, who have no connection with this case at all."

Kyoko was quickly approaching her wits' end. Etsuko's words seemed insane and logical at the same time. No wonder her parents had completely lost control of her.

She glanced at Mrs. Ogata. The poor old woman's face persuaded her to try just once more. "Listen, Etsu," she said, "the apartment at Setagaya isn't the only place where you can do your vigil in memory of your husband. Furthermore, you're not the only one who's been badly hurt by his death. How about considering your parents' feelings, too?"

Etsuko's pale face turned scarlet all of a sudden. "It's easy for you to talk like that," she said, raising her voice to an embarrassingly high pitch in that quiet place. "You're a happily married woman. How could you understand my feelings?"

123

Kyoko was left speechless. She felt she had been slapped in the face.

The wave of emotion leading to Etsuko's outburst seemed to have passed quickly. She covered her face with her hands and quietly began to sob. "I'm sorry—I shouldn't have said that," she muttered. "I didn't think I could ever become so insanely bitter. Please forgive me." She raised her eyes and took Kyoko's hand. "Kyoko, please remain my friend, will you? I need you . . . Please come to see me often in the apartment at Setagaya."

Early in the afternoon the same day, Kirishima was on his way back to the office from lunch. He had almost reached the rear entrance of the Criminal Affairs Division Building, when a young man walked up to him and said, "Excuse me. Are you State Prosecutor Kirishima?"

"Yes. And who are you?" Kirishima could tell by the badge on the man's double-breasted coat that he was a lawyer. But there were three different law societies in Tokyo alone, and it would have been impossible for anyone to know the faces, let alone the names, of all the lawyers in the city.

"I'm Tetsuya Higuchi, Mr. Ogata's junior partner. I'm sure you've already heard about me in connection with the Tsukamoto case." When Kirishima didn't reply, he added, "I've seen you a number of times in action in various courts, Mr. Prosecutor."

"And what's the problem?"

"Haven't you got something to discuss with me?" Higuchi spoke in an even tone.

"Not that I know of."

"I'm sure I'll be questioned, sooner or later. As a lawyer I can predict that much. So I thought I'd try to see you straight away. I don't particularly relish the idea of the police sniffing around me all the time. Besides, I'll have to go to the Kansai district to appear for a client within the next few days, and I don't want anybody to think I'm running away. That's why I decided to contact you now." His lips curled up in a smile that had a trace of sarcasm in it.

"I'm grateful to you for making the effort," Kirishima said pleasantly. "Please come up to my office—I'm prepared to hear whatever you have to say." If he was really going on a trip, he thought, it was preferable to get his story before he left. There was no way of keeping him in Tokyo at this stage.

In Kirishima's office Higuchi took one of the visitors' chairs and began to talk immediately. His voice was smooth and without the slightest trace of tension.

"This is a most unfortunate case," he said. "Well, to put it bluntly, I must be one of your suspects at this stage. I met the victim only once, quite by accident, but in relation to Etsuko Ogata we were rivals, and he beat me. I must admit I hated his guts at the time."

Kirishima gave a short nod and thought the man facing him was making the usual play of being completely honest about the obvious.

"But—and you may well refuse to believe this, Mr. Prosecutor—my real concern was not for my own pride but for Etsuko's happiness. I asked her to marry me partly because I was confident I could make her happy, and partly because I firmly believed this was the way to repay Mr. Ogata for all he had done for me over the years. So it's simply unthinkable that *I* would've done something to land Etsuko and the Ogata family in the depths of despair. Please note this point before anything else." Higuchi spoke as if he were standing behind the bar table, addressing the court.

Kirishima decided to try to jolt him out of his complacency with a nasty question. "Then it wasn't love but a sense of obligation to Mr. Ogata that prompted you to propose to his daughter?"

"Let me answer this by saying that I'm not quite as simple in my emotional make-up as the fellow in the *naniwa-bushi* ballad. For some time past I had entertained the idea that if Etsuko were prepared to become my wife, this would benefit everyone concerned. I also felt some affection towards her, though I can't say it was

125

passionate in any way. Perhaps I could best describe it as a quiet affection based on reason . . . In my opinion, any man who at the age of twenty-nine allows himself to be blinded and demented by love is a little weak in the head."

Kirishima thought Higuchi was the most unlikely person to commit a crime of passion. He was a man whose mind was dominated by reason to such an extent that he was almost as cold as a stone. A man like him, if he were ever to commit a crime, would plan everything to the minutest detail and would always be at least two jumps ahead of his pursuers.

Changing the subject, he asked, "When did you become aware of the existence of Yoshihiro Tsukamoto?"

"I'd suspected for some time that Etsuko was having dates with some other man besides me, but it was near the end of last year that I had the fact confirmed. I met them accidentally in a Chinese restaurant at Akasaka."

"Did you demand an explanation on the spot?"

"No, I wouldn't have done anything so boorish, especially in the presence of other people. As it happened, Etsuko herself insisted on introducing us. I think it was a panic reaction on her part."

"Judging by the behaviour of those two, did you assume their relationship had already passed beyond the stage of normal friendship?"

"Well, yes, I did," Higuchi said sourly.

"And did you withdraw then, realising you had no chance of holding her?"

"No, I didn't. I met Etsuko the following day and told her I'd fight to the end. You'd already know this from her, I'd say."

"What exactly did you mean by the word 'fight'?"

"I thought if I could demonstrate to her he was unsuitable for a partnership for life, she might come to her senses. But I had no intention of taking the wind out of his sails by distorting the facts in any way. That would've been against the spirit of fair play, and in any case, I thought if I did that and Etsuko learnt about it, I'd be automatically disqualified."

"What gave you the impression Tsukamoto was unsuitable for marriage?"

"Purely by accident I came across the fact that he had some special association with a man called Sogo Kumagaya, leader of a right-wing extremist group. I wanted to find out more about this, so after obtaining Mr. Ogata's permission I began to investigate Tsukamoto's background generally."

"And then you reported your findings to Mr. Ogata?"

"Yes. As I'd expected, my investigation confirmed my first impression had been correct. I was now fully convinced this man wasn't fit to become Etsuko's husband. Regardless of my personal feelings, don't you think it was my duty to report my findings to Mr. Ogata?"

"Nevertheless, your personal feelings did enter into it?"

"Mr. Prosecutor, you are at liberty to put your own interpretation on it. But I can assure you that although I told Etsuko I'd fight him to the end, I wouldn't have interfered had I thought there was a fair chance of her achieving happiness by getting married to him. But I was soon convinced a man with such shadows in his past couldn't possibly establish a happy home that would last."

Higuchi pulled a file out of his brief-case and put it on the desk. Then he said, "This is a report by the Teikoku Private Detective Agency. I wouldn't have had the time to look into every detail personally, but I didn't want to leave any gaps either. So I engaged these people to do it for me. Unfortunately, by the time this report was delivered to me, it was too late anyway. My efforts were completely wasted . . . It may be of some use to you, Mr. Prosecutor, so please accept it."

"Thank you—much obliged."

"Of course, you might already have all the facts contained in this report . . ." Higuchi stared at the file for a moment, then despondently shook his head. "No, I'm still convinced he wasn't the sort of man who could've made a woman happy for long, even if he *was* a man of property on a small scale."

"A man of property?" To Kirishima this was an entirely unexpected piece of information. "According to the police he had no property apart from his personal effects, a small insurance policy, and a modest amount in a savings bank account."

"Well, I don't know about his savings account—even the private detective was unable to ascertain what he had in it. But he did find out that Tsukamoto had bought his apartment as a home unit for 3,000,000 yen."

"I thought he was renting it?"

"At first he was. He had paid the usual key money, and for some months continued as a tenant on a monthly rental basis. Then last October he paid the balance of the purchase price and obtained a strata title on the apartment. Where he got the money from I wouldn't know, but details of the actual transaction are all there in that report."

Kirishima flipped through the report and found the figures. He recalled being mildly surprised at Tsukamoto's ability to save up 1,000,000 yen by the age of thirty. Still, a very thrifty young man who had been prepared to earn some extra money in his spare time could have done it. But another 3,000,000 yen? That was just too much. How on earth had he got hold of that kind of money?

Kirishima was fascinated by the question, but Higuchi didn't let him ponder over it for long.

Taking the initiative, he said, "Mr. Prosecutor, I'm not so naive as to think that what I've told you so far has cleared me of all suspicion. Do you mind if I say some more in my defence?"

"Go ahead."

"Let's assume for the moment that *I* am the killer. My obvious purpose in committing this crime was to win back Etsuko. Whether my act would actually achieve this purpose is beside the point. The essential thing is that I was *hoping* to achieve it by killing Tsukamoto. Do you agree so far?"

"Yes, provided you had no other motive."

"But of course I didn't. How could I? As I said before,

128

I only met the man once . . . Now, by killing Tsukamoto I did in fact completely defeat my purpose instead of achieving it. Had I killed him before they were married, at least I would've spared Etsuko some of the pain she's suffering now."

"That may be so, but if you had killed him before the wedding, the suspicion against you would've been much stronger. That might have persuaded you to leave the murder till after the wedding."

"Yes, this is a valid point," Higuchi said, "but it doesn't alter the fact that once Tsukamoto was dead—whether before or after—I automatically came under suspicion. Am I right?"

"Yes."

"Now, can you imagine I'd have any chance at all to win back Etsuko and thereby achieve my purpose while I'm suspected of the murder of her husband? Of course not. That's why any suggestion that *I* am the killer is absurd . . . The actual position is that at least until the killer is caught she won't have anything to do with me. Even if I have the perfect alibi, and this is accepted by the police, I'm sure she still won't be satisfied. And even when the killer *is* caught, she may still retain her doubts, thinking I might have hired him or otherwise pulled some strings behind the scenes . . . In other words, in any further attempt I might make to win Etsuko's favours, this murder will be a definite hindrance to me, not an advantage."

Kirishima was genuinely impressed with Higuchi's reasoning. The man had considerable talent, he thought. He'd be a tough opponent in a court of law.

"Yes, this is a very logical argument," he said. "The only thing is, if all rivals in love based their actions on logic, no lover would ever get killed. But in fact a lot of them do."

"Being a lawyer I'm well aware of that, but I also know the saying, 'make your doctrine suit the case'." Higuchi forced a cold smile. "Mr. Prosecutor, can you imagine me losing my reason in a jealous rage?"

"I wouldn't attempt to form an opinion at this stage

. . . And now, since you're already here, perhaps we could deal with some of the routine questions. Just for the record, could you recall your movements on the evening of February 15?"

"Yes, of course . . . As might be expected, I was rather ill at ease that evening. When I thought of Etsuko entering the bridal suite, I couldn't help feeling a little depressed. So I decided to go to see a show to divert my mind."

"And where did you go?"

"I went to see the Russian film version of *Hamlet* at the Miyukiza. I'm fairly certain it was the final day of screening."

"You didn't have anyone with you?"

"No."

"About what time did you leave the theatre?"

"Oh, it would've been shortly before ten o'clock."

"And what did you do then?"

"Well, since *Hamlet* hadn't done anything to improve my mood, I decided to try a drink. I drove to the Black Rose Bar on the outskirts of Roppongi."

"In your own car?"

"Yes."

"This bar—do you drink there regularly?"

"Yes, though I go there more for the sake of the atmosphere than the liquor. I don't drink very much, but I do enjoy the quiet milieu of that place. I don't like noisy bars."

"What time did you get there?"

"It wasn't quite half past ten."

"Mm-hm. And how long did you stay?"

For the first time Higuchi looked slightly disconcerted. He smiled awkwardly, and said, "This is something I don't feel like talking about, but I don't suppose I've any choice now . . . When I got there, the proprietress was about to close because there was no other customer, and both the barman and the barmaid were off with the flu. She told me she herself didn't feel too good."

"And then?"

"Well, since I was one of her regular customers, she

let me in, and I had a couple of drinks over the next thirty minutes or so . . . There were only the two of us in the bar, and somehow she sensed my mood. It must have matched her own . . ."

"What's the name of the proprietress?"

"Yasuko Yoshimura. She's about my own age . . . I gave her a lift home and, well, ended up spending the night with her . . . It's not the sort of thing I'm very proud of . . ."

Kirishima could hardly keep a straight face. That a single man should make such fuss over a one-night stand. Higuchi was certainly as straight-laced as they came, he thought.

"Where does she live?"

"Oh, about five minutes' walk from Yotsuya station. I don't know the address—I'd never been there before —but I can get it for you."

"And you didn't leave her apartment till the next morning?"

"That's correct."

If this was true, Higuchi had a perfect alibi, Kirishima thought. No wonder he had come forward voluntarily. He wanted to lift the suspicion hanging over him as quickly as possible.

Displaying none of his previous self-confidence now, Higuchi said, "When you establish beyond doubt that I had nothing to do with this crime, will you be prepared to forget what I've told you about staying with that woman?"

"That goes without saying. I couldn't disclose any private matter of this kind unless it was absolutely essential to the case of the prosecution. As a lawyer, you must be well aware of this."

"Yes, of course," Higuchi said hesitantly. "My question wasn't addressed to the prosecutor, but to the private citizen."

"Oh, I see." Now Kirishima understood what Higuchi was driving at. He was afraid his adventure with the bar proprietress might reach Etsuko's ears through Kyoko. Obviously, he hadn't yet given up his ambition to make

131

his senior partner's daughter his wife. "I can assure you the private citizen you're referring to never enters this office. So you're quite safe on that score."

At about the same time, Inspector Yoshioka was facing Sogo Kumagaya in the homicide squad's interrogation room at police headquarters. The old man was dressed in *haori* and *hakama*. A folding fan was held defiantly in his hand.

He glared at Yoshioka, and said, "What do you want from me? I've had some dealings with the security police from time to time, but this is the first time I've had anything to do with the homicide squad. Now, what is it?"

"Haven't you heard about the murder yet?"

"Oh, is it Yoshihiro you're referring to?" The defiant expression disappeared from Kumagaya's wrinkled face. "Indeed I'm saddened by his death ... Though I hadn't been invited to the wedding, I was racking my brains trying to find a suitable marriage gift for him, and then this happened ... All I can do now is pray for the repose of his soul ... Frankly, I don't think I can be of any assistance to you concerning his death, but on this occasion I shall willingly co-operate in whatever way I can."

"Have you any idea who might have killed him?"

"I wouldn't be surprised at all if it was the work of some people in the Communist Party. The study of management is a capitalistic discipline, isn't it?"

Yoshioka heaved a deep sigh without realising it. "Can you tell us about the connection between you and the deceased?"

"Yoshihiro was the son of a man to whom I'm indebted for life."

"Indebted? In what way?"

"Shinnosuke Tsukamoto was the master who opened my eyes and mind. During my formative years I read his *World of Shintoism* so many times I could recite it from memory ... He wrote *We Are His Children* for popular consumption, and indeed it's rather simple in its approach, but *Ruinous Thoughts* is a fine work, perfectly applicable even today. In it he explains with great clarity how both communism and western democracy can destroy the fundamental character of the nation, and in fact predicts the sickness of today's Japanese society."

"I see," Yoshioka said with drooping lips. "Now, could we leave these ideological problems for the moment and talk about your relationship with the victim's father? Was it purely one of master and pupil? Or were you also involved in the revolt just before the end of the war, in which Tsukamoto played a major role?"

Kumagaya nodded gravely. "That's an old story now, so there's no harm in telling you I did take part in the uprising, but only as one of the mob . . . When we failed, the master directed us to go into hiding and work unceasingly for the cause. This, of course, made good sense. You may recall that during the Munich riots in Germany, when Nazi supporters were fired upon by regular soldiers, Hitler himself was one of the first to run . . . As the master stressed at the time, one had to accept temporary shame for the sake of final victory. Throwing one's life away without purpose at that crucial juncture would've been an unforgivable sin against the cause."

"I see. That's why Shinnosuke Tsukamoto turned his back on his followers who were about to throw their lives away by *hara-kiri*, took to his heels and ran like a rabbit? And you—since you were only one of the mob —I suppose you had no problem fading out from the scene?"

Kumagaya replied with studied dignity. "Yes, this is how it would appear to a superficial observer. He wouldn't be able to comprehend the exalted motivation behind our actions. You see, we modelled ourselves on Shikanosuke Yamanaka, the sixteenth-century soldier of the civil wars, whose lifelong ambition was to restore the Amako clan to its former glory . . ."

Yoshioka didn't know what the old man was talking

133

about, and he didn't care. But he was satisfied Kumagaya wasn't putting on an act. This was a rare old bird, in whom the fanatical patriotism of the war years somehow survived to this day. "By the way," he said, "were you on friendly terms with the victim, too?"

"With Yoshihiro? No, there was nothing like that between us. After the master's death I took care of the young fellow for a little while, staying in the background, of course. Those were bad times, and I thought it could be embarrassing for the bereaved family to be openly associated with a man like me . . . And once Yoshihiro became a scholar, I was even more careful to keep a respectable distance."

It was amazing, Yoshioka thought, how fanatical rat-bags like this old man managed to pay due attention to appearances, at the same time as they tried their hardest to swim against the current.

"When did you last meet the victim?"

"It was at the end of last year. I ran into him accidentally in a most unlikely place, and we exchanged a few words without even sitting down."

"And the time before that?"

"If I rightly remember, it was around 1962."

If this was true, Kumagaya would have no connection with the case. Yoshioka felt disappointed, but went on with his questioning. "Were you associated with Tadaaki Tsukamoto in any way?"

"Who's he?"

"He was the victim's younger brother. In his student days he'd been mixed up in various right-wing activities, so I naturally thought he would've run into you at one time or another."

"Aaah, you're talking about Tadaaki Yasuda, aren't you? He used his mother's family name since early child-hood . . . That's why I didn't understand you for a moment, but if you think I'm the one who dragged him down, you're completely wrong!" Kumagaya slammed his folding fan on the table. "I had certainly entertained some hopes of transmitting to him his father's great ideals, but he was an unworthy son. He kept away from me, then went astray, pursuing an evil course. Finally death put an end to his pitiful career . . . I've often blamed myself for not trying a little harder to save him, but now that he's with his father in the other world, he has every opportunity to beg the master's pardon. There wouldn't be any point in raking up his sins now, after all this time . . ."

Yoshioka didn't accept at face value everything the old man had said. There might have been more to his relationship with Tadaaki than he would have the police believe. But so far as the present interview was concerned, there was nothing more to go on.

"One final question then, Mr. Kumagaya," he said. "Just as a matter of formality, would you tell us where you were on the evening of February 15?"

Kumagaya's wrinkled face suddenly turned stiff again, and he glared at the inspector, as at the beginning. "Do you think *I* might have murdered the son of the man to whom I owe so much?" He picked up his fan from the table as if he were going to strike out with it. "I was engaged in debate with my young followers from seven o'clock till after midnight. And if you think I'm not telling the truth, I suggest you go and ask my pupils."

CHAPTER NINE

Kirishima decided to take a personal look at some of the academics who had been associated with the victim. He advised Inspector Yoshioka accordingly, and next morning drove to Chiyoda University with his clerk Kitahara.

At this stage of the investigation the principal task was to sort out all persons who might have had a motive for the crime. And while these days universities were no longer the ivory towers they used to be, they still had a lot of peculiar characters on their staff. A prosecutor was better equipped to deal with such people than a police officer. That was why Kirishima decided to interrogate them personally, and Yoshioka gratefully accepted his ruling.

First Kirishima called on Professor Kuwajima, dean of the Department of Economics. He only had to wait a couple of minutes before the tall, silver-haired professor appeared in the reception room. He radiated gentleness and dignity, as might be expected of an eminent scholar.

"Thank you for sparing the time, Professor," Kirishima said politely.

"It's nothing." He offered Kirishima a chair and a cigarette. "As dean of the department I'm often dragged out to ceremonial functions relating to coming of age, marriage, funerals, ancestral worship and so forth. But frankly, I never thought I'd have to attend the same man's wedding and funeral with only one day between . . . Well, what would you like to know?"

"To begin with, could you tell me something about the victim's move to this university? Who brought him here?"

"I did. Are you aware of the reason for his departure from Kyoraku University?"

"As far as I know, it was precipitated by the death of an unworthy younger brother in a fire."

Kuwajima nodded. "I was told about it by my friend, Professor Suenaga, who was Tsukamoto's immediate superior at Kyoraku. I decided to bring the young man here because I felt there was no sense in allowing him to ruin his promising career over something which was none of his doing. Kyoraku is rather dominated by tradition, but here we have a more forward-looking attitude. We always need new talent on our research staff, and I thought Tsukamoto might prove useful in his particular field."

"Were his colleagues aware of his family affairs?"

"No. Only the vice-chancellor knew about his background. All the others were given the impression Tsukamoto hadn't been able to get on with his professor at Kyoraku, so he came over to us. Of course, he himself could've revealed the truth to someone here. That I wouldn't know."

"And as his dean, what did you think of Tsukamoto's performance as a scholar and teacher?"

"I was completely satisfied with him. He was very keen on research, and this gave some of his colleagues a much needed incentive. He was also popular among the students. To be quite honest with you, one of the weaknesses of our university is that we've too many people on our staff who wish to settle down to a cosy, effortless existence once they reach a certain level. We aren't unique in this, but Tsukamoto did introduce a certain dynamism to his section. This was probably due to his training at Kyoraku as much as to his character."

"How did he get along with his colleagues?"

"Perhaps he was inclined to be a little introverted, but this isn't at all unusual among scholars. He didn't make friends easily, but I don't think he had any special problems of communication either."

"Can you think of anyone who might have had hostile feelings towards him? Forgive me for saying this, but I understand the academic world is by no means free of the usual complexities of human relationships."

"Scholars are human beings, like anyone else," Kuwajima said, forcing a smile. "But perhaps it's true to say that because of their comparative isolation and continuing quest for knowledge, some scholars retain certain childish characteristics—especially petty jealousy—more so than adults in the outside world would. I couldn't say with authority that there was absolutely no ill feeling towards Tsukamoto. But if it did exist, it certainly wasn't ever brought to the surface, and I don't believe it could've possibly had any bearing on his murder. On the other hand, it isn't unthinkable that some of his tardier colleagues secretly sighed with relief when they heard of his death. But that's all I can say."

"I understand," Kirishima said. "Then may I ask you something else? Would you have any knowledge of the victim's financial standing, by any chance?"

"When he came here, I asked him about it as a formality. He told me he owned no real estate and had only about 300,000 yen in savings, but that wasn't anything unusual. Scholars are measured by their talent and capacity for sustained effort, not by their wealth. If he had been ashamed of his modest means, his qualifications as a scholar would've been immediately suspect."

"But we've discovered he had 4,000,000 yen in savings last autumn."

Professor Kuwajima tilted his head in surprise. "This is news to me. I was under the impression Tsukamoto had no talent for making money . . . I wonder if he might have won something on the lottery?"

Professor Araki, head of the business management section, appeared to be a fastidious man. And there was a certain hauteur in his attitude towards Kirishima. He said as little as possible, and his manner was cool and disinterested.

"I know nothing about his private life, so I can't really help you," he said, making it clear from the start he wasn't going to put himself out to assist the investigation.

Kirishima repeated his previous question to the dean by asking Araki what he had thought of Tsukamoto's performance as a scholar.

Araki raised his eyebrows. "Let me see . . . He was certainly very enthusiastic about research, and had plenty of drive—almost to the extent of being carried away by ambition. This, of course, is fairly typical of all young scholars."

There was quite a difference between his assessment and the dean's, Kirishima thought. "Could you give me an example?"

"Well, for one thing, he rushed into print with the results of a rather immature research project of his before it was quite completed. He did that against my advice."

"By the way, can you offer any suggestion regarding his death?"

"None at all, except that the incident has nothing to do with the university."

"What makes you say that?"

"The idea of murder in a university is unthinkable. Furthermore, Tsukamoto appeared to have something to hide. I heard a rumour—though I can't remember where, or from whom—that he had been associated with some person of questionable character in making illegal money. I laughed at the suggestion at the time, saying it was most unlikely. I certainly didn't take it seriously— that's why I can't remember the source of the rumour. But now I wonder if the answer lies in that direction?

139

Perhaps you should follow it up."

"I will," Kirishima said pleasantly. "But supposing there *was* some truth in that rumour, and it had been brought to light before Tsukamoto's death, what would've happened then?"

"It would've been raised at the departmental board meeting. Tsukamoto's problem at Kyoraku University had sprung from something in which he hadn't been personally involved. But any illegal act for which he himself was partly responsible would've automatically meant his dismissal from this university. And then his future as a scholar would've been in jeopardy. Now, I have a lecture to deliver, so please excuse me, will you?"

Araki picked up a book and some notes from his desk and promptly marched out of the room, leaving Kirishima sitting there.

No matter what Araki had said, he seemed to know quite a bit about the mystery surrounding the victim, Kirishima thought. But at this stage there was no way of cornering him.

The next stop was the research room which had lost its master. A short, bespectacled youth stood up and introduced himself in an apprehensive voice.

"I'm Kunio Iwauchi," he said. "I've been working under Mr. Tsukamoto since the end of last year . . . A police officer has already examined this room. I was about to collect the deceased's personal effects and take them to Mrs. Tsukamoto. Then I was going to move out of here. Is there something else you want to look at?"

"No, there's no problem concerning the room itself," Kirishima said, glancing around. It was a drab place. Apart from a couple of desks with chairs, a book-case and a big filing cabinet, there was nothing in it. "I'd like to ask you a few questions if you wouldn't mind."

"What would you like to know, sir? I'm completely bewildered by Mr. Tsukamoto's death . . . Apart from everything else, I've lost my first real opportunity to work under an excellent teacher . . ."

"Have you any idea at all about his murder?"

"I can't imagine why anyone would've wanted to kill

him."

"Did you notice any recent change in Mr. Tsuka-moto's behaviour?"

"If there was any change, it was all for the better. After he got engaged he became much more cheerful. His previous moodiness was completely gone."

"I see . . . Now, tell me this. Was Mr. Tsukamoto engaged in any special research during the time you were with him?"

"What do you mean by 'special'?"

"Well, he might have been doing some pioneering work which produced immediate results of a practical nature."

Iwauchi adjusted the spectacles on his nose. "Business management is a fairly new field of study, therefore research into almost any aspect of it amounts to pioneering, in a sense. But I can't think of a single facet of our research that could've immediately produced profitable results. This may be possible in some technological field, but surely not in business management studies. I really don't think Mr. Tsukamoto's research work could've had any link with his murder."

"I thought so, too, though I know very little about management studies."

"Mr. Tsukamoto did lecture to engineering students, but only on industrial administration . . . The only thing associated with profit that I can think of is his manuscript for a book to be published in the near future. He finished it and handed it to the publisher about ten days before his wedding. It's to have the title, *Understanding I.E.,* and will be published in soft cover and sold at a retail price of 300 yen. The first print will be 8,000 copies. So after tax, the return in royalties will be no more than 220,000 yen. You could hardly call that a profit, con-sidering the amount of work Mr. Tsukamoto put into it."

"I see . . . By the way, we've gained the impression Mr. Tsukamoto didn't get on well with Professor Araki. What do *you* think?"

"I wouldn't know anything about that," Iwauchi said,

blinking a few times.

"I was told in the registrar's office a short while ago that another lecturer in the business management section, a Mr. Nitta, has been away since the day before Mr. Tsukamoto's wedding. I understand his family home is at Tsuchiura?"

"That's right. His father was over seventy and was suffering from an advanced form of asthma . . . I heard he died on the morning of the fifteenth."

"Would you know if there might have been some antagonism between Mr. Tsukamoto and Mr. Nitta?"

"I'm sorry, I wouldn't know anything about that," Iwauchi said.

When it came to human relationships, this assistant certainly became supercautious, Kirishima thought.

After leaving the research room of the Department of Economics, Kirishima and his clerk went to see Kawaji, who worked in the research section of the Department of Law. This was located in the next building.

Since Kawaji had been one of the victim's closest friends, and he worked in a different department, he might be prepared to talk more freely, Kirishima thought, realising at the same time that special care would have to be taken during the questioning. Kawaji was an expert on the Criminal Procedure Code.

But the young lecturer received him eagerly and immediately asked a number of questions which showed his genuine concern.

"How's it going? Have you any clues to the killer yet?"

"None so far. That's why I've come to seek your cooperation."

"I'll certainly do whatever I can to help you. I've been advocating the abolishment of capital punishment, but now I'm not so sure any more. The man who was capable of killing my friend on his wedding night must be a monster, whatever his motive."

"It's the motive we're concerned with at the moment."

Kirishima said. "Have you any suggestion to offer?"

"I haven't the faintest idea, I'm afraid . . . As far as I know, Tsukamoto never did a thing to arouse anyone's displeasure or hatred. Certainly he was a rather unsociable man, not very good at getting along with people, but after a while his gentleness and sincerity showed through."

"But surely we couldn't say nobody has ever had a grudge against him?"

Kawaji held Kirishima's gaze for a while, then answered with a question. "You've met Professor Araki, haven't you?"

Kirishima nodded.

"Well, I was going to tell you this anyway . . . But would you mind keeping the source of your information to yourself?"

"Yes, of course."

"I personally think Professor Araki's hostility towards Tsukamoto was largely a product of misunderstanding. His wife is notorious in university circles, to the extent of being often referred to as a nymphomaniac. Well, Tsukamoto became one of her targets, but he resolutely ignored her advances. So, in retaliation she began to poison her husband's mind with all sorts of phony tales about him . . ."

Kawaji lit a cigarette and got rid of a couple of distasteful puffs. "Of course, the professor knows his wife as well as anybody, so he largely ignores her shallow intrigue. But even so, after hearing the same slander over and over again, he'd naturally start wondering if at least portion of it mightn't be true."

"Yes, that's possible."

"Now, I wouldn't know what she was telling him about Tsukamoto. It could've been that favourite line of spurned women—they accuse the man they fail to land of having tried to seduce them. Or she could've told her husband Tsukamoto had an eye on his chair and was trying to ease him out of it by going over his head to the dean. That's just speculation, of course."

"Are you sure there was nothing between Mrs. Araki

and the victim?"

"Absolutely. Tsukamoto was ultra-conservative where women were concerned. Even *I* became impatient with him over that. Before Etsuko's appearance on the scene he had no girlfriend of any sort. In fact, I was rather stunned by the sudden blossoming of their friendship. I thought the two must have been born under the same star."

Kirishima shifted in his chair and began to scratch the back of his head. "Do you think Professor Araki still has some affection for his wife?"

"Mmm. That's a hard one to answer. Perhaps he has —mixed with dislike, and self-reproach. He's partly responsible for what she is today . . ."

"What d'you mean?"

"This is only hearsay, you understand, but I was told the couple had no children for a long time. Then about ten years ago Mrs. Araki had a boy. They treasured him and raised him with great care. Then one Sunday, soon after the boy's fourth birthday, she had to go out somewhere and left the child at home in her husband's care. Araki was absorbed in some newly received literature, and the boy managed to sneak out of the house. By the time his disappearance was discovered, it was too late. He was found floating face down in the nearby Tamagawa canal."

"I see," Kirishima said. "And that's when she began to change?"

Kawaji nodded. "And the same can be said of her husband. Araki's enthusiasm for his work rapidly declined after the tragedy. His students say behind his back that his lectures are the same year after year, including the jokes he tells . . . He has now reached the stage where his previously established reputation barely supports his position."

Kirishima recalled Araki's hard face and curt manner, and was reminded of numerous similar psychological patterns he had perceived in his work. There were far more people than generally imagined who hid their distress and confusion behind a tough front . . . He decided to change the subject.

"Tsukamoto was far better off financially than we had expected," he said. "Would you have any idea where his extra income came from?"

"Well, public lecture fees and royalties from published work are normal extras for scholars, but none of Tsukamoto's writings has become a best-seller. I'm quite sure he didn't get much out of his books. And I don't think he ever worked for any company in an advisory capacity."

"He purchased the apartment he was living in for 3,000,000 yen."

"I thought he was renting it." Kawaji looked genuinely surprised. "Of course, he could've bought it with a loan raised somewhere, but Tsukamoto always disliked borrowing money—ever since we were students."

Kirishima asked a few more questions but didn't get any further. So far as the actual murder was concerned, Kawaji could do no more than keep repeating that he was baffled.

"Mr. Kawaji, I understand you've been a widower for some time?"

A shadow passed over the young lecturer's face. "Yes," he said, "my wife died in a car accident the year before last. I've never driven a car since."

On his way back from the university Kirishima called at police headquarters to have a talk with Yoshioka.

"A couple of interesting facts have come to light in the meantime," Yoshioka said with an air of urgency, as if he had been waiting for the opportunity to report to Kirishima. "Higuchi's statement to you has been confirmed by the bar proprietress Yoshimura, but it seems the relationship between them goes beyond that of bar keeper and customer."

"Was there a sexual relationship between them prior to the night mentioned by Higuchi?"

"I've no proof of that, but there's ample evidence of a lawyer-client relationship. About two years ago Yasuko Yoshimura obtained a divorce from her wealthy husband on the grounds of his adultery, and with Higuchi's able assistance she finished up with a large amount of settlement money. That's how she could buy the Black Rose Bar."

"Then she must feel indebted to Higuchi?"

"Yes. It's not unthinkable she would've helped him to establish a false alibi."

"What type of woman is she?"

"Quite beautiful in a plump sort of way," Yoshioka said, winking. "This may be an unkind thing to say, but I think she's far more attractive than Mrs. Tsukamoto. And I'm sure any man who managed to get into bed with her would have a pretty good time . . . But she certainly isn't the type of woman a man like Higuchi would want to marry."

"If she's like that, then isn't it possible she'd be prepared to assist Higuchi without any jealousy in his attempts to get himself a suitable wife? The only thing is—Higuchi's statement is most convincing and logical, and in his case rejected love would seem to be far too weak a motive for murder."

"That's true," Yoshioka said, making a glum face. "Still, at this stage at any rate, I'd like to proceed on the assumption that his alibi isn't one hundred percent . . . Now, the second fact to come to light is that there's a rather mysterious man called Hiroshi Watanabe among the victim's relatives."

Kirishima nodded without comment. As he had expected, the inspector hadn't wasted any time digging up Watanabe.

Yoshioka said, "According to Mrs. Tsukamoto, he's one of those intelligent rascals with a dubious look about them. Apparently, he saved Tsukamoto's life when they were children, and has been sponging on him ever since."

"Have you got his address?"

"I've no idea where he is at the moment. Until February 4 he was living in an apartment located about five minutes' walking distance from the victim's apartment."

"Has he been missing since?"

"Not exactly missing, because he moved out of the

apartment in the normal way, but we can't establish his present whereabouts. He just told the caretaker he was going north to take up a new position."

"But hasn't he left a forwarding address?"

"No. He said he'd live in temporary accommodation till he found a suitable flat, and asked the caretaker to forward all his mail to Tsukamoto's address. But so far there's no letter for him there."

"He's a strange bird all right," Kirishima said.

"Oh, I almost forgot—when Watanabe moved into the apartment, Tsukamoto signed as his referee."

"When was that?"

"The tenancy agreement was signed on May 1 last year."

"Wasn't that soon after Tsukamoto himself had moved from Kyoto to Tokyo?"

"Yes . . . It certainly looks fishy to me."

"Have you dug up anything on Watanabe's occupation, or last place of work?"

"I'm afraid I haven't. The caretaker says when he moved in there, he just said he'd be looking for a suitable job, or something like that. But of course, once a university lecturer signed his papers for him, nobody worried about his job any more."

"Hmm. And did he pay his rent properly?"

"Yes. Sometimes he was a few days behind, but generally there was no trouble with him. And he paid up when he moved out."

"Didn't he associate with anyone in that apartment house?"

"No. My man checked this out thoroughly in the hope of getting a clue on him, but apparently Watanabe didn't speak even to his next door neighbour. Well, this is nothing unusual in Tokyo these days . . ." Yoshioka made a sour face. "Anyway, all we know about him is that he lived a very irregular life and was always full of *sake* when he got home. Hardly anybody ever visited him. When he moved in, he had very little luggage, but later bought a few pieces of furniture and some household utensils. Then just before moving out, he sold the

147

lot to a second-hand dealer. He left there with a single suitcase."

Kirishima shook his head. "I'm sure he could tell us an interesting story, if only we could get hold of him."

"Yes . . . I've a feeling he has a criminal record. Of course, the name doesn't mean a thing. Unfortunately, a new tenant has already moved into the apartment, so it'd be virtually impossible to collect fingerprints. Anyway, when Watanabe left, the caretaker did a big clean-up job, even to the extent of changing all the *tatamis* . . . I think the only thing we can do now is ask the Identification Section to make an identikit picture of him."

"Wouldn't the victim's elder brother, or his lawyer, or someone else know something about this man? Surely there must be somebody?" Kirishima no longer could conceal his irritation.

"Well," Yoshioka said sheepishly, "I only received this report a few minutes ago. My men couldn't do much yesterday, with everybody attending the funeral . . . And I feel that even if this Watanabe turns out to be a bad one, it'll be difficult to connect him with the murder. He was supposed to be sponging on Tsukamoto—almost living off him. Why would he want to kill the goose that lays the golden egg? Furthermore, I don't think he had a strong enough hold on Tsukamoto to get him out of that hotel on his wedding night. And suppose it was Tsukamoto who had a hold on Watanabe through knowing something about him, and Watanabe wanted to shut him up? In that case how on earth could Watanabe have extorted money from the victim?"

"You're right. Besides, even if he wanted to kill Tsukamoto, there was no need for him to do it on the wedding night."

Yoshioka nodded. "We've checked on a number of other people apart from Higuchi and Watanabe. I'm afraid none of them would've had a reason to commit this crime . . . And how about your inquiries at the university, Mr. Prosecutor?"

Kirishima gave an account of the various interviews. The longer he went on, the more disappointed the inspector looked.

"I see," Yoshioka said in the end. "Professor Araki and his wife each would've had some sort of a motive. But so far as Mrs. Araki is concerned, I doubt whether she would've been able to lure the victim out of the hotel on that particular night. Moreover, it seems quite impossible for a woman to commit a murder like this all by herself."

"I think so, too. Even if there was something between her and the victim, it's most unlikely he would've been prepared to leave his bride that night just to go to make love to her. Another point is that Mrs. Tsukamoto knew about Mrs. Araki, so even if she did phone that night, there was no need for Tsukamoto to go to great lengths to conceal her existence from his wife. Besides, if Mrs. Araki had been so desperate to hang on to her lover, she would've tried something well before the wedding, wouldn't she? . . . Finally, the person who made the phone call had a male voice."

"Well, that eliminates Mrs. Araki," Yoshioka said. "As for Professor Araki, he was Tsukamoto's immediate superior, and as such was certainly in a position to lure him out of the hotel with the excuse of the exam papers. But why would he have done that? As a jealous husband he should've felt greatly relieved that his wife's real or imagined lover was at last settling down with another woman, much younger than Mrs. Araki. There was no point in killing him . . ."

Kirishima gave a couple of short nods. "And even if Araki believed Tsukamoto had his eyes on his job, that still wouldn't amount to an acceptable motive for murder. After all, the victim was a young lecturer who had only been there a short while and hardly wielded enough influence for Araki to worry about . . ."

Yoshioka gave a deep sigh. "It's confusing all right. On the basis of what we've got to date, there isn't anyone to derive monetary gain from Tsukamoto's death except his wife. And we have no real suspect for the grudge motive either. So what the hell *is* the motive?"

"Well," Kirishima said, "murder is often the end

149

result of some extraordinary psychological process in the killer's mind, which is beyond the understanding of the observer. In such cases it's useless trying to solve the crime by sound reasoning . . . But whatever we are facing here, we must guard against hasty conclusions."

"I understand," Yoshioka said. "I'll try to follow up every clue, however small, as thoroughly as I can."

"I've full confidence in you and your men, Inspector."

CHAPTER TEN

"At last we're getting somewhere," Yoshioka told Kirishima on the phone just before lunch the next day. "We've got the taxi driver who picked up the victim in front of the New Tokyo Hotel. He's employed by the Toyo Taxi Company and has been away from work for the past three days because of his son's illness. He said he was too worried about his son to read the papers."

"Uh-huh. And where did he take the victim?"

"To a lonely spot near the National Railway workshops at Shinagawa."

"Shinagawa?"

"Yes. Apparently, Tsukamoto didn't head for the entrance to the workshops, but stood there looking around, as if waiting for someone to turn up. The taxi driver left immediately, so he can't say what the victim did next . . . A little while ago two of my detectives inspected the exact spot with the driver."

"Can you describe the locality?"

"The railway workshops and stores and a number of marshalling yards take up a large area. It's a place never seen by the general public. At night it becomes almost a

151

no man's land—completely quiet and deserted. There's a big pharmaceutical plant and a number of other factories in the vicinity. All are quiet at night."

"Yes, I think I know the place—I've been through there once," Kirishima said.

"According to the driver, there wasn't a soul around where Tsukamoto got out of the taxi."

"It was the ideal place for murder."

"We'll make a thorough search of the area, though I doubt if we'll find any physical evidence after four days. Apart from everything else, we've had a few showers since . . . I reckon the victim was killed somewhere there, and then the body was taken by car to Kitamicho to be dumped. The obvious intention of the killer was to slow down the investigation."

"Or he might have been disturbed at the workshops, so he knocked out the victim with a *karate* blow and drove him to the other place to finish him off . . . Anyway, even if the chances of finding some clue near the railway workshops are very slim, please have the vicinity thoroughly searched."

"I'll certainly do that," Yoshioka said. "By the way, those railway workshops are in an entirely different direction from Chiyoda University in relation to the New Tokyo Hotel. And at this stage we can't find anyone connected with the National Railway, or living in that area, who was known to the victim. What do *you* think, Mr. Prosecutor?"

Kirishima put his elbows on the desk and cradled the receiver in his hands. "Well, now we have it confirmed it was the victim who told his bride a lie. It would've been absolutely impossible to lure him out to that lonely spot with the excuse of the missing exam papers. But that still leaves us with the question—what *was* the excuse the killer used? To be honest, I've no idea at all at the moment."

"Same here . . . The only thing I can add is that the victim must have trusted the killer, or at least wasn't afraid of him. This is indicated by his willingness to meet the killer in that lonely place, and also by the frontal

152

attack on him."

"I agree. And this means we can just about eliminate any theory based on a threat . . . Well, we can't go on forever discussing this on the phone. But just to make sure we're on the right track—how can you be certain it was Tsukamoto who was picked up by that taxi driver? Couldn't it have been somebody who looked like him?"

Yoshioka replied without the slightest hesitation. "We mixed the victim's photograph with nine others depicting men of similar features and age. The taxi driver picked out Tsukamoto at once. So he must have taken a pretty good look at him."

"Right. This it what I had in mind. Is there anything else for now?"

"Yes. Concerning Watanabe, and how the victim managed to purchase his own apartment, I sent senior detectives to both lawyer Koike and the elder brother."

"I see."

"I'll deal with Koike first. He said he knew from the victim there was a distant relative called Watanabe who gave a lot of trouble. He had caught sight of the man a couple of times but never actually spoken to him. And he didn't know what Watanabe's exact relationship to the Tsukamotos was."

"And what did he say about the money?"

"Nothing much. He claimed he had no detailed knowledge of the victim's financial affairs. He spoke cautiously and tactfully, as might be expected of a lawyer. My man wasn't satisfied and pressed on, but finally got the impression Koike was quite genuine. Koike suggested the modest assets left by Tsukamoto Senior to his widow would've been eaten up completely in the education of the three children, so it was unthinkable the victim's money would've come from that direction."

"Mm-hm. And what did the elder brother have to say?"

"Surprisingly, he didn't know much about Watanabe either."

"That's strange . . ." Kirishima leaned back in his

tilting swivel chair until the phone cord was almost taut, and rested his head against his raised left arm. "He must be related to Watanabe in the same way as his brother. Besides, Watanabe is supposed to have saved his brother's life. If that's true, then isn't it rather odd he doesn't know much about the man?"

"The detective questioned him persistently on that, but didn't get very far with him. Tsukamoto said he was aware of the existence of a man called Watanabe who had lived near the Tsukamoto home during the war and had been one of Yoshihiro's playmates. But he himself had lived in the barracks of a munition factory, doing labour service under the Students' Mobilisation Act at the time. He couldn't remember much of life in and around the Tsukamoto home during that period. It was well after the war that he first heard about Watanabe saving Yoshihiro's life."

"Hm. Did he say what the exact family tie was between Watanabe and the Tsukamotos?"

"He claimed he had no idea. He said he vaguely remembered his mother saying something about it, but links between distant relatives were often very complicated, and he had never personally associated with Watanabe, so over the years he had completely forgotten about him."

This made sense, at least on the face of it, Kirishima thought. He himself had quite a few relatives he couldn't sort out. When it came to relationships like his maternal grandfather's cousin's son, there was hardly any difference between a relative and a complete stranger, and it was impossible to remember the connecting chain. But he still wasn't quite satisfied with Nobumasa Tsukamoto's explanation. Frowning at the receiver, he said, "Nevertheless, if the victim was recently associated with Watanabe, surely this would've reached his elder brother's ear somehow?"

"That's what I thought, too, but he claims that nothing's been mentioned to him, nor has he ever met Watanabe in recent years."

"Did he say when he met him last?"

"He said it was about ten years ago, and if he met him again today he probably wouldn't recognise his face."

"Well, I think he's lying. I simply can't believe the victim never said a word about Watanabe."

"Yeah, I feel the same way, but it may be unwise for us to make up our minds too quickly on this. Some members of the Tsukamoto family attended the victim's wedding, and they're being interviewed at present. Older people often know a lot about complicated family relationships, and we might pick up something from them, with a bit of luck."

"And how did Tsukamoto go on the question of his brother's income?"

"He was pretty vague about that, too. He offered the suggestion that, since his brother had specialised in business management studies, he might have been able to analyse the financial position of various companies and make some extra money with shares."

"These days it takes a professional to make any money out of shares, I'd say."

"I couldn't agree more," Yoshioka said mournfully. "I learnt this at my own cost just recently . . . Anyway, my man took him up on this straight away, and Tsukamoto said, well, if it wasn't shares, his brother might have been involved in commercial transactions—perhaps in the commodity market."

"But you didn't find in the victim's apartment any invoice, receipt, delivery docket or anything else to suggest this, did you?"

"No—nothing."

"I thought so."

"Well, my man asked exactly the same question, and then all of a sudden Tsukamoto flew off the handle and said, 'My brother wasn't a child any more—he didn't have to report to me every time he made some extra money. Furthermore, I didn't care how he made it. As his elder brother, all I want to say is that I don't think he ever obtained any money illegally.' Then he got really nasty and asked how long the detective proposed to pester a sick man like him . . ." Yoshioka's sigh came through clearly on the phone. "He's probably concealing something, but what more can we do at this stage? We haven't got anything on him. And to make matters worse, my man says he's sharp as a razor and has nerves of steel —altogether too clever a bird to be caught with chaff . . ."

Certainly the most difficult people for the police to deal with were intellectuals who also had courage, Kirishima thought. Nobumasa Tsukamoto must have proved just a bit too much for the poor detective. On the other hand, he might have been simply telling the truth all along . . . "And have you gained the impression the Tsukamoto brothers didn't get on with each other?"

"No. According to Koike, they were very close, even if they didn't meet very often because each was busy in his own work. And Koike's opinion has been confirmed by Mrs. Tsukamoto."

"I see . . . Is there anything else?"

"Not at this stage," Yoshioka said. "For the time being I propose to continue on the lines suggested by you the other day."

"Please do that. And we'll have to get together again soon."

Kirishima stretched his fingers after replacing the receiver. He had been on the phone for nearly an hour. Then he folded his arms and drifted into thought without realising he hadn't had his lunch.

Around the same time Kyoko Kirishima visited the victim's apartment at Setagaya. Etsuko was already living in it. She had moved in immediately after the funeral.

Kyoko had phoned her in the morning and become even more anxious about her. Etsuko's voice had been gloomy and lifeless, as if coming from somebody half asleep.

So when Kyoko had finished her shopping at Shibuya, she decided to call on Etsuko before returning home.

Opening the door for her, Etsuko looked as if she had lost some more weight during the night. Her eyes were bloodshot and dull. She had probably hardly slept at all, Kyoko thought.

In the Japanese room, Yoshihiro's photograph in a black frame stood in front of his ashes, and smoke from freshly replaced incense sticks rose wavering into the air.

"Have you had your lunch yet?" Kyoko asked.

"I don't want any."

"What about breakfast?"

"I had something light . . ."

Kyoko knew this was a lie—Etsuko's intonation had been totally unconvincing.

"This is what I was afraid of," Kyoko said. "Here, have some of this." She took some *sushi* out of a packet she had just bought at Shibuya, and then got up again to make the tea.

When Etsuko didn't show any interest in the rice rolls, Kyoko said, "You're not on a hunger strike like those Buddhist monks in Vietnam, are you?"

Finally Etsuko picked up a *sushi* and reluctantly began to eat.

Kyoko kept up the pressure. "If you're going to carry on like this, I'll take you back to your parents, even if I have to put a rope around your neck and drag you all the way."

"I'll be all right," Etsuko said, chewing listlessly. "From now on I'll have regular meals. I just didn't have an appetite this morning . . . You don't have to fly into a panic over every little thing."

"You must keep up your strength, Etsu, otherwise you won't last the distance."

"Yes, I realise that," Etsuko said eagerly. "I know I must last till the trial is over. As a matter of fact, I made my husband a promise only last night."

Making a vow to a dead person wasn't anything unusual, Kyoko thought, but there seemed to be an echo to Etsuko's voice, and for the first time in days she smiled, rather strangely. Somehow, it was frightening.

"Yes, I discussed a lot of things with him last night," Etsuko said. "I'm not lonely any more. He never leaves my side—not like other husbands who have to go to

157

work every day . . ."

Now Kyoko was really worried. She was going to tell Etsuko to stop thinking about her husband and to turn her eyes to the future, but decided to hold her tongue. She realised her advice would have no effect on Etsuko while she was in this mental condition. If anything, it might make her worse.

The door-bell started to ring. Kyoko told Etsuko to continue her meal, and went to open the front door.

It was Koike, Yoshihiro's lawyer. He looked a little surprised to find Kyoko there, but immediately bowed and said, "I appreciate your kindness. It's reassuring to know you're keeping an eye on her. How is she?"

"Well, to be quite frank, I'm a bit worried about her," Kyoko said softly. "I may be wrong, of course, but I think she should be looked at by a specialist."

"D'you mean a psychiatrist?" Koike kept his voice down to make sure Etsuko wouldn't overhear the conversation.

"Yes," Kyoko whispered. "Would you know anyone suitable? Somebody who'd be prepared to make a home call? I thought he could say he came to offer his sympathy as one of her husband's friends, or something like that."

"Hmm. Let me see. I have a cousin who's a psychiatrist—a very competent man, too. His only trouble is he loves gambling. Especially when it comes to horseracing, he gets completely carried away. That's why his relatives say behind his back it's he who needs his head examined . . . Well, perhaps we could talk about this again when we've observed Mrs. Tsukamoto's behaviour for a while." Koike took off his overcoat, then anxiously added, "D'you think she might be too confused at the moment? I have some practical matters to discuss with her."

"No, I don't think she's that bad," Kyoko said. "She should be able to follow you all right. I only suggested the examination because I'm afraid her condition might deteriorate further if she's allowed to brood over her dead husband without any check."

"This is where your companionship may prove very

helpful to her . . . Well, then I'll try to talk to her in your presence, if you wouldn't mind."

Koike went into the Japanese room and once more expressed his sympathy to Etsuko. Then he squatted down in front of Yoshihiro's photograph, lit an incense stick, and prayed for a while with hands joined. Finally he turned to Etsuko again.

"It's too late to do anything about this now," he said, "but I must apologise to you, just the same. I share the responsibility with Mr. Kawaji for making you a widow. If we hadn't told your husband to get the marriage certificate registered at the ward office the same afternoon, you'd be still Miss Ogata today."

"Mr. Koike!" Etsuko's previous absent-mindedness was gone in an instant. Her pale face was alive with feeling. "Please don't say another word about this. I've no regrets at all. On the contrary, I'm glad I could be with him as his legal wife, even if only for a few hours . . ."

Kyoko felt like crying. She thought Etsuko's words had expressed a fusion of joy and sorrow in a delicately crystallised form.

Koike wiped his nose with his handkerchief, then said, in a tremulous voice, "I perfectly understand how you feel—and would like to help you all I can . . . As a lawyer, I can't give you much moral support. Being so busy at the office I couldn't come to see you often, much as I'd like to comfort you every day. But I'm determined to do my bit somehow, so I consulted your brother-in-law yesterday. And he asked me if I'd help you in the matter of your husband's estate . . ."

Kyoko thought it might be too soon to talk about inheritance. But Etsuko's face was expressionless like a *No* mask. No trace of emotion was showing on it now.

". . . This seemed to me a good idea at first, but after considering it last night I decided against it. I thought it'd be different if you had no one else to help you, but you have a lawyer father, so it'd be natural for him to take care of this for you. There was no need for me to poke my nose into it . . . I rang Mr. Ogata not so long ago and mentioned to him Nobumasa Tsukamoto's request and my conclusion. But he said he had no desire to deal with any estate his daughter might inherit—it would only remind him of the tragedy and make him more depressed. All he wanted was see his daughter return home as soon as possible. His answer was very touching . . . I then suggested he might leave the matter to his junior partner or some other young lawyer he could trust. But he said, 'You've been a close friend of the deceased as well as his legal adviser, so I don't see why you shouldn't do it, especially since his brother has asked you.' "

Kyoko could appreciate why Koike was so hesitant. Succession to property was often a troublesome business, with ugly disputes developing even among the closest relatives. On the other hand, from a lawyer's point of view this type of work was much more rewarding financially than, for example, defending somebody in a criminal action. Therefore Koike would run the risk of somebody unfairly accusing him behind his back of trying to exploit the widow of his close friend, even if the money involved was only small.

"I don't want any money," Etsuko muttered. "I'm only interested in Yoshihiro's memory . . ."

"But if you're going to live in this apartment, you'll have to support yourself, and you can't do that without money . . . As his widow, it's the most natural thing for you to inherit his property. This is your right, and you needn't be shy about it, or feel obliged to anyone . . . Frankly, I'm personally against the idea of you living here on your own, but this is what you want to do, isn't it? I understand you don't want to go back to your parents' home for the time being?"

Etsuko nodded and sat up straight. "Mr. Koike, I agree with everything you said. Indeed, why should I be hesitant about having the things my husband left behind? . . . I'm going to take advantage of your kind offer and ask you to look after my interests. I'm prepared to leave everything in your hands."

"Thank you for your confidence—I'll do my best to deserve it," Koike said in a businesslike manner. "I'll prepare the necessary documents straight away and bring them over tomorrow for you to sign. And I think you should meet your brother-in-law in my presence within the next two or three days."

"Yes, I will."

"Mr. Tsukamoto is extremely sympathetic towards you. He sounds as if he wants to relinquish his succession rights in your favour. And so far as the insurance money is concerned, to avoid gift duty he wants to collect it and pay the tax on it, and then quietly transfer the balance into your account."

"Such details are really beyond me—I'll leave them to you. But I do feel my brother-in-law is doing far more for me than normally would be expected of him."

"Well, in my opinion you shouldn't reject his generosity. I'm sure the comparatively small amount of money involved won't make any difference to his financial position . . . But apart from that, there are quite a few other problems to be sorted out, so I think you should meet him as soon as possible."

Etsuko nodded. "Actually, I myself thought of meeting him sometime. At the funeral we had no opportunity to talk—we could only exchange a few words."

"Mr. Tsukamoto said the same thing, as a matter of fact . . . Now, coming back to the question of the inheritance, your husband's estate includes some copyrights, but I'll consult Mr. Kawaji on that." Koike ran his fingers across his forehead, collecting his thoughts. "Oh, yes. I only learnt this the other day—your husband bought this apartment as a home unit and has a clear title to it. I'll try to transfer it to your name as quickly as I can . . . Well, there are a few more minor problems, but we can talk about these some other time. Right now I'm running late for an appointment, so I'd better get going, I suppose." He got up and hurriedly fastened his briefcase. "Will you excuse me now?"

Men and women were certainly different, Kyoko thought philosophically as she let Koike out. The loss of his close friend must have been quite a shock to him, but his reaction to it was positive and logical. He wanted to ease his own sorrow by doing all he could for his friend's widow.

About an hour later, when Kyoko was about to leave, the door-bell rang again. It was Kawaji with a big parcel under his arm.

He spent a long time in prayer in front of Yoshihiro's photograph, then offered Etsuko his sympathy in an elaborate, flowery style. The essence of it was that her dead husband was sure to be pleased she had come over to his apartment to stay and pray for his soul.

Some colour returned to Etsuko's face. She must have been grateful there was somebody who understood how she felt.

But Kyoko wasn't pleased. Kawaji's words had been most considerate, but they might do Etsuko more harm than good by encouraging her in her melodramatic mood. She thought Koike's practical kindness was far more helpful.

"This parcel contains his personal belongings from the research room," Kawaji said. "There may be some more, but since Iwauchi had this lot wrapped up, and I was coming over anyway, I brought it with me."

"Thank you for your kindness," Etsuko whispered.

"Don't mention it . . . And if you feel you can't bear looking at them, I'm quite prepared to take them back . . ."

"No, that won't be necessary," Etsuko said firmly.

Kawaji nodded and then proceeded to unwrap the parcel. Among all the pens, notebooks and half-finished manuscripts there was a snapshot of Etsuko in a small frame. "According to Iwauchi, he kept this in a locked drawer."

Etsuko looked at her picture for a little while, then said in a calm voice, "When I get a bit more settled, I'd like to distribute these things as mementoes among his friends . . . So far as his books are concerned, they'll be of no use to me, so I'd like to give them to the university. Could you look after that for me?"

162

"Yes, of course," Kawaji said. "I'll consult Iwauchi about it, as the subject matter is outside my field . . . And if you've any other problems, please don't hesitate to ask me—I'll be only too happy to assist in any way I can . . ."

For the next twenty minutes or so Kawaji talked about his dead friend, stopping every now and then to comfort Etsuko and to re-state his sympathy for her. Then he got up to leave.

Kyoko decided this was a good opportunity for her to go, too. Etsuko's reference to the traditional distribution of the deceased's belongings as mementoes suggested she was much calmer now than she had been a few hours ago.

"Which way are you heading?" Kyoko asked Kawaji as they reached the street.

"I'm going to Komaba."

"Then I'll give you a lift. I'm going home by taxi, anyway."

"Thank you very much."

She hailed a passing cab, and soon they were on their way. "My husband suggested I should learn to drive before getting tied down with children," Kyoko said. "So I'm taking some lessons at the moment, but I find the rules and regulations much more complicated than expected. Learning them all is almost a task for a legal expert like you."

Kyoko brought up the subject of driving just to say something, but Kawaji responded with unexpected fervour.

"Those driving instructors can be very annoying," he said. "When I went for my driving test some years ago and did rather poorly in the theoretical part, they asked me with a straight face if I was really a lecturer in law at a university. Well, in my opinion, the questions had been put so badly that anyone trained to think logically would've come up with the wrong answers . . ." He didn't seem to be very pleased with the subject, and changed it suddenly. "Incidentally, you wouldn't be the wife of State Prosecutor Kirishima by any chance, would you? As master of ceremonies at the wedding I had to call on you to speak, and I wondered. Kirishima isn't a common family name."

For Kyoko this wasn't a welcome question, but she couldn't avoid answering it now. "Yes, I am," she said, "but Etsuko happens to be my closest friend from way back. My visit to her has absolutely nothing to do with my husband."

A sardonic smile crossed Kawaji's face. "Yes, I'm well aware of that. If I were the killer, I'm sure I wouldn't have to worry about sitting with you in the same taxi, since State Prosecutor Kirishima's business is none of your concern . . ."

If he meant this to be funny, he certainly had a strange sense of humour, Kyoko thought. There must be a weird kink in his character. Suddenly she was a little scared.

Kawaji produced a cigarette and slowly put it between his lips. "I've made a little discovery today," he said, then struck a match and lit the cigarette with elaborate care. "Yesterday I gave your husband various reasons for Professor Araki's possible hostility towards Tsuka-moto . . ."

Kyoko recalled Araki's sour face at the crematorium.

". . . Well, now I've got one more. Araki's father was a professor of economics, too, I've learnt. He did a lot of study on Marxism before and during the war. His interest was purely academic, of course . . ."

Kyoko sucked in her breath. "Are you suggesting Mr. Tsukamoto's father would've . . ."

Kawaji nodded gravely. "His father, whose followers were nicknamed 'Private Political Police', put a special interpretation on Araki's interest. Because of the lunatic atmosphere of those days, the old professor was not only removed from his university post, but was subsequently arrested by intelligence agents of the military. He was supposed to have died of a heart attack while being interrogated, but knowing how those agents operated during the war, I wouldn't be at all surprised if he was tortured to death. His son, the present Professor Araki, was given a rough time, too."

"And he knew that Yoshihiro Tsukamoto was Shinnosuke Tsukamoto's son?"

"I'm not sure about that, but I don't think he did when Tsukamoto moved over to Chiyoda University. The dean of that department disclosed nothing of my friend's background to anyone, and the family name Tsukamoto is quite common." Kawaji drew on his cigarette, then added, "Well, even if Professor Araki did subsequently learn of the connection, to me it's unthinkable he would've wanted to revenge his father's death in this manner after all those years . . ."

CHAPTER ELEVEN

"I see," Kirishima said, making a sour face as he listened to Inspector Yoshioka on the phone the following morning. "I think it's time for me to move in . . . In the meantime, will you check Professor and Mrs. Araki's alibis, just to make sure? . . . Good. We can discuss that later . . ."

He put down the receiver and remained motionless for the next minute, then turned to his clerk Kitahara. "I want you to drive to Shimotakaido immediately."

"That's where Nobumasa Tsukamoto lives, isn't it?" Kirishima nodded.

"Are you issuing a formal request for his appearance?"

"Yes. But before you hand him the summons, take a good look at him, will you? Don't bring him in here unless you think he can stand up to it. Use your own judgment. It may be a bit too much for him in his present condition, though he managed to attend the funeral, so he can't be too bad."

"I'll be careful." Kitahara put on his overcoat and left without further comment.

Kirishima gazed unseeingly at the Tsukamoto file in front of him. A prosecutor's direct summons usually had the desired psychological effect, especially on an intelligent person. "Well, we'll soon see," he muttered to himself.

About two and a half hours later Nobumasa Tsukamoto limped into Kirishima's office in Kitahara's company. He had a scarf wrapped around his neck, and the upturned collar of his overcoat covered part of his ears. After sitting down in one of the visitors' chair, he removed his white flu mask.

"I'm sorry to drag you here in this condition," Kirishima said, "but to solve your brother's murder we urgently need your co-operation . . . How're you feeling?"

"Not too bad, thank you. My injuries are mending well, but this damned flu has hit me pretty hard. I don't seem to be able to shake off the fever . . . With all these unfortunate things happening at the same time, I'm almost inclined to resort to religious magic, though I'm a confirmed atheist." He smiled wryly. His voice was so hoarse, it made Kirishima feel like clearing his own throat all the time. "Anyway, I hope the police will catch that bastard soon. When I think of Etsuko living on her own in that apartment, I feel that tearing him to pieces with my own hands wouldn't be enough for him . . ."

Recalling some of the things Kyoko had told him last night, Kirishima said, "I myself feel genuinely sorry for Mrs. Tsukamoto . . . By the way, I heard you want to forsake your succession rights in her favour. Is that right?"

Nobumasa gave a curt nod. "As might be expected of a prominent prosecutor, you know how to use your ears. Well, the property involved is quite small, and I think she should have the lot, by way of compensation. I'm not short of money at the moment."

"I admire you for your attitude," Kirishima said.

"Are you going to give her the insurance money as well?"

"I'm the beneficiary of that policy, so I'm going to collect the money. But what I do with it afterwards— that's my own business, isn't it?"

"This is not the Tax Office. You can speak freely."

"As I told you before, I want to do as much as I can for her. This should sufficiently answer your question."

"You seem to be very well disposed towards her."

"Yes, I took a liking to her the first time I set eyes on her when Yoshihiro introduced us. She's kind-hearted and intelligent. Actually, at the time I thought she was too good for him. Beauty is only skin deep, as you know . . ." Suddenly his face became gloomy. "Besides, now that Yoshihiro's gone, I've nobody left in the whole world. This loneliness can become depressing, you know. Suppose I achieve something outstanding in my work. There's no one I can share my pleasure with. That's why I want to take good care of Etsuko, and that's why I place value on my relationship with her. She's now my sister-in-law—the only close relative I've got."

"Why don't you get married?"

"Mr. Prosecutor, as you may well imagine, my late father and youngest brother cast a shadow not only on Yoshihiro, but also on me. Every time a suitable marriage proposal cropped up, it came to nothing. On the other hand, the type of women who didn't care about such things proved either unfaithful or impossible to stomach for long. It was always one way or the other. Until now, I've never met anyone like Etsuko . . ."

If he hadn't set his sights so high, surely he could've come to terms with some woman by now, Kirishima thought. But of course, people isolated by misfortune or prejudice often developed a defence mechanism of excessive self-respect. It was common for such people to want to marry someone beyond their reach . . .

Would Nobumasa be thinking of marrying Etsuko sometime in the future? She was now one of those women often described by small-minded people as 'ruined for life'. She was certainly more attainable now than she had been as the maiden daughter of a prominent lawyer, and

Nobumasa seemed to have a special affection for her. It was quite common for a widow to marry her dead husband's younger brother. So why not the elder brother, for a change?

"Perhaps you intend to take care of her permanently from now on?"

"Well, if she returns to her parents' home, I wouldn't be able to do that without offending the Ogata family . . . But I certainly don't want to lose her, if I can help it."

This made his intentions towards Etsuko pretty clear, Kirishima thought. But it was unthinkable he would've murdered his own brother just to get her. Not even an idiot could have hoped with any confidence that the widow would automatically marry him.

"I see," Kirishima said cheerfully, deciding to change the direction of the interview towards the heart of the matter. "Incidentally, I'm still rather surprised by your brother's financial position at the time of his death. Are you sure you've no idea of the source of that 3,000,000 yen he bought his apartment with? In my opinion, it would've been impossible for him to save that much out of his lecturer's salary."

Nobumasa frowned for just a moment, but he must have been prepared for the question because he answered it smoothly. "I've already told the police everything I could think of."

"Unfortunately, your suggestion of share or commodity transactions can't be accepted, simply because there's no trace of such transactions."

"Then he might have won some money on the lottery. If my memory serves me correctly, there's a 3,000,000-yen special prize."

"If he had such rare luck, surely he would've told you about it? Wouldn't it have been natural for him to give you a portion of his win, since you were his closest living relative? Or was there some ill will between you?"

"No, we were very close—much closer than most brothers. So you're probably right in what you say."

"Anyway, winners of the larger lottery prizes can easily be checked out, and we'll do that just to make

sure, but I don't think your brother will be among them."
Kirishima looked at Nobumasa earnestly. "Mr. Tsuka-moto, this is a very important point. If we can find the
source of that money, we may be able to establish the
motive for your brother's murder. You said just a little
while ago that you hoped the police would catch the
killer soon. Well, you can help them by telling me every-thing you can think of—not only things you know for
certain. In other words, I'd like you to speak out without
restraint."

Nobumasa closed his eyes for a while, as if in concen-tration, then said, "I can only think of the obvious
things, I'm afraid . . . Isn't it possible he worked for
some company as a management consultant in his spare
time?"

"Yes, that's possible, but wouldn't a fee of 3,000,000
yen be far too high for this type of service?"

"Not necessarily. If his advice on improved adminis-trative and production methods saved the company
30,000,000 yen a year, he could've easily received ten
percent of that in fees. And for a company with an
annual turnover of, say, 10,000,000,000 yen to effect a
saving of 30,000,000 yen through better management
seems quite reasonable to me."

"With that I agree," Kirishima said. "The only thing
is—I had a quick look at the subject over the past couple
of days, and it seems to me it'd be impossible for one
person alone to prepare a comprehensive efficiency plan.
Usually the preparation of such plan involves the assess-ment of existing management conditions from various
angles, and this requires the combined effort of a number
of people with different specialities—engineering,
accounting, marketing, psychology and so on. Therefore,
even if the fee paid by the company is quite large, the
share of each expert in the team would be only small."

"I see," Nobumasa said. "You're probably right. I
know nothing about management—it's right outside my
field."

"Furthermore, if your brother did provide such a
service, wouldn't the company concerned have sent an

170

executive—or at least a wreath—to the funeral? There was nobody like that present, was there?"

"No, there wasn't . . . It looks as if I'm barking up the wrong tree . . ." He cupped his chin with one hand and fumbled at his walking stick with the other. "Well, how about this then? I know for a fact my brother often got involved in short management courses for businessmen, so there must have been some executives who would've become friendly with him. Now, as you know, in order to raise capital, companies usually make a new share issue or borrow from a bank. But when money is as tight as at present, sometimes they're forced into back-door deals at high interest rates, calculated daily, or have to borrow secretly from some other company with large undeclared reserves. And in such cases there's plenty of scope for the middle man who provides the discreet link between lender and borrower."

Kirishima nodded. "You mean your brother might have acted as a finance broker, utilising his personal connections with executives of various companies?"

"I wouldn't describe it that way because it sounds too professional, and my brother could've only interested himself in such deals in his spare time, if at all. But precisely because he wasn't a professional, the parties concerned could've preferred him, knowing he was trustworthy, and it was in his own interest to keep his mouth shut. Now, suppose he had succeeded in arranging a loan of 3,000,000,000 yen for some major company? A commission of 3,000,000 yen on that would've been only .1 percent—well below the normal figure. I don't think he would've been too shy to accept such a reward if it happened to come his way."

"I see."

"Besides, if he did take part in this kind of deal, it wouldn't be at all strange if he said nothing about it, even to me. People involved in a secret deal must keep it secret—it's as simple as that, especially where the company's credit rating is at stake. And what if the lender or the borrower happened to be a rival of Toho Kasei, the company I work for? In that case Yoshihiro would've made doubly sure I knew nothing of it."

Yes, this theory was plausible enough, Kirishima thought. He had heard stories about the difficulties of raising capital and the involvement of mediators who seemingly had nothing to do with the financial world. So it wasn't unthinkable a lecturer in business management studies would have been doing something similar as a sideline.

Only, as Nobumasa himself had suggested, in investigating such matters the prospect of discovering the truth would be very slim. So, to put it bluntly, the very raising of this subject amounted to an exercise in subtle evasion on his part.

"I follow you," Kirishima said innocently. "I'll certainly look into this. And I hope it won't sound offensive to you if I suggest that, for a person engaged in scientific research, you seem to have a pretty good inside knowledge of company affairs."

"Oh, I wouldn't say that. My information is based on bits and pieces I picked up from Yoshihiro from time to time on business practices generally. But until now it never occurred to me he might have been personally involved in any deal."

"Would you have any other thoughts on the origin of that 3,000,000 yen?"

"Only that I don't think my brother would've made the money by illegal means. Even if he did act as a mediator in the manner I mentioned, this kind of thing's quite acceptable these days."

"I see," Kirishima said evenly. "Then let's move on to the next problem—the one concerning the man called Watanabe." Before Nobumasa could say anything, Kirishima raised his hand and added, "I've been told about your explanation to the police, but frankly, I just can't believe your brother didn't tell you a single thing about this man."

"Well, he certainly didn't say anything recently." Nobumasa's expression grew indignant. "Are you suggesting I lied to the detective?"

Kirishima didn't answer the question. Instead, he said,

"Some of the investigating police officers think the man's name may not be Hiroshi Watanabe at all. In other words, they think your brother told his wife a lie."

For the first time since the start of the interview Nobumasa's feverish face turned noticably paler, and he looked as if he was trying hard to appear unconcerned.

"I can't see how my brother could've told a lie," he said. "I had no personal contact with Watanabe, nor did I have any interest in him, so I'm not surprised my brother didn't bother to talk to me about him."

"Is it true that he's distantly related to you and your brother?"

"Yes, that's true. But I wouldn't know what the exact link is."

Now Kirishima was ready to play his last card. He said, "A minute ago you asked me if I suggested you were telling a lie. To my regret, I now must answer yes to your question. What's more, I've proof you're lying."

Nobumasa gripped his walking stick and nearly rose from the chair. "What the hell are you talking about?"

"The police have interviewed all your relatives who attended your brother's wedding or funeral. Not one of them knows anything about Hiroshi Watanabe. Even if he's only a very distant relation, isn't it strange nobody in the family except you has ever heard of him?" When Nobumasa didn't reply, Kirishima added, "So I can't help reaching the conclusion there's no Hiroshi Watanabe among your relatives. It then follows that you've conspired with your brother in devising an elaborate falsehood about this man."

Nobumasa stared at the floor, biting his lip.

Kirishima's voice grew harsher. "Hiroshi Watanabe—whether the name is real or false, it doesn't really matter. What I want to know is, who *is* this man? What's his connection with you and your brother?"

Nobumasa gave a deep sigh but still didn't answer.

"We've reason to believe this man could be your brother's killer. So I can't understand at all why you're trying to protect him."

Nobumasa looked up, wiping his forehead at the same

173

time. Finally he said, "Mr. Prosecutor, would you give me a couple of days to answer this? I'd need at least till tomorrow afternoon."

"But why can't you answer it now?"

"It concerns a delicate and rather complicated matter, and I'm getting feverish again, and it's interfering with my ability to concentrate . . . But I can assure you Watanabe had absolutely nothing to do with my brother's death."

"That's for me to decide."

"Yes, of course . . . But I've got a splitting headache now, and my mind is becoming confused. I really don't think I can continue this conversation right now . . . But please accept my word I've no intention of absconding. My conscience is perfectly clear. I've nothing to be ashamed of."

"If you've nothing to be ashamed of, then why did you have to tell a lie?"

"Because the matter concerns another person's reputation, though I must admit it may have some influence on my own future, too, depending on the circumstances." Nobumasa spoke firmly, and held Kirishima's gaze with steady eyes. He looked as if he wouldn't budge another inch.

Kirishima thought it would be useless trying to push him any further—it would only stiffen his resistance. It might even make him exercise his constitutional right of silence. Softening his voice somewhat, he said, "I still can't see the difference between telling me today and telling me tomorrow whatever you're going to say . . . Or are you hoping to find a clever excuse during the night?"

"I can assure you, Mr. Prosecutor, I wouldn't underestimate you or the police to that extent. My own experience has taught me how hard it is to maintain a lie for any length of time . . . But suppose your own job as a prosecutor depended on whether or not you disclosed a certain fact? Suppose you knew you'd have to put in your resignation immediately you made that disclosure? In such a situation, would you like to make up your mind

174

on the spot? Or would you prefer an extra day to think about it?"

Kirishima felt these were not the desperate words of a cornered man, but the words of someone who stood firmly on his rights. And in any case, detaining Tsukamoto at this stage was out of the question. He had no choice, really, but to go along with him. And with the assistance of the police he might even have a new card up his sleeve by tomorrow afternoon . . .

"All right, you win," Kirishima said tonelessly. "I'll wait till tomorrow afternoon, much as I dislike the idea. But that's as far as I'm prepared to go, and I hope you won't attempt anything like moving into hospital on the pretext of a relapse. I'd follow you even there if I had to."

"That won't be necessary," Nobumasa said stiffly. "I'll be here tomorrow afternoon, without fail . . . But right now I feel completely exhausted, so will you excuse me?" Without waiting for an answer he got up and began to limp towards the door.

The clerk followed him out into the corridor to show him to the lift.

When Kitahara returned to the office, he said, "Mr. Prosecutor, is it all right to leave him to his own devices, d'you think?"

"There's nothing else I can do at the moment. There wouldn't be any point in having him watched. A clever man like him knows that any attempt to abscond at this late stage would only make matters worse for him. Moreover, I feel he was genuine about needing an extra day to sort things out before giving me the facts on Watanabe. Had his mind been made up not to tell the truth when he came in here, he could've produced a number of convincing lies about Watanabe without any trouble. For example, he could've said the man was an illegitimate son of their late father, and they were covering this up by calling him a distant relative . . . And I simply don't believe he would've murdered his own brother, especially since they were much closer than brothers brought up in a normal happy home. The way he said he had nobody left in the whole world now—I don't think that was an act."

"Well, you'd know best, Mr. Prosecutor," Kitahara said with deliberate scepticism.

Kirishima shot his clerk a glance. "Why? D'you think he might be the killer?"

"Perhaps I shouldn't go that far . . . But I *will* say there are a lot of fishy things about him."

"What a shrewd observer you are," Kirishima said, laughing. "How about making a cup of tea? You could unburden all your suspicions while we're having it. Or can't you speak your mind unless you've got a skinful of *sake* in you?"

"You can laugh all you like, Mr. Prosecutor, but I still say Nobumasa is the only one who could've lured Yoshihiro out of that hotel with some excuse."

"I don't know about being the *only* one, but he certainly would've been in a position to do so."

"Secondly," Kitahara said self-importantly, "the big problem of why that most unsuitable night was chosen for the murder will solve itself straight away if Nobumasa is the killer."

"How?"

"He thought that by pretending he was too ill to attend his own brother's wedding, he'd divert all suspicion from himself. And as a practical consideration, he could've been too weak to commit the crime before that night. His injuries were quite genuine."

"That's one way of looking at it."

Kitahara was undaunted. "Thirdly, Nobumasa is far too interested in Etsuko's welfare. If she had been married to his brother for a long time, I could understand this, but at this stage she's almost a complete stranger to him. Then why is he so generous towards her?"

"You think it's just a camouflage, do you?"

"Well, it's not impossible, is it?"

"Perhaps not," Kirishima said, drawing on his cigarette and maintaining a straight face. "By the way, if he's the murderer, what's his motive? And where does

Watanabe come into the picture?"

Kitahara knitted his eyebrows in concentration. "This is only guess-work, you understand, but what if the Tsukamoto brothers and Watanabe were involved in some mysterious money-making scheme? Alternatively, what if only the brothers were involved, but Watanabe discovered their secret and used it for blackmailing them?"

"Could you cut out the rhetorical questions and get on with it? We haven't got all day, you know."

Ignoring this, Kitahara said, "If Watanabe *was* a blackmailer, the Tsukamoto brothers would've considered him not only a nuisance and a financial drain, but also a constant danger because of his drunkenness. Despite paying him all the time, how could they be sure he wouldn't shoot off his mouth when he was rotten with *sake*?"

"So the brothers wiped him out. Is that it?"

"That's possible, but I rather think Nobumasa did the job alone and hid the body somewhere. Yoshihiro somehow learnt of Nobumasa's crime and was seized with panic, and then it was his turn to be silenced for good, as a safety measure."

"I see," Kirishima said, still enjoying this little diversion. "Your theory is fascinating, but if what you say is right, then why has Nobumasa asked for one extra day? He could never disclose Watanabe's true identity, no matter how long he's given to think about it, according to your theory."

"Well, he mightn't have been able to think up a good enough lie on the spur of the moment. That's not so easy, you know, even for a clever fellow like him, especially when he's already in a state of agitation."

"All right, but he must have realised it'd be much more difficult for him to tell a convincing lie tomorrow than it would've been today. For instance, I might have swallowed a bastard son story today, but I certainly wouldn't do it tomorrow. In fact, if he can spin a yarn I can't pull to pieces, he must be the greatest liar in Japan, and I'll bow to him with total admiration."

177

"I accept this, Mr. Prosecutor," Kitahara said with growing excitement, "but let me support my theory by looking at the brothers' income. Yoshihiro wasn't the only one who made good money, you know. It seems to me Nobumasa is making even more. I realised this for the first time when I went to his place this morning. He has a posh house on a large allotment. It must be worth close to 10,000,000 yen at current prices."

"Is it his own house?"

"I sounded him out on that on the way here, and he said he'd bought it about four years ago, and it was a bit too big for his income."

"Well, a company like Toho Kasei would treat its research workers pretty generously. He'd be on a fairly high salary, and would probably get a special bonus every time he produced something profitable. Furthermore, he could've borrowed some money from the company by using his retirement grant as security . . . Anyway, depending on the outcome of tomorrow's session, I'll probably get the police to check on his financial position."

"Let me see . . ." Kitahara screwed up his ruddy face. "Apart from the house, he's got a brand new de luxe sedan. Of course, once a salary-man reaches a certain classification it's not unusual for him to buy a car on hire purchase. But apart from the question of money—"

"Are you saying that if he used his car, he could've easily committed the crime with a leg and an arm in plaster?"

"Exactly . . . And he made a point of telling me he hadn't used his car since the accident."

"Oh? That's rather suspicious, isn't it?"

At last Kitahara realised Kirishima was making fun of him, but he accepted it in good grace, even entered into the spirit of it. "And while we're on the subject," he said, "let me inform you, Mr. Prosecutor, that there's the inevitable woman behind this crime, and I'm not referring to Etsuko Tsukamoto. The woman I have in mind is gorgeous, rather common, and very nasty."

"How did you find out about her?"

"Kitahara's pretty smart, eh? Well, just as I was walking up to the house, she rushed out with a threatening look on her face. They must have had a lovers' quarrel. When a man associates with this type of gay bird, he can expect plenty of trouble . . ."

"Did he say anything about her?"

"Yes, in response to my diplomatic question, of course. I said, 'The woman who has just left the house— isn't she a beauty?' And he replied that she was beyond shame, or words to that effect . . . I should've stopped her in the first place and asked how much she charged."

"Now, that might have been a bit undignified for a prosecutor's clerk."

"Yes, I suppose so," Kitahara muttered while casually searching for something in his coat pocket. "What's this?" He produced a match-box with *Princess Bar— Ginza* printed on it. "Now, where did I get this from? . . . Oh, I know—I saw it in the visitors' room while waiting for Mr. Tsukamoto to turn up. On the top of it was a cigarette butt with lipstick smeared on it."

Kirishima burst into laughter. "Hey, you! Strictly speaking, that's stealing, you know."

"Well, I've been serving prosecutors for the best part of thirty years, but I've never once seen anyone being arrested for stealing a box of matches . . . Would you like me to take it back?"

"I don't think that'll be necessary. Just don't do it again."

Kitahara carefully put the match-box into a drawer of his desk. "Even a single box of matches is too valuable an item to throw away," he said. "It might come in handy some day."

CHAPTER TWELVE

Around nine o'clock the following morning Etsuko was heading for Nobumasa's home in Koike's car.

When he picked her up he again apologised for causing her the inconvenience. "As I told you on the phone last night, Nobumasa said he must see you this morning, but he looked so ill, I thought perhaps——"

"It's all right," Etsuko said. "Don't worry about it."

"I was called to his house last night, and he talked about some of his plans for the future. After we discussed matters relating to your husband's estate, he said he wanted to tell you something urgently. When I asked him what it was, he said he'd rather tell you first, in my presence . . . Would you have any idea what it might be?"

"No."

"He said he had to go to the Criminal Affairs Division head office early this afternoon, so he'd like us to be there by ten o'clock—that would leave enough time for a full discussion."

"I see."

During the rest of the journey they didn't say much. Koike was concentrating on the heavy morning traffic, and Etsuko seemed to be absorbed in her own thoughts.

Presently Koike said, "We're nearly there."

"Pardon?"

He repeated the words as he turned the car off the main road and into a narrow street on their left. In that area there were still a few vacant allotments, even some vegetable plots. This gave the impression the place was far out of the city centre.

"That's his house over there," Koike said and began to brake. "Hey, what's that?"

The house was the last one in a dead-end street. It was a fairly modern residence with a green wire fence around it. Quite a few people had gathered on the footpath in front of it, and there was a police patrol car parked at the gate. Inside the fence two uniformed policemen moved about with eyes kept to the ground.

Koike stopped the car and turned to Etsuko, his face drained of colour.

"What happened?" she asked. "They haven't arrested him, have they?"

Just then a policeman's head appeared in the car window. "You've some business here, sir?" he asked Koike.

"That's right. But what happened?"

"If you'd like to get out of the car, sir, the detectives will tell you all about it."

As soon as Koike and Etsuko were out of the vehicle, a burly man wearing a black overcoat came up to them.

"Morning," he said morosely. "Who are you?"

"This is Mrs. Etsuko Tsukamoto, Mr. Nobumasa Tsukamoto's sister-in-law. I'm Shoichi Koike, her lawyer. We've an appointment with Mr. Tsukamoto. What's wrong?"

"I'm Chief Detective Nozawa, of the Takaido police station," he said slowly. "Sorry to have to tell you this, but Mr. Tsukamoto has been murdered, probably late last night . . . I must ask you to remain here till Inspector Yoshioka arrives from police headquarters. He won't be long . . ."

181

Kirishima was also on his way to the scene, driving his own car from home. Since it was a Sunday, he had planned to go to the office after lunch, only to see Nobumasa, but a little after half past nine Inspector Yoshioka rang him and told him what had happened.

This was the last thing Kirishima had expected. He wondered if he had failed in his duty by not getting a police guard put on Nobumasa's house, even for that one day. He had been so busy assessing the pros and cons of Nobumasa's possibly absconding, it had never occurred to him the man's life might be in danger. And of course, it wasn't possible to provide police protection for everyone being questioned in a murder case. There had to be some special reason—there just weren't enought policemen to go round.

His conclusion that Nobumasa wouldn't try to evade justice by going into hiding had been correct, but why hadn't he thought of *this?*

I've made a mistake . . . I've made a mistake! . . . As he repeated the words, his anger grew thicker, and so did his determination to get the killer, if it was the last thing he did.

When he pulled up in front of Nobumasa's house, Inspector Yoshioka was already there. His big black squad car was parked next to the patrol car.

"Glad you could come, Mr. Prosecutor," Yoshioka said. "I thought you might have gone away for the weekend."

Kirishima didn't reply. He walked straight through the gate towards the front door.

Yoshioka must have guessed what was on Kirishima's mind by the look on his face. "Nobody could've anticipated this," he said. "And I'm sure it has nothing to do with your summonning him to the office yesterday . . . Anyway, it's most unlikely Nobumasa would've contacted Watanabe to ask him what to tell you today. That would've amounted to saying, 'If you'd like to murder me, your last chance is tonight' . . . No, I really don't think the motive for this crime was to silence Nobumasa. It's probably just a coincidence he was attacked last night."

"The killer could've easily found out he'd been to see me yesterday," Kirishima said dryly.

"Agreed. But even if he did, he wouldn't know what the purpose of the interview was, or what Nobumasa told you. Interviewing a victim's brother is the most natural thing in the world. Why should he have thought it meant any danger to him?"

"Well, let's concentrate on what we've got here," Kirishima said curtly. He decided there was no point in brooding over something that couldn't be undone, even if he felt he was partly responsible.

Yoshioka showed Kirishima into the visitors' room. Nobumasa's corpse was lying face down, about six feet inside the door. There was a narrow purple-coloured bruise around the back of the neck.

"Same technique as before," Yoshioka said. "Stunned him with a blow to the front, then strangled him with a cord. This time he would've had an easier job, I'd say, with the victim in such poor condition."

"What's the preliminary estimate on the time of death?"

Yoshioka pointed to a gas heater in the room. It was still burning, fully turned on. "The closest we can get to it is between 8 p.m. and 11 p.m., and even this could be out, depending on how long the heater's been on. If the killer knows anything at all about forensic medicine, he might have lit it himself to make things a bit harder for us. Or it could've been burning since early in the evening."

Chief Detective Nozawa gave his report in a stilted, lumbering police style. "At about 9.10 a.m. today the charwoman who comes here every morning, a Mrs. Tomi Kosaka, discovered the body of the owner of the house, Nobumasa Tsukamoto, in its present position. She reported the incident on the police emergency line. Immediately upon receiving instructions from police headquarters, I proceeded to the scene, and upon arrival placed several constables on guard around the building. The Takaido police station is only a few hundred yards

from here, so it didn't take me very long to get here . . .
I requested Mrs. Kosaka to remain on the premises.
Subsequently the victim's sister-in-law, Mrs. Etsuko
Tsukamoto, and her lawyer, Shoichi Koike, arrived in a
car, and I requested them, too, to remain on the premises
pending further instructions. At present they're seated in
the living room, situated on the opposite side of the
passageway."

"Thank you," Kirishima said. "We appreciate your
efforts." He wasn't surprised to hear that Etsuko and
Koike were here, since his wife had told him last night
about Koike's visit to the apartment. But he was a little
annoyed they had turned up at such an awkward time—
so soon after the discovery of the crime.

Ignoring the busy fingerprint experts, Kirishima looked
around the room once more. It was neat and clean, but
had the unmistakable drabness of a bachelor's home. A
five-piece lounge suite, a large book-case filled with sets
of various encyclopaedias and art books, and a small
glass cabinet containing foreign wine and spirit bottles—
that was all the furniture. The only decoration was a
large, framed western painting that looked like a printed
reproduction.

On the coffee table were two brandy glasses, a bottle
of Hennessy Three Star cognac, a cigarette box and
lighter, and a large ash-tray with a pile of butts in it.

"This could prove interesting," Yoshioka said, handing a dark green pocket notebook to Kirishima. "It
belongs to Koike, and was left here on the sofa, apparently last night."

"Then this must be his second visit here in less than
twenty-four hours . . . But we can leave this till later.
How about making a start with the woman who discovered the body?"

"Yes, of course," Yoshioka said obligingly. "We can
use the study, if you like."

That was another western-style room. Here the shelves
were loaded with foreign-language originals dealing with
science and technology. There was no fiction or general
literature, or anything on the arts. Kirishima thought the

184

books in the visitors' room must serve only as a decoration.

Soon a fat woman in her mid-forties was ushered in by a policeman. She looked coarse but good-natured, and obviously bewildered. Her small, shiny eyes never stopped blinking.

"Just relax, will you?" Yoshioka told her. "There's nothing for you to worry about."

"Yes," she whispered, but his reassurance didn't seem to have the slightest effect on her.

"You're supposed to come here around nine o'clock each morning. Is that right?"

"Yes . . . I was told to come late in the morning."

"Have you been here every day?"

"Yes, every day, since the master's accident. Before that, I used to come every third day to do the washing and cleaning."

"What about yesterday?"

"Yes, I come yesterday morning . . . When the master had to go out, he told me I could go home earlier, so I finished me washing and cleaning, and left here around two o'clock."

"You left here before Mr. Tsukamoto returned home. Is that right?"

"Yes, that's right."

"What about locking up the house?"

"Yes, I've got a key to the kitchen door at the back. I keep it in me bag all the time . . . The front door can be opened and locked without a key, from the inside. It's a spring lock, or something like that."

"And did you come in through the back door this morning, too?"

"Yes . . . There's a buzzer at the back. I pressed it just to let him know I was here, but I come straight in. The master told me to do it, so he wouldn't have to get up."

"And then?"

"He wasn't in the living room, so I looked into his bedroom. I thought he could be still asleep, you see, but his bed was empty. It hasn't been used at all since yesterday morning . . . He wasn't in the dining room either, so I

185

looked for him in here, and then in the visitors' room
. . ." She opened her little eyes wide, together with her
mouth, and started to take the air in quick gasps. "I've
never been so scared in all me life! Oh my . . .
Namumyohorengekyo . . . Namumyohorengekyo . . ."

"Just leave your prayers till later, will you?" Yoshioka
said testily.

"Yes—yes," she panted.

"Would you have any idea how it happened?"

"No—no, I wouldn't—honest."

Yoshioka glanced at Kirishima. His expression suggested it would be useless going on with her.

Kirishima raised a finger, and said to her, "Now, I
want to ask you something. Yesterday morning, before
the man came to drive Mr. Tsukamoto to the city, was
there a woman in this house?"

"Ah, yes," she said, frowning. "I've seen that woman
a couple of times before yesterday."

"What's her name?"

"I don't know . . . I first seen her early last December.
I gone to the door to answer the bell, and she was there,
and I said, 'Yes?', and she said in a real nasty sort of
way, 'Yes, that's what I'd like to know—who're you?
You must be the charwoman. Well, just step out of my
way then. He's at home, isn't he?' That's what she said,
and then just walked straight past me, as if I wasn't
there . . . She's a nasty piece of work all right—make no
mistake about that."

"Didn't Mr. Tsukamoto tell you anything about her?"

"No—nothing much, but each time she came the
master looked real annoyed afterwards. Yesterday he
said, 'Next time she comes, tell her I'm not home, will
you?' That's what he said."

"Did you hear what they were talking about?"

"No, I never put me nose into other people's business
—I keep out of the way . . . But there was a bit of a
commotion, with shouting and screaming, I can tell you.
I ain't surprised the master was angry. With his accident,
and his flu, and the way his poor younger brother finished
up—he had enough trouble without this hard bitch push-

186

ing her way in here."

"You said there was shouting."

"Yes, plenty of it."

"Well, then you must have overheard something."

"No I didn't—honest."

"Not even a single word?"

Mrs. Kosaka opened her hands and shrugged her shoulders in desperation. "I come here to do me work. I ain't got no spare time to worry about other things when I'm doing me washing and cleaning and cooking. When the water's running from them noisy taps, I can't hear other people talking."

Kirishima ended the questioning with a short nod. The clue to the identity of that woman was locked away in Kitahara's desk, anyway. There was no need to terrorise this poor creature any longer.

In this instance Etsuko was useless as a source of information. Not only did she know very little about Nobumasa; this second shock must have further impaired her powers of reasoning. She just sat there with the empty stare of a doll. Yoshioka must have sensed her state of mind, because he asked only very formal and simple questions. Even to those, her answers could have been summarised in one sentence—she had been brought here by Koike, and she knew nothing about anything concerning this incident.

Kirishima offered her his sympathy in a fairly formal manner. He would have liked to comfort her in a more personal way, but since he was here as an investigating prosecutor, there was a limit to what he could say, especially in the presence of a police officer.

Then came Koike's turn. To begin with, he gave an account of his visit here last night and this morning. He was deadly pale, as might be expected, but didn't lose his composure at any stage. His story was clear and to the point.

"It was about seven o'clock last night when I received a phone call from Nobumasa. He said he'd like to discuss certain things with Etsuko in the morning, but wanted to make some arrangements beforehand, so could I go over

187

to his place straight away. I agreed. After advising Mrs. Tsukamoto on the phone that she'd be expected here in the morning, I came over, arriving just before eight o'clock."

"Were you on your own at home when the victim rang you?" Yoshioka asked.

"No. A young man called Keizo Takei was visiting me at the time. As a matter of fact, it was he who answered the phone. Mr. Takei worked in my legal office as an assistant clerk while studying for his Judicial Training Institute entrance exam. He passed last year and will commence his studies at the institute next April."

"I see. And when you arrived here last night, Nobumasa was on his own in the house?"

"Yes."

"Were you immediately shown into the visitors' room?"

"Yes."

"Was the gas heater on at the time?"

"No. Nobumasa lit it after we went into the room. Then he produced a bottle of cognac and two glasses, and offered me a drink."

"Did the arrangements he referred to on the phone concern his brother's estate?"

"Yes."

"Did the victim tell you he was going to forsake his succession rights?"

"He had indicated that some time ago."

"Then why was there any need to make certain arrangements before meeting Mrs. Tsukamoto?"

Koike hesitated for just a moment before answering. "There are a number of problems concerning Yoshihiro Tsukamoto's estate, and I intend to tell you all about them. But this will require a rather lengthy explanation. I wonder if we could leave it till later? It's clearly a side issue, so far as your present investigation is concerned, and if I go into detail about it now, we'll be here all day."

Yoshioka glanced at Kirishima to gauge his reaction, then said, "Well, we can put it aside for the present, if you promise to tell us all about it later."

"I've already done that," Koike said with just a trace of irritation in his voice.

"Well then, you said the victim had informed you he wanted to tell Mrs. Tsukamoto something in addition to the matter concerning her husband's estate."

"That's correct. And because he considered this other matter very important, he wanted a witness. That's why he specifically asked me to be present during the discussion."

"I see. Have you any idea what this other matter might have been?"

"None whatsoever. I didn't want to pry, as I thought I'd learn about it this morning anyway. Furthermore, I had a hunch it wouldn't involve me as Mrs. Tsukamoto's lawyer."

"Didn't he drop any hint at all? People often do that when they want to be mysterious."

"The only thing he said was that he had to go to the Criminal Affairs Division head office in the afternoon to tell the State Prosecutor something, and he wanted to have a discussion with Mrs. Tsukamoto beforehand. But I don't know if this had any bearing on that other matter."

"Then do you think it might have something to do with Hiroshi Watanabe?"

"I wouldn't hazard a guess. I know next to nothing about Watanabe. I don't even know how much Nobumasa himself knew about him."

"About what time did you leave this house last night?"

"Our discussion took only thirty to forty minutes at the most. I left here straight after that."

"Was there any suggestion he might have been expecting another visitor after you?"

"No, I don't think so. But he must have been still alive around half past nine."

"Why's that?"

"Well, after leaving here I drove straight back to my home at Yoyogi-Uehara, and when I took off my coat I realised I'd left my notebook somewhere. Losing it would've been a great inconvenience to me because I've got a lot of important data in it, including some appointments and the office schedule for the next two weeks. I thought I might have left it here, so I rang Nobumasa to find out. He looked for it, and then told me it was here. This was around twenty past nine, I'd say."

"Are you sure it was Nobumasa you were talking to on the phone?"

Koike nodded. "Absolutely. I've known him for a long time—there was no chance of mistaking someone else's voice for his."

"Was there anybody with you when you made the call?"

"Mr. Takei was still there. We both like playing *go*—we're pretty evenly matched. We'd previously arranged the game for last night. With my wife being away, we had a good opportunity to play a leisurely game. Actually, we were interrupted by Nobumasa's phone call."

"Where's your wife?"

Koike adjusted one of his cuff-links before answering. "I think I mentioned this to the detective when he interviewed me the other day . . . Well, this is rather embarrassing, but the day before Yoshihiro's wedding I had a row with my wife. The upshot of it was that she returned to her parents' home at Kamakura . . . She'll be back . . ."

Yoshioka was suddenly seized by a coughing fit. After a few seconds, he said, "Would you like to tell us what the quarrel was about? You're not obliged to, of course."

"I don't mind," Koike said, smiling. "It had to do with the wedding, in fact. At the last minute my wife suddenly declared she didn't want to go in a kimono to that particular reception, and then began complaining she didn't have a suitable dress to wear. I got mad with her and told her she wasn't the one who was getting married. Well, that was the start of it. Finally she didn't attend the wedding at all, and I certainly lost face over it."

"And she hasn't been back since?" Yoshioka asked as casually as possible.

"No . . . As a matter of fact, I was just going to fetch her this afternoon—after completing the business here . . . My wife is a rather headstrong person, and we've had a similar showdown before. There's no real problem, you know, only on this occasion I've been so busy following Yoshihiro's death—I just haven't had the time to go and get her. And of course, she expects me to do just that— she wouldn't come back on her own steam. Too proud." Koike gave a sardonic cackle.

"I hope it'll work out all right . . . But that means you don't have an alibi for the night of Yoshihiro Tsukamoto's murder, do you?"

Yoshioka's question was sharp as a dagger, but Koike didn't bat an eyelid.

"No, I don't," he said. "But then Yoshihiro's murder was the last thing I would've expected. Following the wedding I went straight home and into bed, after a glass of whisky, because I felt tired . . . Yes, I was on my own all night, but what difference would it make even if my wife had been with me? The testimony of a spouse has little or no value in court, as you know."

To Kirishima's ears Koike's words carried sarcasm and self-scorn in equal proportion, but they seemed to have offended the inspector.

"In that case," Yoshioka said spitefully, "you don't really have an alibi for the night of either of the two murders, do you?"

This time Koike looked as if he was getting fed up with the inspector. He looked Yoshioka in the face, and said, "You're quite correct. But if I'd been the killer, I wouldn't have done the job in such an absurd way . . . Mr. Takei knew I was coming to this house. I also mentioned it to Mrs. Tsukamoto on the phone. Surely if I'd wanted to come here to murder somebody, I wouldn't have told everyone about it . . . Moreover, I left my notebook here, and my fingerprints are all over the place. If I were really the culprit, to do all these things would amount to saying to you, 'Please come and arrest me, Inspector, I'm the killer, you know.' Isn't that right? Being a lawyer, I should know at least that much about how an investigation into a murder is, or should be, conducted."

Koike's sarcasm seemed to conceal genuine indignation. Kirishima felt Yoshioka had gone too far, and deserved what he got.

191

CHAPTER THIRTEEN

The homicide squad detectives now started on a room-by-room search of the house. Kirishima and Yoshioka didn't want to be in the way, so they took Koike with them to the nearby Takaido police station.

"Now you can tell us all about those problems concerning Yoshihiro Tsukamoto's estate," Kirishima said when they had settled down. "I don't mind how long it takes—I've got plenty of time." He had decided to take over the questioning from Yoshioka, because Koike's statement was likely to be crowded with legal references.

"Mr. Prosecutor," Koike said formally, "before I proceed, I must request you to make this an unofficial interview. I've no objection to you taking personal notes, but I wouldn't like my statement to go on record."

"Why's that?"

"Because it could be against the interests of my client. So unless you accept this condition, I can't tell you the story, I'm afraid. I don't think I have to point out to you that as a lawyer I've the right and the duty not to disclose the confidences of a client."

"Who's the client you're referring to?"

"Etsuko Tsukamoto. I have her warrant of attorney to act on her behalf in the matter of her husband's estate."

"I see . . . But as you know, we don't disclose any confidential information unless it's essential to the case of the prosecution."

"Well, even if the facts I'm going to reveal do become essential to your case, I must still insist this interview be kept out of the official records. Otherwise my professional reputation could suffer. Of course, if the police carry out their own investigation on the basis of what I'll tell you, and they uncover the same facts through their own efforts—that'll be no concern of mine."

In other words, his concern was for himself, not for his client, Kirishima thought with distaste. This was characteristic of a certain variety of lawyers practising today. "All right," he said, "your statement will be kept confidential." He motioned to the police shorthand writer to leave the room. "You can go ahead now."

"Thank you," Koike said, obviously pleased he was getting his own way. "Well, the other day, when one of the detectives asked me about Yoshihiro's property, I mentioned copyrights 'and some other rights'. I used these words advisedly."

"Then what you're about to tell me relates to those other rights?"

"That's correct. My answer at the time wasn't quite frank, but it certainly wasn't a lie either. I couldn't have revealed the truth then under any circumstances."

"Are you suggesting the death of Nobumasa Tsukamoto has changed the position?"

"Yes, indeed."

"Then were you legal adviser to Nobumasa as well?"

"No, I wasn't. Had I been, I couldn't have acted for Etsuko Tsukamoto at the same time, since her interests weren't necessarily coinciding with those of Nobumasa. I was legal adviser to Yoshihiro only, but his interests had a bearing on Nobumasa's future."

"Would you mind clarifying that?"

"Yes, of course," Koike said obligingly. "Yoshihiro's estate has a large hidden component—the patent on a manufacturing process relating to some synthetic resin product. I don't know the technical details . . ."

Kirishima controlled his surging excitement. Yoshi-hiro, a business management expert, couldn't have invented a new chemical process. It must have been Nobumasa—he must have done the research on it.

Koike said, "As you probably know, any new invention by a company employee automatically becomes the property of the employer. This is the accepted rule in Japan today. A research worker who wants to retain the benefits of his invention for himself can get around this by resigning from the company, taking up a post at a university, and marking time till he can plausibly claim he's done the research there. Alternatively, he can hide his invention from the company and take out a patent on it in the name of a relative or friend. This sort of thing's done quite often these days . . ."

Kirishima nodded. Now he fully understood why Koike had been so anxious to keep this interview confidential.

Koike's expressive face became a mirror of righteous-ness. "Of course, anyone who deliberately deceives the company which guarantees his livelihood, using its re-search facilities and materials for his personal gain, isn't a very nice person, to put it mildly. However, there would've been nothing improper about Nobumasa using his spare time to help his younger brother with some research work."

Kirishima couldn't help smiling. This fellow could talk his way out of a noose around his neck, he thought. "Since I've promised to keep this discussion off the record, there's no need for you to try to find excuses for Nobumasa. On the other hand, nobody in his right mind would believe a lecturer in economics could've done original research in an unexplored area of resin chem-istry, even with his brother's help."

"That may be so, but while he was in Kyoto, Yoshi-hiro used to lecture regularly on industrial administra-tion in engineering departments of universities other than his own. Because of this, he was perfectly entitled to describe himself as a lecturer in a certain chemical

194

engineering department. And I'm pretty sure that's what he put on the patent application at the time. There was nothing fraudulent about that."

"That's true," Kirishima conceded.

"And Mr. Prosecutor, I have quite a lot of sympathy for Nobumasa, and don't find it at all difficult to justify his action. Normally, if a person of outstanding ability makes a contribution to his company's progress with an important invention like this, he's rewarded by promotion to executive status. So he has the incentive to devote all his energy to the service of that company. But Nobumasa had no hope of promotion."

"Because of his father and younger brother?"

"That's right. A big company like Toho Kasei is very jealous of its reputation. It'd be unthinkable for them to raise to executive rank a man who had a criminal in his family. It's just not done . . . Actually, at one stage Nobumasa's immediate superior considered him as a possible match for his daughter. Because of that, he looked into Nobumasa's family background, and of course the whole thing was immediately dropped . . . When a person comes to the conclusion that no matter how hard he may try, he'll get no reward for his efforts, isn't it natural for him to become rebellious? Personally, I couldn't blame him for what he did."

There was certainly logic in Koike's argument, Kirishima thought. There was nothing more frustrating for an able employee than seeing his prospects of promotion cut off. It was a different story with a man of limited talents, who'd be resigned to a life of mediocrity.

He nodded, and said, "Would you know when the patent application was approved?"

"Approximately two years ago. I can't recall the exact date or the patent number at the moment, but I'll get it for you. All the papers relating to it have been left with me."

"I'd like to see them," Kirishima said. "And has anybody bought the patent?"

"Yes. Yoshihiro entered into a contract with Taiyo Kako for the manufacturing rights. As you probably know, this company recently embarked on a major expansion programme, so it's particularly interested in utilising all new developments in the field. On the other hand, its research staff is still fairly weak compared with Toho Kasei, or its long-time rival, Nisshin Kagaku."

"Were you involved in the signing of the contract?"

"Yes. At the time Yoshihiro was still in Kyoto, so I often had to act on his behalf. On all occasions I handled the matter on a strictly business basis, charging the normal fee. You're welcome to examine the contract and my receipts."

"Yes, I'd like to do that, just as a matter of formality . . . By the way, what annual income did Yoshihiro derive from the patent?"

"He was getting a five percent royalty on sales according to the contract. During the first year, production didn't get properly under way, so he only received a little over 3,000,000 yen, as far as I can remember. But last year he grossed about 20,000,000 yen, and from now on the annual amount is expected to increase further."

"That's a very large income . . . And what happened to the money?"

"Most of it would've gone to Nobumasa, I'd say. Yoshihiro probably received a percentage for lending his name. But this was something arranged between the two brothers, and there was no need for me to concern myself with it, even if I was Yoshihiro's lawyer."

"Isn't it more likely it was a fifty-fifty arrangement? Have you any special reason to think most of this income would've gone to Nobumasa?"

"Yes. I know Nobumasa was thinking of resigning from Toho Kasei and becoming independent. Naturally, he wouldn't have been able to establish a company all on his own. He intended to find a number of investors who'd join him in the venture, but he wanted to have as much financial say as possible. That's why I think that after paying for his house he would've put most of his extra income into savings bank accounts. Yoshihiro was well aware of his brother's plan, and he had a considerable income of his own, so I don't think he would've expected to receive a large share of the royalties from the patent."

"I see . . . Nevertheless, the money he paid for his apartment would've come from his share of royalties, wouldn't it?"

"Well, 3,000,000 yen is fifteen percent of the 20,000,000 yen return for last year. Nobumasa could've given him that much."

"And I assume the matter Nobumasa wanted to discuss with Etsuko this morning would've concerned this patent business?"

"Yes, he was going to tell Etsuko about it. He intended to relinquish his succession rights to Yoshihiro's estate, but so far as the income from the patent was concerned, he expected her to agree to maintaining the existing arrangement. I'm sure Etsuko would've complied with his request without any trouble."

"But as things stand at present, Etsuko still doesn't know anything about this?"

"No. He was going to ask her personally this morning. I was to be there only in case they needed my advice."

"Do you know what percentage of the royalties Nobumasa proposed to pay to Etsuko?"

"Last night he suggested twenty to twenty-five percent of the total after tax. As her lawyer, I considered this a fair offer under the circumstances, and was going to advise Etsuko to accept it."

"Have you any idea where Nobumasa banked his savings?"

"No, I haven't. But my guess is he would've placed it into a number of accounts with various banks, using false names to circumvent the problem of tax and other things."

"How far was he with his plans to set up the company?"

"I've gained the impression he wasn't very far advanced. He seemed to have held discussions with various people from time to time, and he was getting his own capital together, but I think it would've taken at least another year to get the company actually registered, even without making allowances for the present tightness of

197

the money market."

"Has Nobumasa left a will?"

"No, he hasn't, but after the accident he did talk about making one. Once he said, 'Who can guess what may happen next?' Now that I think of it, he might have had a premonition of his death."

"Then it looks as if there'll be no successor to Nobumasa's property?"

"As far as I know, there won't be," Koike said with a sigh.

Kirishima unconsciously shook his head as he thought about it. When a person died without leaving a will, his legal successors were, firstly, the lineal descendant, secondly, the lineal ascendant, thirdly, the brothers and sisters, and as an exception the status of the spouse was recognised under present Japanese law. Assets left without a will came under the jurisdiction of the Court of Family Affairs, which appointed an executor. And if nobody came forward to claim succession rights, after a certain period the estate automatically became Treasury property. Inheriting a distant relative's fortune, as it happened in the United States and some other countries, was unthinkable in Japan without the existence of a will.

Nobumasa had no wife or child, and his parents and brothers were dead, therefore he had no successor to his property. It would pass to the State, and no individual would gain anything from it. Etsuko would be the only person to benefit, in an indirect way. She would inherit the patent under Yoshihiro's name, and with Nobumasa dead, she would naturally retain all the income from it.

Koike seemed to have guessed what Kirishima was thinking, because he said, "Mr. Prosecutor, this *is* a strange situation, isn't it? I was so excited this morning— it just didn't occur to me. Nobumasa certainly had considerable assets, and yet, no one could possibly profit by his death . . . Then what was the motive for this crime? Is there anybody who might have had a very deep-seated grudge against the Tsukamoto brothers? I can't think of anyone . . ."

For Kirishima, this was a riddle to which he had to

198

find an answer, sooner or later. At least Yoshihiro's death could have a connection with the hidden ownership of the patent. Possession of something that produced an income of more than 20,000,000 yen a year might be a strong enough motive for murder. And in theory, the only person who could have had such a motive was Etsuko. This was an inevitable conclusion.

"Are you sure Etsuko Tsukamoto still knows nothing of this patent? Couldn't Yoshihiro have told her about it before his death?"

"I don't think he did," Koike said, frowning. "A few days before the wedding I suggested to Yoshihiro he should disclose the patent to Etsuko. His answer was that if he hurriedly told her about it, she might get the wrong impression about his brother's character. He preferred to explain everything to her during their honeymoon, when they'd have plenty of time to themselves . . . So it's most unlikely he would've told her before his death. Had he died a few days after they'd left on their honeymoon, then I'd say it would've been possible."

"I follow," Kirishima said. "And was there anyone else who knew about the patent—apart from the brothers and yourself?"

"Well, because of the nature of the arrangement, I think they would've kept it to themselves as much as possible. But I couldn't say definitely that no one else knew about it. For example, the people who were going to invest in the new company might have been told. I wouldn't have a clue who they are . . ."

Kirishima leaned back in his chair to cross his legs. "Now, let's get back to where we began," he said. "Had Nobumasa already taken steps to relinquish his succession rights to Yoshihiro's estate?"

"It was arranged between us that I'd prepare the document after completing today's discussion with Etsuko. As you know, a notice of intention to forsake succession has to be lodged with the Court of Family Affairs. I was going to do this sometime after tomorrow."

"Then the position is that Nobumasa's share of Yoshihiro's estate will pass to the State?"

"Well, we'll see about that . . . I'll certainly put up a good fight in Etsuko's interests. I don't see why the Ministry of Finance should get the money."

"Now, this may sound a strange question, but isn't it possible that secretly Yoshihiro looked upon this patent arrangement as an embarrassment rather than an advantage to him?"

"I'm not so sure about that," Koike said, knitting his eyebrows. "When I first heard of it, somehow I didn't think this invention of Nobumasa was anything special. I reckoned it might yield an annual income of 2,000,000 to 3,000,000 yen, and this could be handled without much trouble under the arrangement. But of course, the result was far more spectacular than expected, as I've told you. As time went on, people in industrial circles began to take more and more notice of it . . . Yes, now that I think of it, Yoshihiro did seem increasingly concerned about it. His moodiness over the past six months or so might have had something to do with it."

"That's what I thought," Kirishima said. "If someone in the industry buttonholed him and asked him some searching questions about the more intricate technical details, he would've been hard pressed to conceal his ignorance. At the same time, this could've proved very embarrassing to his brother, too."

"What d'you mean?"

"Well, let me put is this way. Once sales resulting from this invention reached hundreds of millions of yen a year, Toho Kasei, which is a rival of the company that bought the manufacturing rights, would've naturally taken an interest in this product, perhaps to the extent of checking on the inventor's name. While things had been only at the patent application stage, and even later, while no real profit was being made, Toho Kasei probably wouldn't have been aware of it, since the number of new patents taken out annually must be enormous. But once they started to check, they would've been most surprised to find the inventor was a business management expert who had absolutely nothing to do with advanced chemical production techniques. And then they would've discovered that the so-called inventor's elder brother, who was employed by them, was doing research in exactly the same field! . . . Of course, they couldn't have labelled Nobumasa an industrial spy, since he sold a secret which hadn't been stolen but had been produced in his own brain. Still, I can't understand why he stayed with Toho Kasei for two more years after the patent had been issued."

Koike looked up quickly. "I thought I've already given a clear-cut answer to that one. Nobumasa intended to resign when he was ready to set up his own company."

"That may be so," Kirishima said, tilting his head, "but after the first year—when his income from the invention reached something like 1,000,000 yen a month—wouldn't it have been natural and advisable for him to leave Toho Kasei? But he stayed on, right up to his death. This looks a bit odd to me."

Koike nodded, and said, "Yes, it does look rather odd, now that you've drawn attention to it. I just never thought of it before."

This was a reasonable answer, Kirishima thought. As Yoshihiro's legal adviser, Koike's job was to look at and attend to problems as they came up. He wasn't expected to gaze into the future.

After exchanging a few words with Yoshioka, Kirishima decided to bring the interview to an end. "Mr. Koike, thank you for your co-operation. I may have to ask you for your help once again some other time, but this will be all for now . . . Oh—is it all right with you if I borrow the papers relating to the patent?"

"Yes, of course."

"Then Inspector Yoshioka will send a detective along to get them straight away."

"That'll be fine," Koike said and stood up. "Well, Mr. Prosecutor, to be frank with you, I feel a lot better now that I've told you all this. And if at any time you want further clarification on any point, please don't hesitate to contact me. I'll be happy to tell you everything I know. And I certainly wouldn't want you to gain the impression I've tried to take advantage of my long-standing friendship with the Tsukamoto brothers in any way."

Soon afterwards the group of detectives who had searched Nobumasa's house returned to the police station. Their work had produced very little result. Even in the drawer which was supposed to hold all the important papers, all they had found was a post office savings book with about 300,000 yen in it. With the pass-book was an envelope containing nine different seals.

"Judging by these seals," Yoshioka said, "there must be nine more pass-books left with various banks."

"You're probably right," Kirishima agreed. "This is an old technique used for tax evasion. It renders ineffective any raid by taxation officers. But I think in his case the principal purpose was protection against burglary. He was a bachelor, away from home in the daytime, and he had a charwoman who was free to come and go. It would've been unsafe for him to leave pass-books lying around with a lot of money in them. But with seals only, unless the thief knew the name of each bank and the false name in which each account was operated, he had no hope of touching the money."

"Yes, that'll be it. He must have used the post office savings account for his day-to-day needs . . . I'll get the detectives to take those seals and check with every bank in Tokyo, one after another."

"You may be able to avoid some of that work if you carefully check any notebook your men might have found in his house. He could've listed those account numbers somewhere for reference."

"Yes, I'll certainly do that," Yoshioka said. "But there's another problem. Suppose there's someone who knew of at least one of those pass-books. That person could've withdrawn the money from that particular account, provided he or she managed to get hold of the right seal. And then we'd find it pretty hard to trace that money."

"Probably." Kirishima was again getting irritated by the inspector's I'm-so-clever attitude.

After a short pause Yoshioka said, "We'll check out that woman straight away—the one your clerk was talking about. We should be able to do this fairly quickly by going to the Princess Bar. And we'll also investigate Nobumasa Tsukamoto's place of work and all his friends and acquaintances, though I feel there's a definite connection between his murder and his brother's. The method of dealing with the victim would suggest this, for a start."

"Yes, I agree," Kirishima said. "But just to make sure, I'd like you to keep in mind also the possibility of the two incidents being independent . . . My present feeling is that the clue to Nobumasa's murder lies in whatever he was going to tell Etsuko in addition to the matter of the succession rights and the patent."

That afternoon Kyoko rushed to Etsuko's apartment immediately after talking to Kirishima on the phone. He had only given her a bare outline of the morning's happenings, but that was enough to make her once again very anxious about Etsuko.

She pressed the button on the bell, and to her surprise the door was opened by Kawaji.

"Ah, Mrs. Kirishima," he said, looking slightly embarrassed. "You must have heard what happened. It's monstrous . . . Not so long ago Etsuko rang me at my home. She sounded so upset, I immediately dashed over here . . ."

Kyoko was stuck for words. It wasn't any wonder Etsuko was terribly upset, no matter how stout-hearted she was, or that she wanted someone to be with her after this new shock. But why did she ring Kawaji? *Why didn't she ask me?*

But soon Kyoko could see the reason. Etsuko must still be determined to stay in the apartment on her own. She must have guessed that after this second tragedy everybody would implore her again to return to her parents' home. Kawaji was the only one who had supported her from the start in her decision to live here alone. She must feel Kawaji was the only person who really understood how she felt . . .

"Since I arrived, she's calmed down a little," Kawaji whispered as he showed Kyoko in.

Etsuko was in the western room, staring vacantly at the heartbreak doll on the table.

"She's been looking at that doll for the past half hour at least," Kawaji whispered. "I'd like to be able to help her in some way . . ."

Kyoko began to wonder if Kawaji had been harbouring a secret affection for Etsuko for some time past. His attitude towards her seemed to go beyond the bounds of normal sympathy . . . There were many examples of sympathy growing into love, or at least being mistaken for it . . .

"Kyoko, I'm sorry to trouble you all the time," Etsuko said tonelessly.

Kyoko was just about to answer when the door-bell rang again. Kawaji went to see who it was, first closing the paper door behind him.

Then Kyoko heard some voices coming from the entry. It sounded like an argument. Suddenly the paper door slid open again, and a man marched into the room. She had never seen him before.

Etsuko gaped at the man for a few seconds, then said, "Mr. Higuchi . . ."

"Etsuko—you look ill," Higuchi said. "To be completely honest with you, I felt rather awkward about coming here, but I can't put up with this any longer."

"I don't think we've anything to discuss," Etsuko said coldly.

"You just shut up!" Higuchi shouted. He had such a threatening look on his face, Kyoko thought he was going to slap Etsuko across the face. "Isn't it about time you came to your senses? How long d'you think you're going to stay in this place? I've come at your father's request to take you back where you belong. Now, go and get ready to leave!"

"I'm not going anywhere." Etsuko's face became white as a sheet, and her hands began to tremble.

"Are you going to let your father die without looking at him?"

"Let him die? What are you talking about?"

"He's been in very poor health since the day of your wedding, and now he can't get out of bed at all. I don't have to tell you he hasn't been well for a long time. Though he's been saying lately you're no longer his daughter, I know how much he's looking forward to your return . . ."

Etsuko didn't answer. She just kept looking at the floor.

Higuchi seemed to be pleased with his performance so far, because he dropped his voice a little and became more persuasive. "I needn't tell you how worried I've been about you ever since your husband's murder. Then this morning, just as I got back to Tokyo from the Kansai district, a journalist friend of mine, a police reporter on the *Tokyo Shinbun,* told me about the second murder . . . For the sake of Mr. Ogata and yourself, I can't let you go on like this. Don't you see the Tsukamoto family is under a curse? The father died in prison, two of his sons have been murdered, and the third was burnt to death. If you stay in this place any longer, you may be next. Bearing their name's bad enough . . ."

Etsuko went red in the face and was about to say something, but Kawaji cut in.

"The killing of Yoshihiro and his brother has nothing to do with the Tsukamoto family name," he said. "The killer's the one to blame, not the victims."

"You keep out of this if you know what's good for you," Higuchi said threateningly. "A minute ago you put on great airs telling me that nobody was allowed to see Etsuko. But what right do *you* have to be here, anyway?"

"You're the one who has no right to demand she should go with you. Judging by your attitude, you must be Higuchi. I've heard of you, and I think you're disgraceful, chasing after Mrs. Tsukamoto like this."

Higuchi turned red as a beetroot and clenched his fists. But when he looked at Kawaji's athletic figure, he seemed to change his mind. "The saying 'a mean person sees evil in everything' fits you like a glove. I set aside my personal feelings long ago, and I'm quite capable of taking Etsuko home with me in a dignified manner . . . Pardon me for asking this, but I hope your attempts to keep her in this apartment aren't part of some insidious design of yours?"

This was becoming a slanging match, with harsh words being exchanged for harsher ones, Kyoko thought with trepidation. She wondered how she had ever got mixed up in it.

"Even if you happen to be at the fag end of the legal profession," Kawaji told Higuchi, "surely you must know enough about the law to realise your previous words amount to slander?"

"I don't care about that—I meant what I said. What other reason would you have for opposing Etsuko's return to her parents?"

"I just happen to have some respect for her feelings—that's all. And since she's an adult, she doesn't have to obey anyone's instructions, especially yours."

"But can't you see something might happen to her if she's left here alone? This is hardly the time for us to enter into mud-slinging."

"You can stop worrying about Etsuko," Kawaji said sarcastically. "I'll accept the responsibility of looking after her. If I think it's better for her to go back to her parents, I'll have a proper discussion with her and try to convince her with sensible arguments. Lunatic bullying tactics—the kind you tried just before—won't shift her from here, I can assure you."

Higuchi must have thought this wasn't getting him anywhere, because now he ignored Kawaji and turned to Etsuko again. "Etsuko, please come home with me." He loaded his voice with all the sincerity he could muster. "Because you've been among these people for a while, you're becoming a bit odd yourself. Please try to recover your common sense and return to your previous peaceful life again . . . I must insist you come with me. Please don't make it too difficult for me."

"As I told you at the beginning, I'm not going any-where," Etsuko said harshly. "It's you who's going—now."

"Etsuko, I can't let you——"

"This is my home. Please leave quietly, or I'll make a complaint to the police. You're unlawfully intruding."

Higuchi's face turned pale for the first time. Only his eyes were still glowing as he said, "I see. I seem to have lost once again." He glanced at Kawaji, then back at Etsuko. "All right. I'm going. And I'll report your charming words to your father, just as you've uttered them." He turned and walked out of the room, but stopped at the door, and said, "Whatever you do, please don't forget your father. Or don't you have a heart any more?"

CHAPTER FOURTEEN

When Kirishima returned to the office from lunch the next day, he was confronted by the beaming face of his clerk Kitahara.

"Inspector Yoshioka rang a minute ago," Kitahara said. "He's coming over to see you, Mr. Prosecutor. He's got that woman."

Kirishima couldn't help smiling. Ever since Nobumasa's murder, his clerk had kept his mouth shut and looked as if he had no further interest in the human race. The collapse of his theory about Nobumasa being Yoshihiro's killer had been a severe blow to his pride, but now that the match-box he had picked up proved useful, he seemed to have regained some of his self-esteem.

"I'd like to say that getting hold of that box of matches with the Princess Bar printed on it was quite an achievement on your part," Kirishima said. "Unfortunately, I'm in no position to say so on this occasion."

"I perfectly understand, Mr. Prosecutor," Kitahara said demurely. "In the strict sense of the word, it *was* a theft, wasn't it?"

They continued in this bantering fashion until Yoshioka

208

appeared in the doorway.

"The woman in question is a hostess in the Princess Bar," Yoshioka said. "Her name is Toshiko Kikuchi. She requested an interview with you, Mr. Prosecutor, and since I thought this would be an opportunity for Mr. Kitahara to identify her, I've brought her along. She's outside in the waiting room now."

"Did she say why she wanted to see me?" Kirishima was surprised. Most ordinary people wanted to keep away from the prosecutor's office, even when they were resigned to being pestered by the police.

"No, she didn't—she's hard as nails . . . But could I first bring you up to date on some other things?"

"Go ahead."

Yoshioka opened his black police notebook. "We haven't quite finished our investigations at Nobumasa Tsukamoto's place of work, but I've got something here. The chief of the research laboratories, a Dr. Shimagami, said the company recently learnt of Nobumasa's deception concerning the patent."

"Only recently?"

"Yes. It's probably because Toho Kasei is such a big organisation . . . Anyway, Dr. Shimagami said Nobumasa would've been put on the mat immediately on his return to work. And depending on his explanation, he was going to be dismissed or asked to resign."

"I see."

"He said most people in a similar position had at least the decency to go back to a university and work there for a while before applying for a patent, and he was amazed at Nobumasa's impudence . . . He could hardly contain his anger, even though he knew the man was no longer alive."

"Do other members of the staff know about this?" Kirishima asked.

"It looks like it. He certainly wouldn't have been able to stay there any longer . . . As for his relations with other employees, he isolated himself as much as possible—for obvious reasons. He didn't seem to have any friends there. My man questioned his assistants, too, but all they could talk about was the work they were doing. They just about drove him up the wall . . ."

"What about acquaintances of the victim outside Toho Kasei?"

"We're still looking into that, but so far we haven't come across anyone who might have intended to join him in the new company. This suggests his plans were in the fairly early stages, as Koike said."

"Mm-hm."

"Other than this, we did some more work at Chiyoda University, and also took a good look at the Araki couple. On the night of the first murder Professor Araki had an alibi and his wife didn't, and on the night before last it was the other way round . . ."

There were known cases of partners in crime sharing their alibis, but this would hardly apply to the Arakis, Kirishima thought.

Yoshioka consulted his notebook. "On the first night Mrs. Araki was supposed to have stayed at home, but she can't prove this. The professor attended the wedding, then took one of Yoshihiro's assistants for a drinking session. They separated around eleven o'clock. Araki hasn't got a current driver's licence, but Mrs. Araki's speeding around in a flashy sports car."

"And the second occasion?" Kirishima asked, suppressing a yawn.

"Araki was reading a book at home, and Mrs. Araki went to see a play together with a number of other women. She was in company till well after eleven o'clock . . . At any rate, there's no way to connect either of them with the second murder."

"Have you already checked the alibis of all the other possible suspects?"

"Koike's story about playing *go* is confirmed by Takei, the fellow who visited him. Higuchi returned to Tokyo on a plane which left Osaka at eight o'clock yesterday morning. Kawaji spent the night of the second murder in his parents' home, where he now lives. But his room is in a new extension, so he can come and go without passing through the main building. He claims he returned home from the wedding reception around eight o'clock, gave his parents the piece of wedding cake he brought back with him, then went straight to his room and didn't leave the house again till the following morning."

Kirishima nodded without comment. It looked as if the elimination method wouldn't work in this case. The alibis of most people involved were full of holes.

"That's about all I've got at present," Yoshioka said. "Would you like to see Miss Kikuchi now?"

"Don't you want to brief me on her first?"

The inspector sniffed, as if smelling something unpleasant. "You'll know all about her as soon as you look at her . . . We're checking on her sexual relationships at the moment. I'm sure it'll take some considerable time."

Miss Kikuchi was twenty-seven or twenty-eight. Her above-average beauty was spoilt by a hard face and greedy eyes. Judging by her hair, piled high above her head, and her bright red suit with fur collar, she must have worked around the Ginza at one time or another and managed to acquire a certain polish there.

Kitahara's nod confirmed she was the right woman.

After introductions Kirishima said, "I understand you work as a hostess at the Princess Bar."

"I work as a companion," she said delicately.

"Oh, I see. Ever since the Tokyo Olympic Games this word seems to have been in vogue."

"But I happen to be the niece of the manageress, so I'm different from ordinary hostesses."

"Then do you help out at the bar when you're free?"

"That's right."

"And what sort of relationship did you have with Nobumasa Tsukamoto?"

"In legal terms, I was his de-facto wife," she said without moving a muscle in her face.

Kirishima took out his handkerchief and wiped his nose to conceal his surprise. Yoshioka had been absolutely right when he said there was no need for a briefing on her.

211

"In law, a de-facto relationship means the partners are living together as husband and wife, only their marriage hasn't been registered. But you haven't been living with him, have you?"

"Well, then let's say I'm his ex-de-facto wife."

"Are you suggesting you lived with him some time ago?"

"Yes."

"When was that?"

"We separated about last March. We'd lived together for some nine months before that."

"Why did you separate?"

"He threw me out," she said spitefully, then suddenly changed her mind and began to dab her eyes with her handkerchief.

"Why would he do that?"

"I couldn't work it out." She produced a couple of unconvincing sobs in her voice. "He claimed I was having an affair with another man at the same time, or some crap like that. There was no truth in it at all . . . When I thought he might have some other woman besides me, I got really depressed . . . He gave me only 200,000 yen to go away with."

"How did you become friendly with him in the first place?"

"Oh, I don't know—there was no special reason. Just one thing led to another. It's one of those things— happens all the time."

"I see," Kirishima said, folding his arms across his chest. "I understand you visited him on the morning of the day he died. Did you go there a number of times after you separated?"

"Yes."

"Why? Trying to make it up with him?"

"No!" Miss Kikuchi pursed her brightly painted lips. "It was for the sake of the baby."

"What baby?"

"My baby, of course. I was pregnant when he kicked me out, though I wasn't sure of it then because I was in that very early stage . . ."

Kirishima frowned but didn't say anything.

She said, "Around that time he was the only man I was having intercourse with—I can give you my word on that. So the child is definitely his. There's no mistake about that. That's why I tried so hard to reason with him —for the sake of the little mite to be brought into this world. But all he did was try to get out of it by saying the child must belong to some other man . . . After a while I got so desperate, I even thought of committing suicide, wondering how he'd take that. But then I thought he might change his mind once he saw the baby, especially if it looked like him, so I decided to leave it till then."

"And did you give birth to a child?"

"Yes. I thought of an abortion at the time, but I couldn't make up my mind about it quickly enough, and then it was too late. The baby was born on November 16 —a lovely little boy. Because of my occupation, I had to leave him in the care of my parents. And that mean creature insisted the baby wasn't his, right up to his death . . ." Miss Kikuchi covered her eyes with her handkerchief and managed a couple of sobs.

"What was the exact date of your separation?" Kirishima asked.

"I can't remember the day, but it was around the end of last February. I must have become pregnant at the last moment . . ." She sighed, closing her eyes, then quickly looked up at Kirishima. "Are *you* doubting me, too?"

"Well, it was cutting it fine, I must say."

"A mother always knows who the father of her child is," she said indignantly. "As soon as I could move about again, I went to see Nobumasa and asked him to take me back with the baby. When he refused, I got awfully upset —really sick. Finally I told him I'd give up hope of becoming reconciled with him, and begged him almost on my knees at least to acknowledge the child was his. But the heartless wretch just laughed coldly under his ugly nose . . ."

"And when you visited him the day before yesterday— was it to try once again?"

"Yes," she said eagerly. "When I heard about his

brother's death, I got scared something might happen to him, too."

Kirishima found this very revealing, though she obviously wasn't aware of it.

"What was his answer this time?"

"We never got that far. He immediately flew into a rage—I just couldn't cope with him at all." Suddenly she sat up and looked hard at Kirishima. "Mr. Prosecutor, I must ask you something."

"Yes?"

"Now that Nobumasa's dead, can I still sue him for the admission of his fatherhood?"

"You're talking about a suit for recognition after death."

"I heard that since a dead man can't be made a defendant, I must bring a suit against a prosecutor. Is that right?"

"Yes, that's correct."

"Then I'll bring a suit again you, Mr. Prosecutor. Would you please arrange this for me?"

It was obvious what she was after. Even if she could prove she had been Nobumasa's de-facto wife, this wouldn't automatically give her succession rights to his estate. But the boy would inherit everything if he was recognised as his.

"It's not as simple as that," Kirishima told her. "You can't just pick any prosecutor you like. The one mentioned in the relevant clause has the exclusive job of appearing on behalf of dead or absent defendants so that trials can be conducted according the civil court rules. What you want to do is get yourself a lawyer. I can't help you in this."

"Oh, I see. It's altogether too complicated for me . . . But there's one thing I'd like you to remember, Mr. Prosecutor. Anyone who might try to rob my baby of his lawful rights could well be Nobumasa's killer."

"Okay, I'll keep that in mind. But tell me this. Since Nobumasa treated you so cold-heartedly, why didn't you bring a suit against him for recognition while he was alive?"

For the first time Miss Kikuchi looked slightly bewildered, but it only took her a few seconds to regain her presence of mind. "Well," she said, "that was because I thought it'd be better if we could come to an agreement without going to court. Legal action costs a lot of money and time . . . Besides, it's only three months since my baby was born."

"That's fair enough," Kirishima said, admiring her native cunning. "And now, just to change the subject, can you tell me where you were and what you were doing on the night of February 20?"

"February 20? That was last Saturday night, wasn't it? I was in the bar, of course. That's the best night of the week for us. I couldn't afford to miss it—with business being so slack these days."

"About what time did you leave the bar?"

"I was there till after eleven thirty." She raised her eyes and suddenly looked incredulous. "You're not suggesting *I* might have murdered him, are you? Much as I hated him, he was still the father of my child. How could I do a thing like that?"

"It was only a routine question. We check on everybody connected with the victim . . . By the way, have you ever met Nobumasa's younger brother, Yoshihiro?"

"No, never. He came to Tokyo after we separated."

"And what were you doing on the night of February 15—last Monday?"

"I was in the bar. There must be plenty of witnesses to that."

When they finished work that evening, Kirishima invited his clerk Kitahara for a drink.

There was nothing on earth Kitahara loved more than *sake*, and after a few glasses it was impossible to shut him up. Depending on the subject, he could become rather tiresome at times, but there were occasions when Kirishima found his comments on a current investigation quite interesting, even useful. The ruddy-faced old badger had a kind of sixth sense developed over long years of service under many different prosecutors.

Sipping his *sake*, Kitahara said, "Mr. Prosecutor, what d'you think of Miss Kikuchi's story?"

"Well, by raising the matter of recognition after death, she automatically revealed that she, too, had a motive for the crime. So she must have absolute confidence in her alibi."

"Mr. Prosecutor, would you let me offer my opinion on this?"

"Look, you've been with me a number of years now, and you know I think highly of your work. There's no need to beg my permission every time you want to say something. Just say it, for goodness' sake."

Kitahara helped himself to another glass of *sake*. "Well, I think Miss Kikuchi has somebody behind her, who finally decided to get in on the act by putting Nobumasa out of his misery . . . When it comes to things like recognition after death, and filing a suit against the nominal defendant, surely there must be somebody advising her? It couldn't possibly have originated in her own brain-box."

"That's what I think, too."

"It seems pretty obvious to me that Nobumasa chucked her out when he discovered she had another lover somewhere. When you asked her why she didn't sue him for recognition while he was alive, she was at a bit of a loss for a moment, wasn't she? Well, she might have thought she couldn't win that way. Nobumasa might have got hold of some evidence against her that would've put her right out of the running."

"Are you suggesting her lover and adviser are the same person?"

"That's possible, isn't it? The baby may well be his. Or she may not be sure which man has done the trick."

"In most suits for recognition there's a firmly established de-facto relationship at the time the woman becomes pregnant, and that's a great advantage to her. But Miss Kikuchi has a special problem on her hands because of the delicate time factor."

"Perhaps this greedy woman has decided to put everything on the one card. While she was living with Nobumasa she must have become vaguely aware of his assets, including the patent."

"I'm not surprised she used the baby to squeeze some money out of him while he was alive. That's why she kept visiting him. But I'm afraid your idea that she's putting everything on the one card just doesn't make sense."

"But why?" Kitahara opened his eyes wide and calmed himself with another glass of *sake*. "Are you saying there's no conspiracy between Miss Kikuchi and her lover?"

"If those two planned this murder together, then needless to say their motive was to make their child the successor to Nobumasa's money, and in turn put some of that money to their own use. Now, to achieve this, it's essential they win the suit for recognition after death. But as I said before, her case is pretty risky because of the time factor, and if it went to trial, the blood type would naturally come up."

"What if they're sure there's no problem about the blood type?"

"You mean Nobumasa and Miss Kikuchi's lover belong to the same blood group? That may be so, but these days a more refined test is used in forensic medicine. There's very little chance of the two men having exactly the same blood type."

"But Nobumasa's remains were cremated today, weren't they? Then how could his blood type be analysed?"

"Hmmm." Kitahara's idea was based entirely on a guess, but still, it couldn't be completely ignored, Kirishima thought. "All right. Supposing your theory is correct so far, then how do you fit Yoshihiro's murder into it?"

"Mr. Prosecutor," Kitahara said theatrically, "I don't think my pride could stand another blow, such as it suffered when my theory about Nobumasa being the killer collapsed so shamefully. But if I have the excuse of being drunk, perhaps I can take the risk. Then may I pause here for a moment?" He emptied his glass, refilled it from the bottle, and promptly emptied it once more. "I think the registration of the marriage certificate on the day of the wedding created an unexpected situation for Miss Kikuchi and her partner. The normal thing would've been to get it registered the next day at the earliest."

Kirishima looked at Kitahara out of the corner of his eye. "You mean, if the marriage hadn't been legally established before Yoshihiro's death, the patent registered in his name would've automatically reverted to Nobumasa, and then if he died next . . . You think they had this all worked out?"

"Yes. Why not? Though I must concede one weak point. My theory doesn't answer your basic question— why did they chose the wedding night for the murder? Well, perhaps Miss Kikuchi didn't know about the wedding till the last minute. That doesn't sound so odd, does it?"

Kirishima knitted his brows but found it rather hard to think. Was it the *sake*? Kitahara seemed to have been doing all the drinking . . . This latest theory of his was certainly much smarter than the one about Nobumasa being the killer. Even so, there were several holes in it. For example, how did Miss Kikuchi's partner manage to lure Yoshihiro out of the hotel?

"The police are checking on Miss Kikuchi's environment and friends. Let's wait for their report, shall we? The thing that bothers me most at the moment is this Hiroshi Watanabe. Nobumasa knew something about him. He couldn't make up his mind whether he should disclose it to me . . ."

Kitahara kept picking with his chopsticks at the meat and vegetable pieces in the *sukiyaki* in front of him. He nodded politely every now and then, but made no comment.

". . . Nobumasa tried to tell Etsuko something before seeing me again. He wanted to explain something to her before disclosing it to me. And whichever way I look at it, it must have been something to do with Watanabe . . . If this man has no connection with Etsuko, then why did Nobumasa feel he had to tell Etsuko about him? This is

218

the part I can't work out . . ."

Kirishima fell silent but his thought processes didn't stop. Once again he drew the conclusion the existence of Watanabe, whoever he was, couldn't be a factor important enough to have precipitated the death of the Tsukamoto brothers . . . Nobumasa had said the matter concerned another man's reputation. Could that person be Yoshihiro? If so, it was easy to see why he had wanted to explain it to Etsuko before making it public by disclosing it to the authorities. But what could've had such an important bearing on Yoshihiro's reputation, even after his death?

"Mr. Prosecutor!" Kitahara yelled out.

"For goodness' sake, what is it? You don't have to shout." He thought his clerk was beginning to look very drunk. It was time to end the session.

"I've come up with a fantastic idea."

"Yes?"

"How can we be sure the man who married Etsuko was really Yoshihiro Tsukamoto?"

Kirishima was dumbfounded. Kitahara had produced a few surprises during the evening, but this was the king of them all.

"What are you talking about? His corpse didn't have the face blown off it."

"No, I wasn't thinking of that. What I'm wondering is whether it was really his younger brother, Tadaaki, who was burnt to death at that hot spring inn? Suppose it was Yoshihiro who died in the fire? This would've given Tadaaki—a man wanted for murder—the chance of a lifetime, wouldn't it? He could assume Yoshihiro's identity and start a new life, escaping justice forever. So far as his features were concerned, he could've got around that by undergoing plastic surgery, ostensibly to get the burns to his face fixed up. Anyway, they must have resembled each other because they were brothers . . ."

"You're unlucky," Kirishima said, chuckling. "This time your bomb just didn't go off. Yoshihiro was a university lecturer. An imposter could've never hoped to cope with that. He might have been able to get away with a few lectures, using some notes left behind by the deceased, or reading out of a book. But how could he have written a thesis on industrial management, or have his own book published? That would've been impossible. And everyone at Chiyoda University confirmed Yoshihiro had been a competent and ambitious man, keen on research."

Kitahara lowered his head and sighed. "Ah, well, it was a good try . . . I must have had too much to drink—dreaming up rubbish like that. Please don't hold it against me, Mr. Prosecutor."

Just then a thought flashed through Kirishima's mind. He stood up quickly.

"This is the end of our little session, by the look of things," Kitahara mumbled with resignation.

"Not at all," Kirishima said brightly. "You just go on drinking while I ring Inspector Yoshioka. You've given me an idea."

Kitahara screwed up his face, now purple after several bottles of *sake*. "Ha. You must be poking fun at me again, Mr. Prosecutor."

"No, I'm not. I'm going to tell Yoshioka to get the police records on that fire at the hot spring inn."

CHAPTER FIFTEEN

Nothing happened for the next two days, and this gave Kirishima an opportunity to clean up a number of small jobs he had on his plate.

He was about to leave for home around six o'clock in the evening when his phone rang. The caller was Higuchi.

"Would you have dinner with me?" Higuchi asked without any preliminaries.

"Dinner—with you?" Kirishima was amazed at Higuchi's brazenness.

"I don't propose to *take* you to dinner, Mr. Prosecutor —since I'm involved in a case you're investigating. What I had in mind was to go Dutch with you."

"Why your sudden interest in me?"

"I've got a story to tell you. It may be useful to you."

After a moment's thought Kirishima said, "I'd like to listen to your story, but I'd rather not have dinner with you. Can't you come up to my office?"

"Not unless you promise to make it an unofficial interview. I wish to co-operate with you as much as possible, but I can't afford to take the risk of being charged with false accusation or slander."

Kirishima tightened his hold on the receiver. "Then are you going to accuse somebody of murder?"

"I haven't got sufficient evidence for that. That's why I'm asking for an informal interview. All I can say is that I've some information which may be helpful to you, and that I hope these two murders will be solved as quickly as possible."

"Mm-hm. And where are you now?"

"Not far from your office."

"All right. Come up then. I'll send my clerk home straight away."

"Thank you, Mr. Prosecutor," Higuchi said coldly. "I'll be there in five minutes."

Kitahara was already putting on his overcoat. He had listened to Kirishima talking on the phone, of course. Diplomatically concealing his disappointment, he said, "I'd better be going then, Mr. Prosecutor . . ."

Higuchi arrived within the next couple of minutes. He had the expression of a boxer about to go into the ring.

"I'd like to make it clear from the start, Mr. Prosecutor, that I'm not doing this out of personal prejudice. I'm indebted to Mr. Ogata, as you know, and I find it upsetting to look at him in his present condition. I'm also concerned about Etsuko. But I can assure you my move has absolutely nothing to do with any future chance I may have to marry Etsuko."

Kirishima couldn't decide for the moment whether Higuchi was sincere, or just clever at putting on an act. He certainly sounded very serious.

Higuchi said, "If Etsuko is allowed to remain the way she is now, she may end up losing her mind altogether. Already she appears to have completely exhausted her nervous energy. And to make matters worse, she seems to be surrounded at the moment by people who, in my opinion, are accelerating her progress towards a nervous breakdown. I can't help seeing her as a lamb surrounded by wolves."

"Wolves?" Kirishima thought of Kyoko's frequent visits to Etsuko. "Whom are you describing as wolves?"

"I'm talking about Yoshihiro Tsukamoto's friends. As

222

you know, birds of a feather flock together. Some impossible people have been hanging around her since her husband's death."

"Is this the information you wanted to convey to me?"

"Yes. I've serious doubts about these people. Not only do they allow her to live in that apartment on her own, but they seem to paralyse her reasoning powers. I can't help interpreting this as part of some wicked plot."

"You seem to be very confident and rather excited, but unless you get down to facts, you'll make little impression on me."

"I appreciate that," Higuchi said. "I was about to go into detail. You may find some of this a little tedious, but I don't want to leave out anything that might help to uncover the truth and bring Etsuko back to her senses."

"I see. Please start," Kirishima said curtly.

Higuchi leaned forward and stuck out his chin. "First I'll talk about university lecturer Kawaji. He's opposed to Etsuko returning to her parents' home, and is obviously trying to win her favours. Only a short while ago he was shedding tears over his friend's death, but already he's after the widow. It's incredible he's got the nerve to do this."

"Your assessment of Kawaji doesn't seem completely impartial to me."

"But Mr. Prosecutor, can you exclude the possibility that he's been secretly in love with Etsuko for some time past? He might have calculated that if Yoshihiro died, he'd be able to get her as well as her money. Since he was one of Yoshihiro's closest friends, isn't it possible he knew about the patent?"

"Well, it's not unthinkable . . ."

"Furthermore, it was he and Koike who insisted the marriage certificate should be registered on the day of the wedding. Was it to ensure Etsuko became legal successor to Yoshihiro's property on the very day, so he could murder him the same night, before she was touched? If this was his plot, then we've no trouble explaining why he committed the crime on the wedding night."

"But I don't think Kawaji could've been one-hundred-percent sure Etsuko would marry him."

"Who can be one-hundred-percent sure of anything? Most gamblers would be happy with a ninety-percent chance. And Kawaji must have thought his chances were as good as that."

"What makes you think so?"

"Look, it's only common sense that when a woman becomes a widow, at least for the first week or so her contacts with members of the opposite sex are very limited. Well, of those few men with access to Etsuko during that first week, who d'you think could be planning to marry her? Nobumasa Tsukamoto is out, because he's dead. Koike's out, too, because he's already married. And as I previously pointed out to you, until the killer gets caught, Etsuko won't have anything to do with me. That leaves Kawaji . . ." For a couple of seconds Higuchi stared at the polished top of Kirishima's desk, looking very bitter. "Admittedly, there's no guarantee Etsuko will marry any of the men now around her. But if Kawaji can successfully pretend he's the only person who understands her, and manages to draw her under his influence, he'll certainly have a big advantage over anyone else."

Higuchi was a talented man, Kirishima thought. Disregarding the basic truth or falsehood of his argument, each sentence he uttered was completely logical.

Higuchi said, "I can easily understand why Kawaji is opposed to the idea of Etsuko returning to her parents' home. He wants her to remain under his influence as long as possible. Once Etsuko goes back to her parents, he won't be able to do as he likes."

Kirishima nodded. "I must admit your argument is very persuasive. Have you any other reason to suspect Kawaji?"

"Yes, I have. He must be very anxious to get hold of some money in a hurry, I'd say."

"Is that so?"

"Yes. According to my information, when Kawaji's father retired from some company, he started up a trade journal in partnership with a couple of friends. It was going well for a while, but last year the business was hit by the general wave of recession, and it's been in dire straits since. He's been forced to mortgage his house up to the roof-top."

"In other words, Kawaji himself has no financial problem, but to save his father he must get hold of a fairly large sum of money?"

"That's right. It's quite possible he has already borrowed a considerable amount from Yoshihiro."

It was not at all unusual for businessmen to mortgage their houses in order to raise funds, so it was impossible for Kirishima to judge on the available information whether Kawaji's father was really in trouble. He felt he had to take Higuchi's story with a grain of salt, but neither could he completely ignore it.

Apart from that, he was amazed how Higuchi could have ferreted out all this information about Kawaji in such a short time, regardless of whether he had been motivated by a sense of justice or a tenacity of purpose.

Kirishima said, "I'm grateful to you for offering this information. But just a few minutes ago you used the word 'wolf' in the plural. This suggests to me Kawaji isn't the only one you suspect of these murders."

"I'm sure it'd be much simpler for everyone concerned if there was only one suspect," Higuchi said with some reluctance. "But to be quite honest, I can't get rid of my doubts about another man—Koike. Besides, it'd be unfair to Kawaji to single him out and ignore the information I can offer on Koike . . . Do you know anything about his wife?"

"I haven't met her," Kirishima said evasively.

"Neither have I, but according to information supplied to me, she comes from a noble family which was ruined by the war. Her father was a baron, or something like that. About seven years ago she won a talent quest and was subsequently promoted by a film company as a new star. But she didn't have much luck on the screen, and later switched to fashion modelling."

"Hmm."

"In short, for several years she lived in a world of

vainglorious glamour. Perhaps because of this, she has an extremely high opinion of herself and is twice as extravagant as any other well-to-do young woman—so I understand. She's supposed to be a very beautiful woman of good education, so I'm not surprised Koike fell for her . . ."

"Are you suggesting Koike's now sorry he married her?"

"No, I'm not. He seems to be still crazy about her. But because she happens to be such an expensive plaything, he never stops complaining about his pocket being always empty. As a matter of fact, I've heard in legal circles that he's been trying to boost his income in some questionable ways. So it's not unreasonable to suspect he might have tried to take advantage somehow of the Tsukamoto brothers' shady patent deal."

"How do you know about the patent?"

"Koike mentioned it to Mr. Ogata, and I was told by him."

"Ah, I see . . . We're looking into that right now, but the fact is, Koike himself volunteered the information on the patent immediately after the second murder, and he had a justifiable reason not to disclose it earlier. Even if he'd been charging excessive fees for handling the patent application and its subsequent leasing to that chemical company, it would've been illogical for him not to reveal this, because he knew we'd find out about it anyway."

Higuchi tilted his head and twisted his mouth at the corners. "Mr. Prosecutor, I'll be very surprised if his charges aren't in accordance with the standard scale of fees. But how can you be sure there isn't a hidden contract alongside the official one for the licence on the patent?"

"Hidden contract?"

"Yes. It's a very common thing these days. The company may pay a five-percent royalty on gross sales under the official contract, but has an arrangement with the owner of the patent to pay an extra one percent under the table. The purpose of this, of course, is tax evasion. Once the owner's income from the patent reaches tens of millions of yen, his tax becomes staggeringly high . . . Naturally, the company has to 'lose' in its accounts the amount paid out secretly, and there's a limit to what it can do. But a big company with a huge turnover wouldn't have any trouble concealing even as much as a couple of hundred million yen a year."

"But to me it's unthinkable the Tsukamoto brothers would've left the negotiation of such an important contract entirely to Koike, and knew nothing of a hidden contract."

"I'm not suggesting that," Higuchi said. "What I'm saying is that if by any chance Koike had diverted to his own purpose part of the money flowing from the hidden contract, this would've been difficult to detect. And now that both brothers are dead, and Etsuko knows nothing about this hidden contract, all the return from it will naturally go into Koike's pocket."

Kirishima could hardly conceal his admiration for Higuchi's logic. This man would be a formidable opponent in court, he thought. Shifting in his chair, he said, "But for a lawyer this would be a very dangerous thing to do, don't you think? If ever that hidden contract came to the surface, he'd be ruined. Furthermore, there's no evidence a hidden contract does exist, is there?"

"I've no evidence of it, and I don't think I could obtain it. Very few companies would reveal such a thing, even under official pressure."

Kirishima thought hard for a little while, then said, "There are certain aspects of your theory which don't help to convince me Koike's the killer, I'm afraid. For example, why didn't he pay attention to the money Nobumasa had already saved up before his death? And another thing. If there's a hidden contract, according to your estimate, the income from it is only about one-fifth of the income from the official contract. If he'd kept the whole patent business completely to himself at this stage —and there was no real need for him to reveal it to anyone, not even to Etsuko—he would've been able to divert the whole of that income to his own use, at least for the time being. If he was prepared to go to the trouble of killing two people for money, then why did he throw away this unique opportunity?"

"Yes, I see what you mean," Higuchi said, and bit his lip.

"Also, as a lawyer, Koike must have been well aware that Nobumasa's estate would pass to the State. Then why didn't he persuade him before killing him to make a will, naming Etsuko as his heir? Koike knew Nobumasa was fond of Etsuko—it would've been worth at least a try . . . Alternatively, why didn't he murder Nobumasa first, so that his property would go to Yoshihiro instead of the State, *then* kill Yoshihiro? In both cases Etsuko would've been the sole successor, and this would've given Koike ample opportunity to milk her . . . No, I think it would've been most illogical for Koike to kill two people for the income from that hidden contract alone, and ignore all the other opportunities to grab some money."

Higuchi appeared to be at a loss. He said, "Well, Mr. Prosecutor, as I told you at the start, I haven't come here to lay a firm charge against Koike, or Kawaji, for that matter. I simply wanted to tell you what I know about them, thinking this might help you with your investigations." He stood up and looked Kirishima in the face. "Thank you very much for giving me your valuable time . . . And if I happen to get hold of some additional information, I hope you'll allow me to come to see you again."

It wasn't till the following evening that Inspector Yoshioka had something new to report to Kirishima.

"We've managed to piece together an almost complete picture of Nobumasa's assets," Yoshioka said, looking rather tired, for a change. Since he specialised in the detection of crimes of violence, this type of financial investigation must have been rather a strain on him.

"Thank you very much for your efforts, Inspector," Kirishima said.

"I'll give you a complete list of amounts in the various banks in a written report later. For now I only want to point out that, according to Koike, the total income received to date from the patent would've been around 23,000,000 yen. Nobumasa's tax for the current year hasn't been paid, so after deducting from the total last year's tax, the cost of his new house, and the percentage he paid to Yoshihiro, the balance should be around 10,000,000 yen. Well, the total of his savings is just over 9,500,000 yen, which is near enough. The difference of less than 500,000 yen doesn't upset our calculations."

"Then it doesn't look as if Koike charged excessive fees, does it?"

"No, we've found no trace of that. For transacting the whole patent business, including the licence contract, he charged a fee of 500,000 yen, and wrote a receipt for it. I think his fee was very modest—he must have been influenced by his friendship with the brothers. And there's no suggestion he might've got hold of the 500,000 yen unaccounted for."

"Anyway, it's unthinkable he would've murdered his friends for that amount of money."

"That's what I think, too," Yoshioka said. "Now, regarding Miss Kikuchi, at the time of separating from Nobumasa she had another lover all right."

"Could you find out anything about him?"

"His name is Mikio Yamazaki, and he seems to be a leading light of the terrorist group Sekishinkai, which was in the news recently. But we don't know his present whereabouts, or whether his affair with Miss Kikuchi's still alive."

"Could this fellow have some knowledge of the law, d'you think?"

"He might know a bit about commercial law, but I doubt very much if he'd have more than an amateur's idea about laws generally. Anyway, I've asked some officers at Section 4 to check him out, so I'll get something on him soon . . ." Yoshioka opened his brief-case and began rummaging through it. "Now, regarding the fire at the hot spring resort, I've finally managed to get an outline on that. The building gutted was the Shinsenkan Inn at Kuboyama hot spring resort, which is about a two-

229

hour bus ride from Tottori City. Here's a report sent to us by the Tottori police."

Kirishima eagerly looked through the report. After about five minutes, he said, "According to this, the dead man's body was so badly charred, it was unrecognisable."

"Yes. The immediate cause of death was suffocation by smoke, and the cause of the fire was an electric short-circuit. There seemed to be no suspicious circumstances."

"It says here that while investigating the identity of the victim, police found that he had entered a fictitious name and address into the hotel register, which survived the fire because it was locked in the office safe. But once they learnt the victim had come to visit Yoshihiro Tsuka-moto and stayed overnight in a room next to Yoshihiro's, they could identify him as soon as Yoshihiro regained consciousness."

"Obviously, Yoshihiro admitted the man visiting him was his younger brother."

"Wait a minute," Kirishima said, "there's something strange here. It says that on the basis of Yoshihiro's statement, police were able to locate Tadaaki's picture among police photographs of wanted criminals, and they showed this picture to all members of the staff at the inn. But no one could definitely identify it as the picture of the guest who had died in the fire."

Yoshioka pouted and shrugged his shoulders. "D'you think this is so important? The photograph was probably pretty old. And since Tadaaki had been in hiding for quite a while, his features must have changed somewhat. On top of that, he would've tried to change his appearance deliberately by wearing glasses, or something like that . . . No, I wouldn't attach too much importance to this."

"You may be right," Kirishima said sleepily. He closed the report and stared at its cover for a while, then began to mutter, as if talking to himself. "The problem that bothers me is the true identity of this man Watanabe. He might have been in possession of some secret of the Tsukamoto brothers. If Nobumasa had been determined not to disclose Watanabe's true identity under any cir-

230

cumstances, he would've thought up a suitable lie on the spot. But instead, he asked me for a day's grace. He must have done this because he wanted to explain to Etsuko something about Watanabe before revealing it to me. And since Etsuko had no personal connection with Watanabe, there's only one answer. Watanabe must have had some special relationship with Yoshihiro—quite apart from saving his life in childhood—which adversely affected Yoshihiro's reputation. That's what Nobumasa wanted to tell Etsuko before disclosing it to me . . ."

"I see," Yoshioka whispered, careful not to interrupt Kirishima's train of thought.

". . . What could that be—the thing that affected Yoshihiro's reputation? It needn't have been anything illegal. It probably wasn't. When a person murders somebody, or commits a robbery, or engages in drug trafficking, the last thing he worries about is his good reputation . . . And since Nobumasa was prepared to disclose this thing affecting Yoshihiro's reputation to Etsuko, he must have been fairly confident Etsuko wouldn't condemn Yoshihiro for it. Otherwise he would've kept silent about it, especially at this stage, so soon after Yoshihiro's death . . . Etsuko already knew about their father and youngest brother, so it must have been something Yoshihiro was personally responsible for . . . He must have done something wrong—and there's only one thing I can think of."

"Would it have something to do with the fire at the inn?" Yoshioka asked.

"Yes."

"But according to this report, there's no suggestion that Yoshihiro disposed of his troublesome brother. The Tottori police are satisfied there was no murder or arson committed. It was an accident caused by faulty electric wiring. And if Yoshihiro escaped without stopping to try to save his brother, that's still understandable in the circumstances. He himself was nearly burnt to death. Who could blame him for thinking of his own skin first?"

"As I told you before," Kirishima said, "I'm not suggesting Yoshihiro murdered his brother. But I feel he could've nevertheless disposed of him, in a sense."

"In a sense? In what sense?" Yoshioka gaped at Kirishima, leaning forward in his chair.

Just then the phone rang. Kitahara answered it. "Hallo . . . Yes . . . Yes, he's here . . . *What*?" Now he was gaping, too, as he replaced the receiver. "Watanabe's just been arrested in Mrs. Tsukamoto's apartment . . . He tried to assault her . . ."

CHAPTER SIXTEEN

Kirishima and Yoshioka immediately drove to police headquarters. And a patrol car carrying Watanabe was speeding towards the same destination. It was followed by Koike's car, which had Etsuko in it.

From the brief telephone message it sounded as if Koike had called at Etsuko's apartment by chance, and helped to arrest Watanabe.

While they were waiting for the patrol car, Kirishima told Yoshioka the rest of his theory about Watanabe's true identity, but very soon a policeman reported the arrival of the vehicle. Yoshioka dashed out of the room, and was back in a couple of minutes.

"The lad's already getting the treatment from five detectives," he said with satisfaction. "This 'fireworks' style of questioning is our usual welcome for the tough ones. It's pretty effective, too. Even the most hardened criminals get rattled. It makes them feel they've just reached the first corner of hell . . . Well, in the meantime, would you like to see Mrs.Tsukamoto and Koike?"

Kirishima nodded, and Yoshioka went to fetch them. Etsuko looked pale but surprisingly calm. Koike's eyes were slightly bloodshot. He was obviously proud of himself. Yoshioka asked him to give an outline of the incident.

"I ran into that man purely by accident," he said. "I went to visit Etsuko because I had some papers for her to sign. I rang the bell, but nobody answered it. Then I discovered the door wasn't locked. I poked my head in and noticed something was wrong. Then I walked in and saw Watanabe in the western room. He was about to assault Etsuko. I knew the police were looking for him, and I myself had very strong suspicions, so I didn't waste any time—I went for him."

"Did you have a fight?" Yoshioka asked.

"Of a sort. First he was stunned by my sudden appearance, then tried to knock me down and get away, but I ran after him. We finished up wrestling on the stairs, while Etsuko rang the police emergency number . . . He hit me a few times, but I managed to hold him till the police arrived."

"We really appreciate your help."

"Don't mention it," Koike said, laughing. "If it wasn't for this, I would've missed the thrill of driving at breakneck speed and going through red lights behind the patrol car without collecting a ticket . . . But seriously, if Watanabe is the killer, I'll have the satisfaction of having done something for my dead friends. I'm glad now I had to play so many sports in my student days. I used to think it was a waste of time."

Yoshioka turned to Etsuko. "Mrs. Tsukamoto, how did he try to assault you?"

"I'm not sure that he did," she said hesitantly. "I was having a cup of tea when the bell rang. I went to the door and asked who it was without opening it. I did this because I've become rather nervous over the past ten days."

"It was a very sensible thing to do . . . And what did he say?"

"He said he had an express letter for me, and I had to sign for it."

"Yes, every second burglar pretends to be a postman

these days. I know what happened. You opened the door a little, and he put a foot in it and forced it wide open."

"That's right."

"And what happened next?"

"I never could put that man's face out of my mind, and now he was staring at me all of a sudden. I thought I was having a nightmare . . . I started to scream . . . He covered my mouth with his hand, pushed me inside, and said I had nothing to worry about—he only came to see me because he had something to tell me . . . He kept talking about my late husband, but I was so scared and excited—I didn't really listen to him. The only thing I can recall clearly is that he said we weren't complete strangers."

"I see," Yoshioka said. "This doesn't sound like an unlawful assault to me. The story must have got inflated by the time it reached us . . . And have you any idea what his real purpose might have been? Perhaps he came to ask you for some money?"

"I wouldn't know . . . I was in such a panic at the time—I was ready to bite him if he tried anything queer . . . He put a hand on my shoulder and said something like 'Sit down and relax—I want to talk to you quietly'. I pushed his hand off and tried to get away from him, and that's when Mr. Koike arrived . . ."

Kirishima remembered Kyoko worrying about Etsuko's mental state, and thought there seemed to be nothing wrong with her. And he decided Watanabe hadn't tried to harm her either. It looked as if his intention had been misinterpreted through force of circumstances.

A detective appeared in the doorway, and said, "Chief, he's a lot tougher than we thought. We aren't getting anywhere with him. All we get is 'I don't know', and now he says he'll shut up altogether unless we take him straight to a prosecutor."

Yoshioka looked a bit deflated, following his boast about their infallible 'fireworks' method. He turned to Kirishima, rather sheepishly, and said, "What d'you think, Mr. Prosecutor?"

235

It was very rare for a prosecutor to do the initial questioning of a suspect, although there were quite a few arrogant characters who demanded this. Usually they were people who either believed or pretended they were big time—until the police cut them down to size. But Kirishima felt this man had something else on his mind.

"All right, bring him in," he said, and turned to Koike and Etsuko. "Mr. Koike, thank you very much for your co-operation . . . Mrs. Tsukamoto, I'm glad you didn't get hurt . . ."

Etsuko looked at him steadily. She had this strange glow in her eyes again. For some reason, her stare always made him embarrassed. He bowed lightly and busied himself with his brief-case till she was well out of the room.

The man in the interrogation room was completely surrounded by detectives when Kirishima and Yoshioka entered. He was comfortably stretched out in a chair, wearing a flashy tweed suit. There was a faint smile on his sallow, shiny face. Kirishima noticed his protruding dirty-yellow teeth, and a knife scar all the way down his left cheek. The man looked unpleasant, to say the least.

Yoshioka made a small gesture like a back-handed slap, and the detectives immediately filed out of the room, leaving only the uniformed guard there.

Kirishima sat down opposite the man, and said, "I'm State Prosecutor Saburo Kirishima. I understand you wanted to talk to a prosecutor."

The man leaned over the table and carefully examined the badge on Kirishima's coat lapel. "You seem to be the genuine article," he said. "All right. Since things have come to this, I'll tell you all you want to know."

"To begin with, tell me your name."

"Hiroshi Watanabe. You must already know this."

"I want to hear your real name."

"That's it."

"I thought you were going to tell me everything?" Kirishima creased his forehead in mock concern. "It

236

looks as if *I* have to tell *you* what your real name is. Well, you're Tadaaki Yasuda. You're one of the three Tsukamoto brothers, only your family name has been changed by deed poll to Yasuda."

"I'm overwhelmed," the man said impudently. "You're a genius—and I'm back where I started. But never mind. It was good fun while it lasted."

"I'm not interested in your sense of fun. I want you to give me the facts."

"Well, the grim facts are that at present I've got no money, no job, and no fixed address."

"We'll soon take care of that," Kirishima said, casting Yoshioka a meaningful glance. "But first tell us what happened at the hot spring resort. Obviously, it wasn't you who got burnt to death, as your brother claimed. Who was it?"

"I thought you would've guessed by now."

"Was it Hiroshi Watanabe?"

"Touché!"

"That's how you could assume his identity?"

"Touché!"

"What was your connection with Watanabe?"

"He was a mate of mine. We were about the same age, though he used to call me big brother."

"Was he on the run, too?"

"No, but we kept in touch. So when I went down with pneumonia, I sent for him."

"This was while you were in hiding after killing a man?"

"I killed a man all right, but let's get one thing straight, Mr. Prosecutor. He too had a knife in his hand. It was a clear case of self-defence."

"You can tell me that yarn later. Right now I want to know when you sent for Watanabe."

"It was at the end of the year before last. I don't remember the date, but it was about four days before his death."

"So it was Watanabe who went to see Yoshihiro at your request?"

"Yeah. Being on the run, I'd just about used up all my

237

dough, and then this pneumonia got me. I was really down . . . Watanabe was pretty hard up, too. Getting to Nagoya was all he could manage . . . Yoshihiro was my only hope. I'd given him plenty of trouble before, so he wasn't very keen on me, I can tell you. And anyway, I didn't fancy crawling to him. But you know how it is— pride must be sacrificed for the belly . . . Nobumasa was a hard bastard—it was no use crawling to him. But Yoshihiro was always a bit of a sucker, rather soft-hearted, so I figured I might be able to touch him."

"What did you do?"

"I thought he'd come good if I sent word to him I was hovering between life and death. Mind, this time I didn't have to exaggerate too much . . . Anyway, I got Watanabe to look him up."

"Did you send him a letter?"

"First I wanted to write him a long one, describing all my aches and pains. But then I thought, how could anybody about to give up the ghost write a long letter? So I put down just a few lines, asking Yoshihiro to listen to Watanabe. Without that he would've never believed him."

"And Watanabe followed your brother to the hot spring resort?"

"That's right. He first went to Yoshihiro's flat at Kyoto, where somebody told him where he was. He sent me a card from there, saying he was going after Yoshihiro up to Tottori. It was pretty decent of him not to let his mate down."

"Did you hear from him again before he died?"

"No, not a word. I knew nothing about the fire either, so I started gritting my teeth in bed, thinking he might have shot through with the money he got from Yoshihiro . . . I had a terrific fever, too, just then. My yarn about being on the verge of death got that close to the truth, it didn't matter . . ."

"But how was it you knew nothing of the fire? You must have seen it in the newspapers?"

"Ahh, come off it. If I'd enough money for a newspaper just then, I would've bought a piece of bread with it. Anyway, the hot spring resort was a long way from Nagoya. If the local paper had anything at all on it, it would've been a couple of lines in a corner. I would've missed it for sure."

"And how did you eventually get out of your troubles?"

"Just by chance I was saved by a member of Gimeikai, a right-wing terrorist mob operating in Nagoya. This mob has some connection with a crazy old joker called Kumagaya, who was once being looked after by my late father. That's how I was given help."

"Did you meet Kumagaya?"

"No, but because I used him as a reference, Gimeikai asked him about me, and he wrote back, giving them the dope on me."

"So you settled down in the care of Gimeikai?"

"Yeah . . . And after I got better, I couldn't just run out on them, so I worked for them on and off till the following spring."

"And how did you come to assume Watanabe's identity?"

"I'm about to tell you that . . . While I was in Nagoya, the one thing that kept bothering me was Watanabe's whereabouts. I wondered what happened to him, and whether he had managed to touch Yoshihiro for the dough. Well, just around that time the police grabbed a heap of fire-arms, and the president of Gimeikai was arrested, so things were getting a bit hot for me there. Anyway, I couldn't have gone on sponging on them forever, though as I said, I *was* doing some work for them." Tadaaki quickly looked up at Kirishima. "No, it's not what *you* think, Mr. Prosecutor—it wasn't anything crooked."

"Never mind that. You can tell me about that later."

"Okay . . . So I made up my mind to see Yoshihiro in Kyoto. It was the middle of last April, I think. When I got there I was told he'd already shifted to Tokyo, and also that he'd lost his younger brother in a fire. Well, when I heard that, I was winded, I can tell you. Then I checked around for a bit. Sure enough, I was supposed

239

to be dead."

"And that's when you guessed what happened?"

"I only had a rough idea then. I knew Watanabe would've given a false name and address at the inn. He never was a great one for law and order."

"And then you saw your big chance, huh? With you officially dead, you'd have no more worries about the police, but you'd be nicely set up to extort money from your brother?"

"I don't like that word, Mr. Prosecutor," Tadaaki said indignantly. "I only went to see Yoshihiro to find out what it was all about."

"And what did he tell you?"

"He'd been naturally flustered when Watanabe turned up. But since that hot spring resort was in such a remote place up in the mountains, with only one bus a day, he couldn't have sent him on his way, even if he wanted to. So he got the next room for him, and said he'd think about my message during the night."

"I see. And that was the night of the fire?"

"That's right. I wouldn't be surprised if Watanabe got sozzled during the evening. For once he didn't have to worry about his own pocket. He could put it all on Yoshihiro's slate. Being blind drunk—that's probably why he couldn't get out when the fire broke out. If it had been me instead of him, my brother would've at least tried to do something, I should hope . . ."

"But why did your brother tell a lie?"

"Well, he said he'd been a bit crazy with pain at the time, being so badly burnt, so he just told that yarn to the police on a sudden impulse, thinking it might be a good thing for me. But I reckon he must have thought it'd be pretty convenient for him, too . . ."

That was understandable, Kirishima thought, following all the heartbreak Yoshihiro had to suffer, and all the things he had to miss because of Tadaaki. Whenever a man's family background was being investigated, his dead relatives wouldn't be looked at so closely as the ones still alive. For years Yoshihiro must have been longing to shake off the shackles of his past. That was why

240

this spontaneous lie had popped out. But he hadn't told a lie under oath, so he hadn't committed perjury. At worst, what he had done was an offence under Clause 103 of the Criminal Code, referring to the sheltering of wanted criminals. But he would've been exempted from punishment under Clause 105, because Tadaaki was his blood relation.

Then so far as the law was concerned, there had been nothing for Yoshihiro to worry about, Kirishima thought. Nevertheless, if his deceit had ever come to light, it would have ruined his reputation and put an end to his university career. Now it wasn't difficult to understand why Nobumasa had been so concerned about this, even after Yoshihiro's death, or why he had wanted to explain it all to Etsuko before revealing it to anyone else, especially since he had been so fond of her.

"And did you pretend you didn't like the idea, or that you thought he'd done something unfair to you?"

"Not really, but he offered anyway to take care of my troubles for a while. He said when he heard I was seriously ill, he was worried about me, but all Watanabe had told him was that I was in Nagoya, so he couldn't locate me."

"Did Nobumasa know all about this?"

"Ah, yes."

"You must have gone to see him, too, for a little handout?"

"That would've been a bloody waste of time. In fact, he warned me through Yoshihiro to keep out of his way if I knew what was good for me. So I made myself scarce, as far as he was concerned. It was no good playing around with that bastard—he was too dangerous. I never met him once after coming up to Tokyo."

"You were quite happy to concentrate on Yoshihiro, hey? But why did you move out of your apartment shortly before the wedding?"

"That was because . . ." Tadaaki began to bite the corner of his lower lip where the knife scar ran into it. "Well, ever since Yoshihiro had started going out with this Etsuko dame, he was getting more and more sour towards me . . . I suppose it was partly my fault— being too dependent on him."

"I can sympathise with him," Kirishima said. "Anyone trying to win the affection of a decent girl would feel awkward about a man like you hanging around all the time."

"You don't seem to have a very high opinion of me, Mr. Prosecutor. You make my heart bleed . . . But anyway, Yoshihiro was gradually getting real mad with me. He started to say stupid things like 'How long are you going to keep on ruining my life?' What crap! But finally I thought I'd better give him a break."

"Now, wasn't that really decent of you? I knew there was some goodness left in you somewhere. Or did you think he might get mad enough to cut your money off altogether, even tell the police about you?"

"He wouldn't have had the guts to do that, don't worry . . . But as I was saying, I'd made up my mind to go away somewhere anyway, and then out of the blue came this chance to go to Hong Kong as a stowaway. I asked Yoshihiro about it, and he said he'd cough up the dough for the passage."

"Who helped to arrange your trip to Hong Kong?"

"Sorry, I can't tell you that. If I do that now, I might get snicked when I come out of jail. For the same reason, I can't even tell you what I was going to do in Hong Kong."

"What makes you think you'll ever come out of jail?"

Tadaaki nearly jumped to his feet. "Now, Mr. Prosecutor, you're making it a bit hot, aren't you? You know I wouldn't get more than five years at the outside for doing in somebody in a fight, even if I couldn't prove he started it, which he did . . . Or are you thinking that *I* might have killed my brothers?"

"That I can't tell you at this stage."

"Aah, come off it—you can't be serious."

"When were you due to leave for Hong Kong?"

"It was supposed to be the thirteenth or fourteenth of this month. But since it wasn't a regular trip, there was every chance the date would be changed at the last moment. So to make sure, I checked out of the apartment about a week in advance and was standing by, staying at a mate's place."

"And how's it you're still in Tokyo, after all this elaborate preparation?"

"That's a sad story, Mr. Prosecutor," Tadaaki said, running his fingers through his dirty hair. "You see, Yoshihiro only gave me 400,000 yen, and the ticket itself was about 300,000, leaving just enough for spending on the trip. But I would've liked to have a little fling in Hong Kong before getting down to business, so I tried to swell my dough with a couple of flutters at the cycle races . . ."

"And you lost all the money?"

Tadaaki gave a painful sigh. "I'm usually pretty lucky that way, so it wasn't an unreasonable proposition at all. But somehow, that bloody day I was just out of luck . . . And to make things worse, the departure date got put off, and that made me pretty nervous, and that's no good when you're going for a flutter . . . To cut a long story short, I'll just have to start this stowaway stunt all over again."

"I don't think you ever intended to go in the first place. Wasn't it just a gimmick to squeeze a nice fat sum out of your brother?"

"Oh, rubbish! I wouldn't do a thing like that."

"And what were you doing on the night of February 15?"

"That evening I still had enough dough left to pay for the ticket. I met the man who'd arranged the trip—that was around seven o'clock—and he told me the ship now wouldn't leave till the twentieth because of some unexpected trouble. That made me real browned off, so I went to watch a picture at Shinjuku, just to do something. I thought, once I was in Hong Kong I wouldn't be able to see any more blue movies, so I might as well make the best of it while I was here."

"And where did you stay that night?"

"After I came out of the theatre, I picked up a bird. I knew she was a professional—just judging by her manner—but still, I thought she'd be good enough to give me a memory of my last days in Japan . . ."

"You don't have to find excuses for everything . . . And did you stay in an inn overnight?"

"Yes. It's around Shinjuku Sankocho, that former blue-light district. It's all set up with a number of small rooms above the bar. Very hush-hush . . ." Tadaaki bared his yellow teeth in a lewd grin. "D'you want to take a look at the place, Mr. Prosecutor? I'll show it to you, if you like."

"What's the woman's name?"

"You don't expect me to remember that, do you? She wouldn't be using her real name anyway. But somebody in the bar might be able to tell you who she is."

"When did you learn about Yoshihiro's murder?"

"I couldn't be bothered reading the papers just then— I was too depressed because I was losing dough all the time. On the afternoon of the seventeenth—I'd just lost another 10,000 on the cycles and was kicking myself— that's when a mate of mine told me he'd read it in the paper."

"And what did you do?"

"I didn't do anything. There was nothing I could do, was there? I couldn't have gone to Yoshihiro's funeral— that was out. And my dough was dwindling so fast . . . I did everything I could think of, trying to recover it somehow by the twentieth, but it was no good . . ."

"And since then you've been hanging around Tokyo?"

"Yeah."

"Didn't you go to see Nobumasa and ask him for help?"

"As I told you before, I valued my nut too much for that."

"Then what did you do on the evening of February 20?"

"By that day my finances were in terrible shape, so I thought I might be able to make something on *pachinko*. I went from one parlour to another, and was game enough to stick it out till closing time, but once again— no luck."

"Is that why you went to see Mrs. Tsukamoto today? To ask her for some money?"

Tadaaki stuck out his chest and looked at Kirishima with hurt dignity. "It was nothing like that, Mr. Prosecutor, I can assure you. The fact is—my death certificate was registered without my knowledge, or permission, and I'm still very much alive, as you can see. So naturally, I too have certain succession rights to my brothers' estates. Of course, it'd be a different story if *I* had murdered them. But I'm the one who knows best I didn't."

"Then did you go to see Mrs. Tsukamoto to demand a share of the property left by your brothers?"

"Well, since I had a false identity I wasn't really in a position to make an open claim. Actually, I was prepared to call it quits if she coughed up just enough dough for another passage to Hong Kong. Because of my brothers' deaths, it was becoming hard for me in any case to carry on in Japan, and I was told there'd be another chance to slip off to that Chinatown at the end of this month . . . Then suddenly this queer bastard jumped on me out of nowhere, and I've finished up here. Well, of all the unlucky days I've had in the past three weeks, this is the worst, I must say." Tadaaki gave a sigh that almost whistled. "Now that things have come to this, I just don't feel like battling on, to tell you the truth. I might as well sit it out in jail for a few years . . . But could you give me an idea, Mr. Prosecutor, how to re-establish my true identity? I'm sure even you'd find it inconvenient to prosecute a dead man."

Now it was Kirishima's turn to sigh. Throughout the questioning Tadaaki had acted like a lame duck that reached the end of its tether, but he was nothing of the sort. He had a purpose in disclosing everything so candidly. The punishment for killing somebody in a knife duel certainly wouldn't be more than a few years in jail. It was hardly something he would worry about unduly when he knew very well that, on completing his sentence, he would inherit a large property left behind by his two brothers.

"By the way," Kirishima said, "why did you insist on

telling *me* all this, instead of the police?"

Tadaaki laughed insolently, and said, "Obviously, once it comes to a legal problem like the recovery of my identity, it's much better to consult a prosecutor than a dumb detective. Besides, there's always a rough one in any bunch of cops. I might have collected a punch or two if I'd told them a story like this. They're pretty excitable, you know, these cops. On the other hand, a prosecutor is usually a gentleman who's prepared to listen to a tale quietly, without fuss, as you did."

CHAPTER SEVENTEEN

It looked as if the Tsukamoto murder case had taken a sudden turn, and was heading for a solution. Tadaaki Yasuda, alias Hiroshi Watanabe, was officially despatched by the police to the State Prosecutor's Office on the evening of February 27. The warrant was based on three charges of murder.

There was no problem at all about the first one because Tadaaki readily admitted it. The man he had stabbed to death was a gangster by the name of Morita. It had happened about two years ago, and Tadaaki had been on the wanted-for-murder list ever since. The evidence against him on this particular charge was almost complete.

As for the murders of Yoshihiro and Nobumasa Tsukamoto, Tadaaki flatly denied he had anything to do with them. And since there was no direct evidence available, Inspector Yoshioka was having a hard time, though he had managed to collect a heap of circumstantial evidence.

The fact that Tadaaki was partially addicted to heroin had made things look bad for him from the start. Groups of dark blue needle marks had been found on both his arms, and a packet of dope and several needles turned up among his belongings.

Drug addicts were known to be great liars, and they often did absurd things when crazed with yearning. According to Yoshioka, it wasn't at all unthinkable Tadaaki had murdered his two brothers simply to obtain money to buy heroin.

Secondly, one of Tadaaki's criminal associates lived near the National Railway workshops at Shinagawa, the assumed scene of Yoshihiro's murder. The Black Cat Bar in that vicinity was a rendezvous for the gang this associate belonged to. In fact, Tadaaki had negotiated the illegal passage to Hong Kong in that bar. In other words, he was well acquainted with that rather out-of-the-way part of Tokyo.

Also, many leading questions by the police had established that Tadaaki had a good knowledge of at least the appearance of Nobumasa's house. But when he was pressed on that, he didn't get flustered. He even managed to put on his impudent smile when he said, "I've never been inside his house, and that's the truth. But I did get as far as his front gate a number of times—only to turn back each time. I felt like having a talk with Nobumasa about Yoshihiro's death, and I wanted to get some dough out of him, too, even if I had to crawl up him. But then I thought of his temper, and the danger of him squealing on me to the police, and I changed my mind—right in front of his gate."

Another thing indicating a motive was that Tadaaki seemed to have some knowledge of the patent. Of course, if he had somehow become suspicious, he could have easily learnt the truth simply by checking at the Patent Office.

As for alibis, the police could find nothing to substantiate Tadaaki's statement. Playing *pachinko* in various parlours on the night of February 20 amounted to nothing. Unless he collected all the bonuses, no one in those parlours would remember his face.

In relation to the night of February 15, there *was* a bar

with little rooms above it in the former blue-light district. But the owner insisted the rooms were strictly for the use of his staff, and not for any illegal purpose, and he had never set eyes on Tadaaki or the woman. Though his statement wasn't reliable, it certainly didn't help Tadaaki, who later claimed the woman had paid for the room.

In his official report on evidence and motive, Inspector Yoshioka offered the following theory:

Tadaaki lost the money he needed for the secret passage to Hong Kong by gambling at the cycle races and elsewhere. It was essential for him to obtain more money from Yoshihiro before the latter left on his honeymoon trip. With some excuse he lured Yoshihiro to the National Railway workshops at Shinagawa on the night of February 15. By this time Yoshihiro was utterly disgusted with Tadaaki's gutlessness and selfishness, and refused to help him. Under the influence of heroin Tadaaki was seized by a murderous impulse. Unexpectedly he hit his brother in the stomach, strangled him, and took all his money. Because he had associations in that area and was afraid of being traced, he moved the body by car to the bank of the irrigation canal at Kitamicho, and dumped it . . . The money taken from Yoshihiro wasn't enough for the passage. After hanging around Tokyo for a few days, Tadaaki decided to ask Nobumasa for help, calling at his house on the night of February 20. Nobumasa not only refused to give him any money, but abused him and possibly assaulted him, revealing also that he suspected him of Yoshihiro's murder. Fright and anger made up Tadaaki's mind to murder Nobumasa as well . . . Tadaaki realised he would inherit his brothers' property, including the patent, and even if he had to spend a few years in jail for killing Morita, he would be able to live in luxury for the rest of his life. He thought this was a better proposition than escaping to Hong Kong . . . Tadaaki pretended to be a weakling to arouse sympathy, but during the interrogation he unintentionally revealed himself as a confident and arrogant person with strong nerves. He didn't appear to be insane or feeble-minded.

While Tadaaki was in custody under prosecutor's warrant, he was continually questioned by Kirishima, but steadfastly denied killing his brothers.

Many drug addicts confessed after they had been deprived of heroin for some time. But Tadaaki stuck to his story of innocence, even though he was showing obvious drug withdrawal symptoms. By the end of the third day he was in bad shape. The colour of his face turned to a dirty grey, his eyes had a vacant stare, and he suffered occasional light fits, with greasy sweat oozing out of him.

The sight and smell of him was nauseating, even to Kirishima who was used to this sort of thing. "Are you in pain?" he asked, unconsciously holding his breath.

"You must be kidding," Tadaaki groaned, still managing a pathetic smile. "I knew the stuff was dragging me down, but I couldn't give it up, though I tried a couple of times . . . Now I have to kiss goodbye to it, like it or not . . . And I won't be going back on it when I come out of jail, that's for sure . . . I'll be a respectable person for a change, with a company of my own, carrying out my dead brother's will . . ."

This man had fantastic nerves, Kirishima thought. Just dreaming about the money he was going to get hold of after leaving jail seemed to enable him to bear all the agony of drug withdrawal. No wonder it was hard to get anywhere with him. And Yoshioka wasn't coming up with any new evidence either. What he had produced so far wasn't nearly enough to justify an indictment.

On March 3 Kirishima again spent the whole morning with Tadaaki without getting an inch further. This was the fourth day of Tadaaki's detention under a prosecutor's warrant, which was limited by law to ten days. An extension of a further ten days could be obtained from the court, but a more convenient course of action was to proceed against him on the charge of killing Morita, and prosecute him later for the murder of his two brothers. But Kirishima would have naturally preferred to dispose of all three charges in the one hearing.

After returning Tadaaki to his cell, Kirishima wasted

an hour re-reading Yoshioka's lengthy report. There were too many things in it that didn't satisfy him. Yoshioka seemed to interpret everything to suit his own purpose.

For example, he offered a plausible theory on Tadaaki's reason for luring Yoshihiro out of the hotel on the very night of the wedding. But to substantiate it, he would have had to prove—and he couldn't—that Tadaaki had lost the last of his money between the evening of the fourteenth and the evening of the fifteenth. Had he run out of money before then, obviously he wouldn't have left it till the wedding night to see Yoshihiro.

Also, Yoshioka didn't explain how Tadaaki knew about the patent. It was most unlikely that either Nobumasa or Yoshihiro would have disclosed such a secret to a troublesome brother. And it was out of the question that Koike would have told him about it, since the two knew each other only by sight. During questioning Tadaaki himself mentioned that Yoshihiro seemed to have had plenty of money in recent months, and he wondered where it all came from.

If Tadaaki had in fact known the secret of the patent for some time, then perhaps it would make sense that he had murdered Yoshihiro—and subsequently Nobumasa—in order to succeed to it. But if that was so, surely he would have planned Yoshihiro's murder well in advance, and wouldn't have picked the worst night—the wedding night—for it.

In his frustration Kirishima decided to re-think the whole case from the very beginning. After returning from lunch he flopped down into his chair, and for the next couple of hours the world around him just didn't exist. And then suddenly he hit on an idea. It was so fantastic, he decided not to mention it even to Yoshioka. Instead, he ordered Kitahara to go to the Patent Office and make a routine check of all documents on file carrying Yoshihiro's name.

Kitahara got back just before six o'clock. With a sour face he handed the result of his tedious labours to Kirishima. He found this newly developed secretiveness of the boss rather distasteful, if not downright humiliating.

Kirishima ran his eyes over Kitahara's notes. And then he knew that the solution to the Tsukamoto murder case was at last in sight.

That evening Kyoko found Kirishima very uncommunicative, even sullen. They had finished dinner and were drinking their coffee, and he just kept looking through her as if she didn't exist. But by now, after four months of marriage, she was getting used to his occasional 'strange periods'. She knew they had nothing to do with moodiness.

"Saburo," she said brightly, "you're breaking the contract."

"Hm?"

At last he was looking at her, not through her, but still wasn't with her.

"When we got married you said a prosecutor was so busy, he just had to take work home at times. But you promised always to keep your work in the study."

"Ah, yes, I remember," Kirishima said, still miles away.

"But you look more like a prosecutor than a husband right now."

"Oh—sorry." Now he knew what she was talking about, and that she wasn't really complaining. This was her way of trying to cheer him up. But at the moment he had too big a problem on his mind. "Incidentally, how's Etsuko?"

"Under normal circumstances she'd probably feel relieved the suspect is safely under lock and key, but that's not the case this time, I'm afraid. While she thought he was Watanabe, a distant relative she had nothing to do with, it wasn't so bad. But now she knows the man who's supposed to have murdered his brothers is her own brother-in-law. This must have been another tremendous shock to her—the third in a row. In less than two weeks she's fallen from the heights of happiness to the depths of despair. She must feel she's landed straight in hell . . ."

"I can well imagine how she feels," Kirishima said absently.

"Saburo, I want to ask you something." Kyoko looked very serious. "Of course, you don't have to answer if you don't want to."

"I probably won't."

"Well, I'm going to ask, just the same . . . Do you really believe Tadaaki murdered his brothers?"

Kirishima looked at her enigmatically and remained silent. Then slowly he shook his head.

"Thank you—that's very generous of you," Kyoko said a little waspishly. "That's what I thought, too."

Kirishima couldn't help bursting into laughter. "The marvellous hindsighted wisdom of women."

Ignoring this, Kyoko said, "I'm beginning to think Higuchi was right in saying the Tsukamoto family is under a curse. But I wouldn't again attempt to persuade Etsuko to go back to her parents. I'm sure it would only make things worse . . . And talking about making things worse—Higuchi's been at her ever since. He came to see her once more, but she promptly sent him on his way without even opening the door. Now he keeps ringing her, but he only makes her despise him all the more."

"I thought he would've given up by now . . ." Suddenly Kirishima's sluggish face seemed to come alive, and his eyes began to glow with excitement. "Kyoko, it's my turn now to ask something."

"Yes?"

"D'you think you could persuade Etsuko to control her dislike for Higuchi for a little while, and perhaps behave so he'd think he still had a chance with her?"

"What on earth are you talking about?"

"Just pretending would be good enough," Kirishima said eagerly. "She'd be able to act like that for a little while, wouldn't she?"

"No, she wouldn't. In her present mental condition she couldn't put on an act if her life depended on it." Kyoko fixed her husband with an icy stare. "Would you please explain what's on your mind?"

"I can't," Kirishima said defensively. "This is such a

253

delicate matter, I wouldn't dare talk about it to anyone. It concerns a clue I've come across, but that's all I can tell you . . . I've already said too much—enough to wreck my plan if it gets out . . ."

"Are you suggesting Etsuko should do some kind of detective work for you? That's out of the question, I assure you. Obviously, you haven't been married long enough to understand a woman's mind."

Kirishima sighed heavily and fell into silence.

For the first time in days Kirishima looked at Kitahara with a cheerful expression. It was Saturday morning, March 7.

"At last I've made up my mind," Kirishima said. "On Monday I'll commit Tadaaki for trial on the charge of unlawfully killing Morita . . . Well, that completes the first stage of the job, and I think I'm going to take it easy over the weekend. I feel I need a rest before going into battle again next week . . . But what about tonight? Are you free?"

Kitahara's eyes flared up and his white teeth appeared in a broad grin. "Mr. Prosecutor, when it comes to a drink, I'm always available, as you know. Would you like me to make a booking somewhere, just to make sure we get in?"

"No, don't bother," Kirishima said. "Tonight I'd like to do things on a slightly grander scale than usual. I have in mind driving to Izu and staying there overnight. There's a very good inn in a quiet spot just beyond Ito . . . But don't look at me like that. I'm not going to claim expenses for this trip, so you can relax."

"It's all right. I'm just a bit awed—not used to these grand affairs. I'll give my wife a ring straight away . . . Would you mind talking to her, Mr. Prosecutor? She can become a bit of a nuisance when she gets jealous." Kitahara reached for the phone, but his hand stopped half way, then slowly returned into his pocket. "Incidentally, is Mrs. Kirishima coming with us, by any chance?"

"Yes."

Kitahara's face suddenly looked a little paler. Nervously he began to lick his lips. "Mr. Prosecutor," he muttered, "there's something I forgot for a moment . . . I've had a gastric problem since early this morning . . . It's very unfortunate . . ."

"Every time you want to get out of something, your belly seems to go funny. You must have a permanent psycho-gastric condition. But just relax, will you? Though my wife will be with us, she won't be doing the driving on this occasion. One of my cousins will be behind the wheel, and he happens to be a racing driver. He's captain of a university car club, and he came tops in last year's All Japan Student Rally. His driving skill is beyond question, I'd say . . . How's your belly-ache now? Has it stopped yet?"

"Well—in fact—yes, it seems to have stopped already."

Kirishima smothered a gust of laughter. "I don't really blame you. I myself still get a bit nervous when my wife's behind the wheel. She's improving though, slowly . . . By the way, I've also invited Inspector Yoshioka. He's been working very hard during the past three weeks. I thought he, too, deserved a little consideration . . ."

Shortly after four o'clock that afternoon Kawaji called at Koike's home at Yoyogi-Uehara.

Koike didn't attempt to conceal his annoyance. "Where did you hide Etsuko, anyway?" he asked testily. "You and I are supposed to be close friends, and I happen to be her legal adviser, too. I thought you'd accord me the courtesy of at least advising me before spiriting her away. As it was, I made several futile attempts to contact her yesterday."

"I'm sorry about that," Kawaji said contritely. "I wouldn't have been able to explain it all to you on the phone . . . What happened was that the night before last she rang me and asked me in a half-crazed voice to go to her apartment. I rushed over in a panic, and she told me between crying fits that even Kyoko was deserting her

255

now—telling her some awful things—and she had lost faith in people altogether."

"Kyoko? She's Prosecutor Kirishima's wife, isn't she? Did she urge Etsuko again to go back to her parents?"

"That wouldn't have been so bad, but apparently, she advised her to make peace with Higuchi."

Koike raised his eyebrows. "That's funny . . . Was that her own idea, d'you think?"

"I'm not sure," Kawaji said hesitantly. "I don't think it would've been inspired by her husband—unless he's getting really desperate . . . Anyway, there's a tutor in the psychiatric section of our Department of Medicine who lives not far from Etsuko's apartment. I rang him and asked him to come over and have a look at her. Then yesterday I took her to the university hospital because it happened to be the professor's visiting day . . . To be quite frank, I just didn't have time to contact you."

"It's all right—I'm not complaining, but what was the result of the examination?"

"Fortunately, there's nothing seriously wrong with her. There's no question of any mental illness. The professor said she was suffering from a hypersensitiveness caused by the number of shocks she had to absorb in the past fortnight. He estimated that, provided she was placed in quiet surroundings, she'd completely recover in approximately twenty days."

"I'm glad to hear that. And where did you take her?"

"I discussed the matter with the professor, and came to the conclusion that to leave her on her own in that apartment wouldn't be any good for her. You see, Higuchi kept ringing her all the time. And there was another call from somebody who, according to Etsuko, sounded like a middle-aged woman saying, 'it serves you right' or 'I told you so'. I wonder if it might have been Mrs. Araki? Well, with all these phone calls bothering her all the time, she would've had absolutely no chance of recovering from this hypersensitiveness. On the other hand, she resolutely refused to return to her parents' home. It seemed that in the circumstances a change of climate would probably be the best thing for her. D'you think I've done the right thing?"

"Yes, I'd say so. This seems to be the best solution. And where did you take her?"

"I was racking my brains for a while, but then I remembered my uncle had a villa at Toyoura, in Southern Izu. There's nobody living there at the moment except the couple who look after the place, and they don't even have the phone connected. So finally I came up with the idea of hiding her there for a while. She readily accepted my offer, and after obtaining Mr. Ogata's permission I took her there. She was very impressed with the place and told me her stay there would give her an opportunity to think about the future."

"That sounds encouraging," Koike said.

"By the way—are you free tonight?"

"Let me see . . . Yes, I've nothing special on."

"Then how about driving out there to have a look at her? It's not a bad spot, you know. I'm sure you'd enjoy the fresh air, and perhaps a nice piece of fish. And if you've something to discuss with Etsuko, you can do it there without interruption . . . I'd appreciate a lift . . . Or would it be unfair to your wife, d'you think?"

"No, that's no problem at all," Koike said sourly. "She seems to have developed a new affection for her parents. She's spent the last few weeks with them. She returned once, but soon went back again with the excuse that her mother was ill."

"Well, then it's all the better for you to get out of the house. It's not much fun staying at home on your own on a Saturday night, is it?"

"You're dead right . . . Okay, I'll drive you out there." Koike felt for his car key in his pocket. "Then we might as well make a start straight away. I have some papers in the car I'd like her to sign."

Kawaji eagerly agreed, and in less than ten minutes they were on their way. With no women around, it didn't take them long to get going. Both seemed to be in a light-hearted mood as the car nosed its way through the Tokyo traffic.

"You can follow the usual route till we reach Ito,"

Kawaji said, studying the road map. "From there I'll direct you."

Once they had passed through the outskirts of Tokyo, Koike relaxed a little, and said, "Just between you and me, why would Mrs. Kirishima come up with the idea of bringing Etsuko and Higuchi closer together?"

Kawaji folded his arms in the passenger seat. "Well, this is only a wild guess, of course—and Etsuko gets so excited whenever I touch on this subject—but I have a feeling Kirishima thinks that Miss Kikuchi, the bar hostess, might hold the key to the murder of the Tsukamoto brothers."

"That woman also came to see me one day," Koike said, keeping his eyes on the road. "She's a dreadful bitch . . ."

"I understand she seems to have a remarkably detailed knowledge of the law. So I wouldn't be at all surprised if Kirishima has come to the conclusion she has a lawyer behind her. Her ex-lover is the leader of a mob of petty gangsters, and can't be located. On the other hand, Higuchi has represented a few other members of the gang in recent months. It's not unlikely there's a connection there somewhere—maybe a very close connection."

Koike said, "I heard that in his Judicial Training Institute days Higuchi had the nickname, Bradawl the Tick. He was sharp and penetrating like a bradawl, and once he got hold of something he stuck to it like a tick . . . Or was his nickname Bradawl the Thick? Wait a minute —I'm not sure now. Perhaps it *was* 'thick', suggesting he had a very thick skin . . ."

They laughed together and then remained quiet for a while. The car entered the Yokohama Highway.

When Kawaji spoke again he sounded a little embarrassed. "I might as well tell you this now," he said. "A couple of days ago I made a very important decision. When the time comes, I'm going to propose to Etsuko. I mentioned this to Mr. Ogata when I saw him the other day about taking Etsuko to my uncle's villa."

"Well, well," Koike said, tilting his head in surprise. "I'm sure it'll be an excellent thing for Etsuko . . . I'm not so sure about you, though. You're going to marry your friend's widow, largely on the basis of friendship and a sense of responsibility. I think this is something you'd want to consider very carefully. You must make sure you won't regret it in the future."

"I'm not being carried away by mere sympathy for her," Kawaji said firmly. "I'm genuinely fond of her, and I admire her courage, kind-heartedness, intelligence, and some other important qualities. In addition, I've lost my wife in an accident, as you know. So I thought Etsuko and I are in much the same boat, both being saddled with unhappy memories. Somehow it seems natural for us to comfort one another and start a new life together."

"I see . . . And what did Mr. Ogata have to say about this?"

"He said it depended entirely on his daughter—he no longer had any influence over her. I told him I heard he'd prefer a lawyer for a son-in-law, and I'd be prepared to leave the university and go into private practice."

"You must be madly in love with her, by the look of things. I'll bet Mr. Ogata was taken aback . . . Well, those who know you well won't think for a moment you're trying to marry her for her money." Koike blinked demurely.

"I'm sure some people will say nasty things about me," Kawaji said. "But I'm ready for that. The truth of the matter is—if I'd been so keen on making money, I wouldn't have chosen a university career in the first place."

Silence followed, but Koike's last comments must have been playing on Kawaji's mind, because suddenly he said, "Talking about money, I'd act more cautiously if I were you."

"What d'you mean?"

"Well, you're handling Etsuko's inheritance, and you've obtained her power of attorney, which means you can sign things on her behalf if you want to, and do anything you like without telling her. Now, personally I'm not concerned about this, since I know you're an honest man. But the fact is, she was in a state of shock and couldn't have exercised her judgment properly when she signed that power of attorney for you. Some people might start whispering when they learn about this. I know the legal position is perfectly above board, but wouldn't this nevertheless make you feel slightly uncomfortable?"

"You think some people might accuse me of securing her power of attorney while she was unable to use her reason, in order to exploit her?"

"Yes. Mr. Ogata hinted at something like that, and I know for a fact Higuchi is already spreading a story about you."

"This is ridiculous," Koike said indignantly. "Now I know why they call him Bradawl the Tick. He knows very well it's against the unwritten rules to speak ill of a fellow lawyer in the matter of fees. If a lawyer had to worry all the time about what other people might say about his fees, he couldn't carry on at all . . . Anyhow, Etsuko's father himself is a lawyer, and so far as Yoshihiro's estate is concerned, everything—including the patent—has been disclosed to the police and to Prosecutor Kirishima. This is like a job in a glass case, with no room at all for manoeuvres behind the scenes. My sole purpose is to assist the widow of a close friend. I'm doing this for Etsuko out of the goodness of my heart, so to speak."

"I fully appreciate that," Kawaji said. "But wouldn't it be wise not to do anything positive about her inheritance, at least for the time being—until things sort themselves out? Especially after that awful Miss Kikuchi stormed into your office the other day."

"My instinct tells me she won't win that suit for recognition."

"That may be so, but there's another problem, too. If Tadaaki is found not guilty of his brothers' murders, he'll have succession rights to their property, too . . . When troublesome problems like these surround the settlement of an estate, wouldn't it be advisable for you to tear up that power of attorney and ask Etsuko for another one at a later date?"

"You don't sound like a lawyer at all," Koike said with contempt. "Since this is such a complicated business, Etsuko needs a legal adviser all the more. Or are you thinking of going into legal practice straight away and representing her interests? If so, I'll willingly withdraw. But you can't leave the university so quickly, can you?"

"That's true," Kawaji said in a low voice. "But you can understand how I feel, can't you? I've a sincere desire to do everything possible in Etsuko's best interests."

"Huh. Then why didn't you tell me this right at the start? In your indirect way, you make it sound as if there was something fishy about me."

"I'm sorry if I gave you that impression . . ." Kawaji cast a cold glance at Koike's profile. "Incidentally, what's the latest about the other one?"

"What other one? What are you talking about?"

"I'm sure you know what I mean," Kawaji said. There was a frozen smile on his face.

At about the same time, Kirishima and his party were having early dinner in the Kiyokan Inn at Ooiso. It was a bit noisy, being right on the street, but Kyoko had recommended the special fish they served there, and the men were in no position to question her authority in such things.

Inspector Yoshioka looked happily relaxed, but the one most delighted with the solid floor under him was Kitahara, as might be expected after the car ride. He had already managed to empty several glasses of *sake* in his subtly inconspicuous way, and was just about reaching the talkative stage.

"Mr. Prosecutor," he said, "even from the back seat I could appreciate your cousin's marvellous driving skill . . . There was just one thing that bothered me a little. Every now and then he speeded ahead, overtaking a number of other cars, then suddenly slowed down till the same cars were ahead of us again. He seemed to be doing this all the time. I wonder if the motor was giving him

261

trouble?"

"No, it wasn't that," Kirishima said with a poker face. "You may already know this, but a rally is a competition based on driving over a given distance at a certain average speed per hour. Unless a contestant passes through a checkpoint at a set time, he loses points. And my cousin is practising this all the time."

"Aah? So that's what it was?" Kitahara nodded several times in appreciation.

Kyoko had been away for a few minutes to freshen up. On her return to the room she said, "I've paid the bill."

They stubbed out their cigarettes and stood up.

As they were leaving the inn, Yoshioka grinned happily, and said to Kirishima, "I'll sure enjoy that fishing tomorrow, Mr. Prosecutor."

It was completely dark now. Koike's car had just passed through Ito City.

"Oh, I almost forgot to tell you," Kawaji said. "The lawyer we were talking about could be in this city right now."

"What lawyer? Are you talking about Higuchi?"

"Mm-hm. Mr. Ogata rang me around midday and said Higuchi was going to stay at the Kanzeso Inn at Ito."

Koike looked at Kawaji out of the corner of his eye. He seemed genuinely surprised. "But he knew nothing of Etsuko's whereabouts, did he? He must be using a private detective to keep an eye on her all the time . . . This man really fills me with awe. I heard about his obstinacy before now, but I didn't realise he was as dogged as that. I don't envy you—having him for a rival."

"You must be joking," Kawaji said scornfully. "He's no rival. Etsuko despises him. I've got no worries about him. He may be very clever in other things, but in this instance he's only making a fool of himself."

"Well, if you have that much confidence in yourself, then you shouldn't have any problems."

"Wait, that's the turn-off—on your right . . . Sorry, I

should've warned you before."

Koike turned the wheel sharply and just made it.

Away from the highway the road soon became a meandering mountain path, sending up clouds of dust behind them. They passed between a couple of thickets and then came upon a stretch of road that was only wide enough for one car at a time. There was a steep rock face along one side, and a sheer drop of at least fifty yards into a gorge along the other.

As the headlights knifed into the darkness, Koike said, "This is an awful road . . . How much further is it?"

"Not very far now," Kawaji said encouragingly. "But drive slowly, won't you?"

A little later the road widened again to double tracks. It must have been the place for vehicles to pass each other.

"Could you stop for a minute?" Kawaji asked.

"What's the matter?" Koike put his foot on the brake.

"I'd like to water the pony . . . There's a beautiful view from here in the daytime. We're about thirty minutes' walking distance from my uncle's villa."

Kawaji spoke casually. The darkness concealed the pallor and stiffness of his face.

The car carrying Kirishima's party was slowly moving up the same mountain road. Sitting in the front passenger seat, Kirishima watched the car's powerful headlights probing the darkness. His lips were tight and hard, and he kept glancing at the luminous dial of his wrist-watch.

There was a strange, stifling atmosphere inside the vehicle. Kitahara was looking around restlessly and asked for the fourth time how much further they had to go. Even Inspector Yoshioka seemed a little impatient. Kyoko sat in her place quietly. Only her eyelids fluttered every now and then.

Once more Kirishima looked at his watch carefully, then gave his cousin a nudge with his knee. The driving ace nodded and lowered his foot on the accelerator. The car leapt forward with a groan and began to negotiate the narrow, winding mountain path at *kamikaze* speed, leaving billowing dust in its wake.

"Holy smoke!" Kitahara yelled out. "Mr. Prosecutor, there's a deep gorge on one side! . . . Hey, what's going on? . . . Is this supposed to be a car rally? . . ."

Kirishima didn't answer. The car was hurling itself through the darkness, held on to the road by the skill of the driver. As it took the curves left to right and right to left, Kitahara heard the tyres whining in protest. He stared for a while with bulging eyes, but finally covered his face with his hands.

Before long the headlights picked out a car parked right at the edge of the gorge . . . and then the figures of two men, locked in struggle.

The driver slammed on the brakes. The vehicle skidded on the loose gravel and veered sideways as it came to a halt. Almost in the same instant Kirishima swung the door open and jumped out.

Just then one of the struggling men knocked the other down with a *karate* chop and tried to dart away. But the second man tackled him like a Rugby player and brought him to the ground. They were rolling together now, only a couple feet from the brink of the precipice.

Kirishima and Yoshioka were sprinting towards them, side by side.

Then one of the combatants broke free and kicked out viciously at the other before starting to run. The man on the ground yelled out in pain but at the same time picked up a fair-sized stone and threw it after the other, hitting him right behind the knee. The escapee lost his balance for a moment, but then started running again with a limp. Inspector Yoshioka caught up with him and grabbed him by the arm. As the man slashed out with his free hand, the inspector dodged and without apparent effort threw him over his shoulder in a remarkable demonstration of judo skill.

Kirishima helped the other man on the ground to his feet. "Are you all right?" he asked.

"I'm okay," he gasped. "Just a few bruises . . ."

By this time Kyoko reached them, and Kirishima left

264

the injured man in her care.

Snapping the handcuffs shut on his prey, Yoshioka was also panting. "Well, Mr. Prosecutor," he said, "I must say this is a catch beyond my wildest dreams, though you did promise good fishing for the weekend."

"So you've set a trap for me?" said the man in the handcuffs, his chest rising and falling, his eyes shining in the dark. "Nice work."

"You've been pretty clever, too," Kirishima said with biting sarcasm. "You've been caught in the act by none other than a police officer . . . Shoichi Koike, I charge you with the attempted murder of Tatsuo Kawaji."

CHAPTER EIGHTEEN

On Monday, March 9, Tadaaki Yasuda was committed for trial, charged with the unlawful killing of Morita. And on the same day Kirishima began the examination of suspect Koike.

The police had delivered Koike into Kirishima's hands the previous afternoon. The accompanying report listed three charges: the murder of Yoshihiro Tsukamoto, the murder of Nobumasa Tsukamoto, and the attempted murder of Tatsuo Kawaji.

During the initial questioning by police Koike had first tried to deny even the third charge. Almost frothing at the mouth, he violently argued it was he who had been unexpectedly attacked by Kawaji, who must have been seized by some mad impulse. But after several hours of non-stop interrogation he finally realised the futility of his stand. And once he admitted the third offence, it would have been impossible for him to hold out for long on the other two, despite his shrewdness and his legal training.

When facing Kirishima, Koike made a new attempt to deny his guilt, and when that didn't work, he tried the right of silence. But as Kirishima relentlessly went on exposing the cracks, Koike gradually lost confidence and began to cave in.

In the end he broke into an eerie chuckle and told Kirishima to save his breath. He made a full confession, then began to boast about the subtlety of his plot, displaying arrogance and vanity typical of intelligent criminals.

By the end of the week Kirishima had more than enough evidence to commit Koike for trial on all three charges.

Koike's own pride had ensured for him speedy progress into the hangman's noose.

Kyoko knew from experience that the only way to change the prosecutor back into a husband was to let him tell her all about the case, even if secretly she would have preferred him to go to bed with her and say nothing. Furthermore, she knew that for this ceremonial occasion it was essential he should have close at hand a liberal supply of best-quality imported brandy.

Toying with his glass in his absent-minded way, Kirishima said, "The two people who've done the greatest job in this case are Kawaji and you . . . You managed to persuade Kawaji to act as a decoy for us, and he did his part with amazing skill and courage. Without that scene on the mountain road I don't know how this case would've ended up. I had no concrete evidence against Koike."

"You're wrong again," Kyoko said teasingly. "The one who's done the greatest job is, of course, you—the inimitably brilliant State Prosecutor Saburo Kirishima. Hurray."

Kirishima made no attempt at false modesty. He slowly emptied his glass, and said, "The two most baffling aspects of this case were related to Yoshihiro's murder. The first one was: what excuse did the killer use to lure Yoshihiro out of the hotel? And the second: why did he have to commit the crime on that most unsuitable night?"

"What was the excuse?" Kyoko asked with simulated enthusiasm.

"To make it safe, the killer had to use an excuse that would've been most inconvenient for Yoshihiro to disclose to Etsuko. So it had to be connected with something Yoshihiro had kept hidden from Etsuko. In the early stages of the investigation I couldn't work out what that secret might be."

"Was it Tadaaki's change of identity?"

"That's right. Yoshihiro didn't tell Etsuko about the patent either, but he intended to explain this to her during their honeymoon. In any case, the patent could hardly have created a situation urgent enough for him to rush out of the hotel in the middle of his wedding night . . . I'll come back to this patent business a little later." Kirishima held out his empty glass to Kyoko. "Now, if the excuse concerned Tadaaki, then the natural thing to assume was that Tadaaki himself was the killer. This is what I thought at one stage, but then I realised it didn't make sense."

"Why?"

"Well, the only possible excuse Tadaaki could've used was that the date of his departure for Hong Kong was very close and he was short of money again. But would this have been enough to get Yoshihiro out of the hotel to some lonely place nominated by Tadaaki? Of course not. Yoshihiro had the upper hand because he was the one to hand out the money. He could've easily told Tadaaki to come to the hotel lobby, or some nearby coffee shop, if he wanted the cash."

"And then Yoshihiro would've only had to be away for ten or fifteen minutes—hardly long enough to make Etsuko suspicious. He wouldn't have needed an elaborate lie, like the missing exam papers."

"Correct. So I came to the conclusion it wasn't Tadaaki who had lured Yoshihiro out of the hotel. If it was somebody else, then Yoshihiro's panicky act didn't look quite so strange. For example, the killer might have told him on the phone that Tadaaki was causing a disturbance somewhere, or making a nuisance of himself."

"But what *was* the excuse he used?"

"Koike confessed he had told Yoshihiro a yarn that went something like this: 'Some time after you left for the hotel, there was a phone call for you at the wedding reception. I took the call, and it was Tadaaki. He said he had to see you urgently, and if you were no longer at the reception, he'd just have to force his way into your hotel suite. I thought this would be terrible, so I rushed to where he said he was. He claims he's been unlucky in gambling and urgently needs 100,000 yen. I'd be prepared to give it to him on your behalf, but I hardly have anything on me, and I can't get hold of any money till the banks open in the morning. So the only thing I can suggest is that you slip out to see him.' "

Kyoko frowned and pursed her lips. "But why didn't Yoshihiro tell Koike to come to the hotel and get the money from him?"

"He did tell him that, as a matter of fact, but Koike managed to persuade him to go by saying that Tadaaki was blind drunk, and it was impossible to tell what he might do next. And to make sure, Koike added that the fellows in the gambling den were very annoyed with Tadaaki and wouldn't let him go till he cleared his debt —they even threatened to put a few more knife scars into his face. So it'd be dangerous to leave him there on his own . . . This is what Koike told Yoshihiro on the phone, and you must remember Yoshihiro had absolute confidence in him."

"I see."

"Now, Yoshihiro had sufficient money on him to give Tadaaki 100,000 yen. He probably thought he'd ask Nobumasa to send him some money by telegraphic transfer to Kyoto. So he told Etsuko the lie about the missing exam papers and then rushed out of the hotel, intending to return straight after meeting his brother. Of course, Koike was waiting for him, ready to kill him. That's the story in a nutshell."

"Yes, this makes sense," Kyoko said, inching a little closer to Kirishima. "Yoshihiro must have thought that by giving Tadaaki the money there and then, his brother wouldn't pester them on their honeymoon but would be safely out of the way in a ship bound for Hong Kong."

Kirishima nodded and took another sip at his brandy. "Well, once I got this far, identifying Koike as the killer was easy. Who could've known that Watanabe was in fact Tadaaki, and who would've been in a position to lure Yoshihiro out of the hotel with an excuse about Tadaaki? Any schoolboy could've worked this out without much trouble. But recognising the killer and proving him guilty are two entirely different things."

"And why did Koike choose the wedding night?"

"You should've asked this in conjunction with the question: why did he make sure the marriage certificate was registered—and thereby Etsuko became legal successor to Yoshihiro's property—before committing the murder? The answer, of course, is that Koike wanted to ensure, first, that Etsuko would inherit Yoshihiro's assets, and second, that Yoshihiro would die before disclosing the patent business to Etsuko, so that Koike could defraud her with the aid of the power of attorney."

"I suppose it was a reasonable assumption on Koike's part that Yoshihiro wouldn't start talking about the patent business straight after their arrival at the wedding suite?"

"That's right. Of course, it would've been different in the case of an impotent bridegroom, who might have wanted to delay the humiliating moment as long as possible."

"I don't think Yoshihiro would've come into that category—not if he was anything like you," Kyoko said, smirking. "But didn't you at one stage think Koike was innocent despite your earlier theory about his guilt?"

"Yes, I did. I thought, since he had volunteered the information about the patent immediately after Nobumasa's death, he couldn't have aimed at milking Etsuko. So he had no motive for either murder . . . At that time I felt I'd reached a dead-end. But then somehow I hit on the idea there might be a second patent registered in Yoshihiro's name."

270

"Oh, I see!"

"This immediately explained why Nobumasa had stayed on at Toho Kasei, even after the first patent had started to produce a large income. He was obviously working on a second and third research project, and needed the continued use of the company's laboratory facilities . . . I felt such a fool for not recognising this."

"You're being too severe on yourself," Kyoko said, running a caressing finger down Kirishima's back. "The patent you knew about was itself producing an annual income of some 20,000,000 yen—which is no chickenfeed. And by disclosing this, Koike cleverly threw you off the scent."

"And just to make things a little more difficult for me, he left untouched all the money already in Nobumasa's savings accounts . . . Yes, Koike was clever all right. He disclosed one patent so he could hide two others behind it . . . Anyhow, by sending Kitahara to the Patent Office I managed to find out that the patent of another new synthetic resin was already registered in Yoshihiro's name. And according to an expert I consulted, this second patent has an even greater potential than the first."

Kyoko shook her head in wonder. "What a beautiful dream of riches it must have been for Koike. Isn't it a shame you had to spoil it for him? With the power of attorney in his hands, he could've done what he liked with Etsuko's inheritance, or the income from it. He could've been milking her with impunity for the rest of her life."

"He told me he intended to take out a third patent in his own name, after the excitement over the two murders had died down. For this the documentation was already in his hands. It would've given him a large legitimate income, eliminating the need to run even the slightest risk. Meanwhile, Etsuko and everyone else would've been convinced he was a fine, honest lawyer, and a good friend . . . Of course, if Yoshihiro had revealed the secret of the patents to Etsuko before their marriage, Koike's plan would've immediately collapsed, and the

271

Tsukamoto brothers could well be alive today. But as Yoshihiro's legal adviser, Koike had no difficulty in convincing him it'd be safer to keep the patent business to himself till after the wedding. And that's why Koike had to murder Yoshihiro so soon after the wedding—before the couple left on their honeymoon and were in a position to have long, intimate discussions about their personal affairs and their common future."

Kyoko was now so close to Kirishima—it was only a matter of time before she could make the final move onto his lap. To conceal her artful progress till the very last moment, she maintained a nonchalant expression, and said, "But why did you have to be so secretive about this latest discovery of yours? You acted as if disclosing it to me could've precipitated a third world war."

"Oh, come now. Isn't this obvious to you?" Kirishima indignantly emptied his glass for emphasis. "If Koike had somehow got wind of my discovery, everything would've fallen through. He would've had time to produce the plausible excuse that he hadn't bothered to mention the second patent because it hadn't reached the income-producing stage . . . In any case, even when I was finally convinced he was the killer, I had no way of pinning him down because he had been so careful not to make up an unwise alibi for either night. That's why I eventually came up with the desperate idea of setting a trap for him. I wanted to draw him out—make him feel he was in danger—so he'd do something rash. Now you can understand, I hope, why I thought of Higuchi in the first place, knowing how keen he was to prove himself to Etsuko."

"You silly," Kyoko said, sliding half-way onto Kirishima's lap, "Mr. Higuchi wouldn't have had the guts to take on a dangerous role like this! That's why I suggested Mr. Kawaji, with his athletic physique and fierce looks . . . It was very decent of him to accept this challenge to avenge his best friend. But he must have been really scared when that critical moment arrived." Kyoko shuddered, as if to demonstrate Kawaji's state of terror, and at the same time firmly established herself on Kirishima's lap. "When you think of it, he had to provoke Koike sufficiently to bring a murderous attack upon himself. The thought of us following in a car would've been small comfort to him when he got out of Koike's vehicle."

"Yes, I was worrying about him all the way, as a matter of fact. When I got his phone call from Ooiso, I felt better, but not for long. After we passed through Ito City, cold sweat was starting to break out all over me . . . Koike confessed he had no intention of killing Kawaji when they set out on the trip. Even when Kawaji told him he wanted to marry Etsuko and go into private practice, Koike was still merely annoyed. Then Kawaji suggested he should tear up the power of attorney obtained from Etsuko, and this made Koike scared and furious at the same time. He was wondering if Kawaji had seen through his deception. But when Kawaji came out with the question about the second patent, Koike was no longer in doubt. He knew the only way to eliminate this new danger to his plan was to eliminate Kawaji . . ."

"He must have thought Yoshihiro had disclosed the secret of the patents to Mr. Kawaji, his best friend."

"That's exactly what he thought. And although he managed to answer Kawaji's awkward question by saying that the second patent certificate hadn't been delivered to him yet, he felt he had to get rid of Kawaji while the opportunity was there . . . He thought nobody knew they were on a country trip together, and considered it a godsend Higuchi happened to be in the same area, trying to locate Etsuko. He figured that with a little luck he might be able to divert police suspicion onto Higuchi, especially if the latter was deprived of an alibi for the evening. At worst, he could make Kawaji's death look like an accident . . . Koike told me he had worked this out between Ito City and the turn-off to the mountain road."

"It must have been an agonising experience for Mr. Kawaji to walk from that car to the brink of the precipice. Knowing he'd be attacked from behind within the next minute must have been more unnerving than being taken by surprise." Kyoko shuddered again and put her arms around Kirishima's neck as if to seek comfort from a frightening thought.

"Yes," Kirishima said, finding it difficult to finish his brandy with Kyoko in the way, "Koike must have found the situation irresistible . . . Well, my guess is Kawaji will receive his just reward for his courage, sooner or later."

"I hope so, too," Kyoko said, snuggling up against Kirishima's chest.

Now Kirishima gave up all hope of another drink. He put his glass on the coffee table, and said, "There's not much more I can tell you. The police investigation has revealed that Koike has been in serious financial difficulties for some time. His wife is a spendthrift, and he himself is all for show. No wonder they were rushing headlong into bankruptcy. His unsuccessful attempts to make some quick money on the commodity market only made matters worse . . . And then suddenly he saw two geese laying golden eggs, and decided to grab one for himself."

"The fatter one," Kyoko said, testing Kirishima's whiskers with her cheek.

But Kirishima didn't seem to be aware of his wife's legitimate advances after weeks of complete neglect. In fact, his expression was changing from serious to outright morose. "The Chief was furious with me," he muttered.

"But why?"

"He said he didn't like the unorthodox way I had conducted this case."

"And what did *you* say?"

"I told him I agreed the way I'd nailed the killer was perhaps unusual, but I couldn't see anything wrong with it. I was having a restful weekend in company with Yoshioka and Kitahara. Then quite unexpectedly I was confronted with Koike's attempt to kill another man. I couldn't just watch from a distance because it happened to be the weekend and the office wouldn't open till Monday! That's what I said, and added that if the Chief thought I'd broken the rules, I'd tender my resignation forthwith."

"You didn't!"

"Yes I did. And then the Chief said my trouble was I was resignation-happy. I'd do much better if, instead of acting like a touchy maiden, I just observed the rules. Then suddenly he put on that inimitable grin of his, and said, 'As head of the Criminal Affairs Division, I've adequately condemned your rash action. And now, speaking as Renji Sanada, your friend, I'd like to thank you for what you did. I do this on behalf of Mr. Ogata, who has helped me so often over the years . . . Incidentally, I notice that Inspector Yoshioka, who was supposed to be enjoying a happy weekend away from his chores, was carrying handcuffs in his pocket. He must have a *Samurai* complex—never forgetting war in peace.' "

Kirishima burst into laughter, and Kyoko thought with some chagrin that her husband should have been an actor.

"Well, that's that," Kirishima said, now ready to succumb to his wife's charms.

Kyoko was going to say something, but changed her mind. She pulled his head down and stretched her neck till their lips could meet. The brandy on his breath didn't bother her. She was used to it.

It was May 12, and the freshness of an early summer was in the air.

Kirishima had to go to a nearby city on official business. He was expected to be away for several days, and Kyoko thought this would be an excellent opportunity for her to go with Etsuko on a short trip to Hakone. The change of scenery would do Etsuko good. Perhaps it would help her forget those terrible days in February.

Not that there was anything seriously wrong with Etsuko. She seemed to possess fantastic powers of recovery. In fact, Kyoko felt her friend was already on the mend.

This was confirmed as soon as they set out on the trip. While riding in the express train to Yumoto, Etsuko was humming a tune in rhythm with the click-clack of the carriage wheels. When they began their journey in the cable car from Gora, with fresh green mountains on either side and a vivid blue sky above, Etsuko sighed, her eyes shining, "Oh, how beautiful." There were young couples, including some newly-weds, in the same car, but Etsuko showed no sign of being jealous of their happiness.

They passed through Owakudani and, reaching the shores of Ashinoko, took an excursion boat for Moto-hakone. Snow-capped Mount Fuji was mirrored in the still water. It was a breath-taking view.

Kyoko stood at the stern, watching the white foam behind the boat, when she heard Etsuko call her name. She turned and saw that the previous cheerful expression was gone from her friend's face. She wasn't sure, but it looked as if Etsuko's eyes were shining with held-back tears. Then she noticed a cardboard box in Etsuko's hands, apparently taken from her travelling bag, which lay open on the deck beside her.

"What's that?" Kyoko asked.

Etsuko walked up to her with the box and opened it. Inside was the sad-faced black Kewpie doll, holding its broken heart. She took it out and placed it on the deck, and switched it on.

The two women watched in silence as large tear-drops began to fall from the doll's eyes, while its hands were desperately trying to put together the two halves of its broken heart.

Then Etsuko switched off the doll and put it back into the box. She produced a black ribbon from her handbag and carefully tied up the box with it.

Kyoko was looking on wide-eyed, wondering what Etsuko was trying to do. She didn't have to wait long for an answer.

"I don't think I need this doll any more," Etsuko whispered and pushed the box off the deck into the foaming white water.

The box disappeared in an instant, but for a while Etsuko kept staring at the endless wake behind the boat. When finally she turned to Kyoko again, she was smiling.

Kyoko took hold of Etsuko's hands and smiled with her. She knew it wouldn't be long before her friend's surname would change again.

ABOUT THE AUTHOR

Akimitsu Takagi was born in 1920 in Aomori, a northern city on the main island of Japan. He was educated at First High School, Tokyo, and at Kyoto University. Graduating as an engineer, he joined the Nakajima Aircraft Company. After World War II, a fortune teller predicted his destiny lay in writing.

He had his first novel, *The Tattoo Murder Case*, published in 1948, and was immediately recognised as a talented mystery writer. His early work was largely confined to the classic detective story, but by 1960 he was probing deeper into human nature and was beginning to base his novels on real incidents, and often on personal experience. His popularity made him a bestselling author.

Although he had no formal legal training, he won the admiration of professionals for his knowledge of Japanese criminal law. Mr. Takagi, a lover of classical music, wrote all his novels while listening to records. He died in 1995.